"Were you often a therapist for your family clients?" Fox asked.

"Only the smart ones," Kelsey replied.

The sassy smile on her lips tempted him like nothing else. His palm was on her arm and he was leaning in before he caught himself. At the last minute, he brushed a kiss on the baby's head and retreated to his desk.

He was too comfortable around her. It was as if he'd been caught in a happy-family web that grew stronger with every passing day. With any luck, she had no idea where his thoughts had led or how desperately he was trying to tamp down his desire for her.

They were employer and employee. Colleagues. She was already an asset to the business and that would only be more valuable with time. He couldn't screw that up, or risk everything he'd worked for to explore this physical attraction.

* * *

The Coltons of Roaring Springs:
Family and true love are under siege

* * *

If you're on Twitter, tell us what you think of Harlequin Romantic Suspense!
#harlequinromsuspense

Dear Reader,

Colorado is a beautiful and rugged part of the world and has always been one of my favorite places. In Roaring Springs, renowned horse breeder Fox Colton has built his ideal life and a prosperous business at the Crooked C Ranch. He thrives on the long hours, the hard work and the solitude.

Until someone leaves a baby boy on his doorstep.

His solitude shattered, Fox is overwhelmed by all the things he doesn't know about caring for a baby. Thankfully, Kelsey Lauder, the equine geneticist he'd planned to hire as his new assistant, is also an expert with babies and children. Determined to find the baby's true father, they embark on a search that turns everything Fox thought he knew about his past and himself inside out.

With all the trouble brewing in and around Roaring Springs these days, Fox and Kelsey have their hands full balancing the baby and long-buried secrets with new desires and increasing danger. I hope you enjoy their story.

Live the adventure!

Regan Black

COLTON FAMILY SHOWDOWN

Regan Black

HARLEQUIN® ROMANTIC SUSPENSE

Special thanks and acknowledgment are given to Regan Black for her contribution to The Coltons of Roaring Springs miniseries.

ISBN-13: 978-1-335-66217-0

Colton Family Showdown

This edition published by arrangement with Harlequin Books S.A.

For questions and comments about the quality of this book, please contact us at CustomerService@Harlequin.com.

Printed in U.S.A.

Regan Black, a *USA TODAY* bestselling author, writes award-winning, action-packed novels featuring kick-butt heroines and the sexy heroes who fall in love with them. Raised in the Midwest and California, she and her family, along with their adopted greyhound, two arrogant cats and a quirky finch, reside in the South Carolina Lowcountry, where the rich blend of legend, romance and history fuels her imagination.

Books by Regan Black

Harlequin Romantic Suspense

The Coltons of Roaring Springs

Colton Family Showdown

The Riley Code

A Soldier's Honor

Escape Club Heroes

Safe in His Sight
A Stranger She Can Trust
Protecting Her Secret Son
Braving the Heat

The Coltons of Shadow Creek

Killer Colton Christmas
"Special Agent Cowboy"

The Coltons of Red Ridge

Colton P.I. Protector

Visit the Author Profile page at Harlequin.com for more titles.

With big thanks and warm hugs to the whole team at Harlequin Romantic Suspense for inviting me into the Colton world and making me feel like part of the family.

Chapter 1

Evening was going toward dark and Fox Colton whistled as he pulled up to the big red barn that meant everything to him. The home he needed and the work he loved under one classic metal roof. He'd never tire of that sense of accomplishment. He'd made something out of nothing with more than forty good acres of the Crooked C ranch. A prime opportunity had become a thriving horse-breeding business.

There were days when it seemed too good to be true.

Against the deepening sky, the barn stood out in silhouette. Fox was weary, but in a way that filled him with immense satisfaction. It had been a long couple of days making sure things ran smoothly on both his brother's side of the ranch and his own. Wyatt was rightly preoccupied with his wife, Bailey, as she delivered their new son, Hudson Earl Colton.

Once he'd finished the ranch work last night, he'd gone to the hospital and waited with the rest of the family, trying to cover his uneasiness with quiet confidence that his sister-in-law and the baby would be just fine. Turned out having been on hand for his mares through countless foals didn't actually make waiting for a new niece or nephew less stressful. But seeing the stars in Wyatt's eyes as he held his son made being there worth it.

Fox picked up his phone, intending to give his brother a text update on the day's activities at the ranch before he went inside. There were a slew of emails waiting for his attention and as soon as he dipped a toe into that water, he'd be sunk for the night. It was one of the best perks of loving his work.

Instead, when he opened the messaging app, he found another baby picture from the proud daddy. Fox chuckled. He could hardly blame Wyatt. The newborn was unquestionably adorable. He sent back a quick aww in reply and then added the ranch update. The recent challenges of a murder victim, a dead bull and a barn fire on the Crooked C had left Wyatt and Fox, along with their hired crew and the Roaring Springs law enforcement, on high alert for anything out of the ordinary.

Pocketing his phone, Fox hopped out of the truck and started for the house. He had a thick burger on his mind for dinner, after a shower and a change of clothes. Inside the door, he pulled off his work boots and ducked into the office for his laptop. He could clear out his email in-box while the meat cooked.

A sticky note on the laptop keyboard caught his attention, and he sat down at his desk, scolding himself for forgetting. He quickly confirmed an interview appointment for tomorrow afternoon with an equine geneticist.

Fox wasn't particularly in the market for an assistant, though business was booming and he was fielding inquiries from other ranchers looking for bloodstock advice. He leaned back in the chair and stretched his arms overhead, rereading the original query. Maybe it was time to think about expanding. Kelsey Lauder had presented a compelling argument for creating the position and her résumé in equine research impressed him. It never hurt business to extend a courtesy and frankly, he was eager to talk with someone who understood both the science and artistry of horse breeding.

Last season he'd lost three foals to premature delivery, well below the average considering the number of mares he'd bred. Risk of the job, of course, but it was never pleasant for the herd or the crew. Each time, they'd sent off the standard lab tests and worked through each layer of cleanup protocols and herd management. With breeding season done and the herd settled for fall, now was the time to dive deeper into the genetic material if he hoped to find something helpful there. Would Miss Lauder be interested in that sort of research?

His stomach rumbled loudly and Fox realized he'd spent nearly two hours at his desk and still needed that shower and dinner. Closing his laptop, he headed upstairs.

The two-bedroom house he'd built into the second story of the barn was simple and functional and suited him to a tee. When he looked around, he imagined his mom, Dana, beaming with pride at the relaxed and lived-in style. It was certainly easier to conjure that image after his little sister Sloane's recent visit. She was the spitting image of their mom, though she had no real recollection of their parents. He and his sister had been raised as Coltons, formally adopted by Russ and Mara, Dana's older sister, after a car crash left them orphans when they were young. Sloane only remembered their second family and there were times when her simpler memories made Fox a little jealous.

Leaving the laptop on the kitchen table, he went straight for the bathroom. He dumped his dirty clothes in the hamper and stepped into the shower, letting the hot spray wash the workday down the drain. Feeling better, he went to his room and pulled on flannel pants and a long-sleeved T-shirt.

Checking the clock, he decided it was too late for a heavy meal, so he heated up a bowl of leftover vegetable soup and sat down to finish clearing his email before turning in for the night. He fell down a rabbit hole of research, reading through a comprehensive report on an herbal supplement found to ease the adverse symptoms of hormonal swings in broodmares.

The sound of a car engine nearby brought him back with a start. He ignored it. A few of the ranch hands had active social lives. As long as the work was done well, the crew could do as they pleased with their personal time. With a sigh, he realized it was after midnight and the horses needed him fresh in a few hours. He switched over from his emails to the breeding log for this season and confirmed which mares were slated for pregnancy verification tests this week.

At last, he closed the laptop and called it a day. Everything else would have to wait until morning. He turned out the lights in the kitchen and padded through the dark hallway to his bedroom.

His head barely touched the pillow when he heard tires on the gravel drive. That car was too close to be headed to the bunkhouse. Fox froze, listening as he reached for his cell phone. After the trouble of the previous months, he couldn't help being on edge.

When he'd remodeled and repurposed the barn, he'd added a low porch to the front door. One of the wood planks on the second step had been squeaky from the start and when he heard that sound, he was up and out of bed.

Any of the ranch hands would've called to let him know about a problem, not just shown up. Phone in hand, he sprinted for the stairs and the front door, grabbing his shotgun on the way. He'd defend his property and let the sheriff sort it out later.

When Fox opened the door, the car was a blur in the night, driving away without headlights. Odds were good the driver would hit a tree or slide off into a ditch, making the sheriff's work easier. He started out the door, shotgun to his shoulder, and nearly tripped over a bulky object on his welcome mat.

A bag. A baby's *diaper* bag. He only recognized the gear because he'd seen plenty of it while Wyatt and Bailey prepared for their son. Next to that was a baby carrier, complete with a sleeping baby, the pacifier loose in his mouth.

Fox flipped the safety and lowered the shotgun. "What the hell?"

The baby gave a start, arms and legs going stiff and his eyes popping open to stare at Fox. His little mouth tugged the pacifier back in tight.

Fox looked around, dumbfounded. “Ha, ha,” he said. He had no idea why anyone would use a real baby in a prank, much less to prank *him*, but he was ready for the stunt to be over. “You got me,” he called a little louder.

No reply.

He rubbed one bare foot against his calf. Prank or not, the night was too cold to stand out here without warmer clothing.

“You can’t be here,” he said to the baby. The infant was bundled up, but he couldn’t just leave it out here. “You’re not mine.”

The baby didn’t care about Fox’s denial.

He hauled both baby and bag inside, out of the chill. The diaper bag and car seat contraption were in shades of blue, decorated with airplanes, trucks and trains in various bright colors.

“Safe bet is you’re a boy.” This wasn’t one of his foals, so it wasn’t his job to confirm or deny the fact. “You’re not mine,” he repeated. No way had he fathered a baby without knowing. Hell, he hadn’t even been with a woman in over a year. That was a hard fact to face, even in the privacy of his own head. So who would dump a child on his doorstep? “Are you Wyatt’s?” he wondered.

Naturally, the baby didn’t answer, just kept staring up at him. Fox studied the tiny face, unable to see any obvious resemblance between the baby and anyone he knew.

He’d just seen Wyatt’s newborn. This little guy was too big to be brand-new. Weren’t people supposed to abandon newborns at fire stations or orphanages? How old was the baby? And how had he wound up on Fox’s doorstep? He called the bunkhouse, but no one there had seen any vehicles that didn't belong to the Crooked C.

"Whoever you belong to, you can't stay here." Fox had no intention of having fatherhood forced on him. Considering his troubled childhood, he'd ruled it out way back in college. Possibly even before that. Not that the baby cared.

He locked the front door again and started upstairs. Should he leave the little guy alone? His sister would know. He pulled out his phone and started to call and remembered she was out of town with her family. Checking the straps, Fox decided the baby was secure in the seat. It would only take him a minute to change. "Wait here." He darted up the stairs, found a pair of jeans and came back to find the baby, eyes wide, calmly taking in the change of scenery.

What did babies see?

He knew how and when horses developed vision, but he'd never bothered to think about the same growth and development in humans.

He sat on the bench next to the door and pulled on his boots. "Come on." He picked up the car seat. "Oof, you've got some heft. Good for you." Slinging the diaper bag over his shoulder, he picked up his keys. "The police will know what to do with you."

Tucking the diaper bag behind the front passenger seat, he wrestled the car seat into place in the back, securing it with the seat belt. He didn't think he had it quite right, but it should do for the short, careful drive into town.

The baby was quiet on the ride and seemed happy enough when Fox carried him, seat and all, into the police department looking for his cousin, Sheriff Trey

Colton. If this was a prank, someone was about to get busted.

"Is Trey around?" he asked the officer manning the front desk.

"Come on back, Fox." Trey waved him into his office, then did a double take when he saw what his cousin was carrying. "Whoa. Who's this?"

"That's what I'd like to know." Fox set the carrier on the sheriff's desk and the diaper bag in the chair. "I found him on my porch."

"When?"

"Less than half an hour ago. I loaded him up and came straight here."

"Why?"

Why? Fox gawked at Trey. His cousin was clearly overtired if he couldn't come to his own conclusions on that score. "So you could handle it. Bringing him here seemed better than calling you out to the ranch."

Eyes trained on the baby, Trey rocked the baby seat. "No one's reported a missing child."

"Well, let me be the first," Fox muttered, planting his hands on his hips. "He isn't mine."

The sheriff arched an eyebrow and pinned his cousin with a hard stare. "Why else would he be on *your* porch?"

"Your guess is as good as mine," he retorted. "I haven't been with anyone." He could feel his cheeks burning with the admission. "Not in a time frame that would have this result."

He should've just had that vasectomy a few years ago after his sister had gotten pregnant. Sure she was happy now, but all her talk of cousins and playdates had terrified him. He was *not* father material. Fox didn't expect her to remember that part of their childhood. Better if she didn't. If only he'd followed through then, he wouldn't have to endure the judgment on Trey's face now.

"It's not my kid," he insisted.

"He's a cute little guy." With a put-upon sigh, Trey unbuckled the baby and lifted him from the seat. "Look for a note," he told Fox.

Why hadn't he thought of that? "No note here."

"Check the diaper bag," Trey said patiently, cuddling the baby like a pro. That too was empty of anything as helpful as identification or a note. "Was there anything else with him?"

"No."

"Sounds like you've got a real mystery on your hands," the sheriff said.

"No." Fox stepped back. "*You* do. He isn't my kid. I can't keep him." Just the thought of having a child in his care made his palms sweat. "I can't keep him," he repeated.

The baby wriggled in Trey's arms, making happy gurgling sounds that made the sheriff smile. "Your front doorstep isn't exactly well-known or easy to get to," he said.

"Oh, my." Deputy Sheriff Daria Bloom walked in. "What a sweet face."

Was everyone on the graveyard shift tonight? With her athletic grace, striking features and golden-brown eyes framed by a cap of short dark hair, she always struck Fox as more of a model than a law enforcement officer. Of course, her real career choice was more than evident since she'd taken the lead on the Avalanche Killer case.

She stepped closer to the baby. "You're a cutie, aren't you?" she crooned.

The baby smiled at her and his pacifier fell out of his mouth to the floor. She picked it up. "What's his name?"

"I wish I knew," Fox said.

"What are you talking about?" Daria frowned, but the expression melted into a smile when the baby reached for her. She let him catch her finger in his tiny hand.

"Fox found him on his doorstep and is certain he isn't the father."

"Your house isn't exactly easy access," Daria replied.

"I said the same thing," the sheriff murmured. The baby's attention went to the star on his navy blue uniform shirt. "Someone went out of their way for you to have him, Fox."

"But he cannot possibly be mine," Fox insisted. "Isn't there someone you call when this happens?"

Daria backed toward the door, the pacifier clutched in her hand. "I'll go wash this."

"I can call child services," Trey offered. "If you're sure that's the route you want to go."

Child services. "Foster care?" Fox rolled his shoulders, trying to release the sudden pinch between his shoulder blades. "Is that the only option?"

"No note, no identification, no reported lost baby." Trey shrugged as he nestled the baby back into the car seat. "I'm afraid that's the best I can do," he said. "It's standard procedure."

Fox stared at the baby. Standard procedure would have landed him and his sister in foster care after their parents died. At that time, his family had stepped up and his aunt and uncle adopted them, given them family roots and the Colton name.

He rubbed at his forehead. “No.” The sheriff was right, his house wasn’t easily accessible, which meant someone had gone to some trouble to leave the baby with him. And been careful enough not to be seen.

“No what?” Trey asked.

“No foster care,” he said, making the decision as the words left his mouth. “There’s been a mistake, clearly.” This was *not* his child. “But I’ll take care of him until I can track down the person he belongs to.” Maybe one of the hands at the Crooked C was the father and whoever had dropped off the baby chose Fox’s porch in an effort to be discreet. His red barn was certainly easier to find in the dark and fewer people would be around.

“We’ll keep an eye out here, too,” the sheriff promised.

Daria returned with the pacifier. “All clean. You should get one of those leash thingies for it. And maybe call a pediatrician in the morning. Just to make sure he’s okay.”

He figured there were a lot of “shoulds” in his immediate future. Fox would ask his sister about the pacifier leash and all the rest. He almost swore. Those questions would have to wait until Sloane and her family returned. For now, the internet would have to suffice.

“I’ll check into it,” he said, trying not to snap. The deputy sheriff was only trying to help. He started to leave and stopped short. “Can someone check the car seat thing? I may not have it installed right. I was in a hurry.”

"On it," Daria volunteered. At the truck, she made the proper adjustments to the base and got the baby seat locked in for the ride back home. "It occurs to me you may have another problem, Fox."

Super. "What's that?"

She gently closed the door. "I admit the Avalanche Killer is foremost on my mind."

As she was lead on the case, that made perfect sense to Fox. He knew what it was like to get lost in solving a problem, in the lab or on the ranch. Another reason not to add a baby to his list of responsibilities.

"Playing a dangerous 'what if' game here," she began. "But *if* the baby's mother has been taken, the killer might have dropped the baby on the nearest doorstep."

Great. Like he didn't have enough to worry about. "You're welcome to come out and take a look around. I heard a car on the gravel and a squeak on my porch step."

"That's all?"

Her disappointment didn't come close to matching his frustration.

"The driver drove off without lights. I didn't hear a crash or see anything on my way into town, but that's a hard road to navigate in the dark."

"I'll come by tomorrow."

With a nod, Fox climbed into the driver's seat and headed for home, *with a baby.* How on earth had this happened? Though his first run at fatherhood was definitely temporary, he found it utterly terrifying.

With sunset painting the horizon in vivid golds and deep indigo, Kelsey Lauder paused at the end of the gravel drive that led to the big red barn. Finally, she'd reached the offices of Foxworth Colton. Two hours late, but she was here.

Being late embarrassed her—so unprofessional—but showing up with her cheeks on fire would make it worse. Everyone who'd learned to drive understood car trouble was never convenient. She'd done all she could to keep Mr. Colton informed with a call to his office that went straight to voice mail and sending a quick email reiterating that she would arrive as soon as possible.

Leaving her car on the side of the road, hazard lights flashing, she'd taken only her purse, eager to move quickly, still hopeful she might be close to on time for her interview. A rideshare service wasn't an option and although she'd caught a ride with a trucker heading into Roaring Springs with a load of produce, she'd had to hike the last couple of miles to the ranch.

Having made a practice of looking for life's silver linings, she found the first hopeful glimmer in that sunset and the second in the long hike that led farther away from the town and main roads. She appreciated distance and privacy, having had so little of it in labs and dorms.

Her extended, up-close look at the southern acreage of the Crooked C ranch was even better than she'd expected. Kelsey had done her research online and been thoroughly impressed by the articles and professional pictures, but in person, the property was far more than photogenic spin. She soaked up layer after layer of beautiful views, gorgeous horses, fenced pastures, well-kept barns and buildings and wide-open fields framed by the rugged mountains.

For years she'd been on a quest to achieve her top personal goals of peace and safety. Those warm feelings enveloped her almost from her first step onto the property, as if the ranch itself was gladly accepting her, buffering her from anything untoward. Small fantasies like that buoyed her spirit from one endeavor to the next as she searched for the place where she could sink deep roots.

Would it be here in Roaring Springs breeding quarter horses at the renowned Crooked C? She was about to knock on her idol's door and find out.

Her nerves jumping, Kelsey pressed her hand to her belly. She paused under the shade of a big tree and pulled out her hair tie. She brushed out her long strawberry-blond hair until the strands were tangle-free again, then she wound it back into a bun to keep it out of her face. She might be late, but she *would* nail this interview.

Since graduating from college and defending her master's thesis in equine genetics, she'd been bumping along from one internship or short-term study to the next. Not a bad system and it had given her time to figure out which facets of her degrees she wanted to put to use. She enjoyed lab work, but missed the hands-on, day-to-day interaction with the horses. It had been years since she'd been present for foaling. With a little luck and some quick talking, she'd be assisting Mr. Colton with that very thing come springtime.

As ready as ever, she marched toward the big barn and up onto the porch, under the sign with the Crooked C Quarter Horses logo. Drawing in a deep breath, she rang the doorbell. Waited several long moments. There was no answer. He could be out, working directly with his mares or just tending to the needs of a forty-acre ranch. Horses didn't keep the same cushy hours as those of the labs she'd been working in.

She knocked, determined to reschedule if he didn't have time to speak with her this evening. In all of the pictures and interviews she'd read, Fox struck her as a decent, kind man. She'd studied recordings of talks he'd given at various program events. The man came across as focused and purposeful, smart as a whip and humble about it. Genuine. If he couldn't speak with her tonight, surely he could recommend a towing service and repair shop. And maybe, in the way of many communities, the repair shop would point her toward an affordable motel.

Roaring Springs was known for excellent skiing, a summer film festival, the resort atmosphere and the spa that catered to A-list celebrities. Kelsey didn't have that kind of money to toss around. Not even for one night.

She rang the doorbell one last time, her mind spinning with new plans and possibilities. If Mr. Colton didn't answer, she'd write a note and tuck it into the door and head down to the nearest barn. Was it better to go in search of someone who could help her or sit here like a lost puppy awaiting his return?

Suddenly, her spiraling thoughts were interrupted by the unmistakable sound of a baby crying. Oh, no. Had all her ringing and knocking woken up the child? One of the first life rules she'd learned was never to wake a sleeping baby.

Way to make a good first impression.

The sounds of wailing increased, as if someone was slowly turning up the volume on a baby monitor. Then the door swung opened and a frazzled cowboy with glazed blue eyes and a miserable baby in his arms stared blankly at her.

Mr. Foxworth Colton. He was taller than she'd anticipated, making her feel shorter than ever. His brown hair, highlighted by hours out in the sun, fell into his eyes and his chambray shirt, half-untucked, was wrinkled and damp in places from the baby's tears or worse. Either he'd grown a beard since the last photo she'd seen or he hadn't shaved in several days. Nothing in his bio had mentioned a wife or children. He had several siblings, though he didn't look anything like a content uncle at the moment.

When her gaze collided with his, she thought the man might burst into tears, too. The baby, a little boy she assumed based on the red airplanes on his sleeper, stared at her with big blue eyes in a wet red face. He hiccupped, then dropped his head to the cowboy's shoulder and resumed his protest. Sympathy welled up within her for both of them.

"Mr. Colton?" She pitched her voice just loud enough to be heard over the squalling.

"Yes."

"I don't mean to interrupt. I'm Kelsey Lauder. We had an interview—"

He closed his eyes. His lips moved, in prayer or curse, she couldn't know. Shifting the baby to his left arm, he offered her his right hand, but the baby's displeasure continued. "I forgot all about it." He winced as the baby arched and screeched louder still.

"I'd invite you in, but the smart move is to come back another day. Can you email me with a few options?"

Technically, yes. "Um…is your wife out?" she asked

instead. The idea of hiking back to her car in the dark held zero appeal.

"Not married. This is..." His voice trailed off as he gently rocked the baby in his arm in a fruitless attempt to settle him. "Well, there isn't an easy explanation."

She'd come prepared to prove herself an asset to his horse breeding program. How to offer help with the baby without overstepping or offending? "I've had some experience with kids." His dark eyebrows lifted. Skepticism or hope? "Lots of younger siblings," she explained.

"There were a couple of stints as a nanny on your résumé," he recalled.

"You're right." Babysitting and child care were the jobs she'd been most qualified for during her high school and college years. She moved back and invited him onto the porch. "It's cooler out here," she said.

"Aren't babies supposed to be kept warm?" he asked, stepping out.

The squirming baby had lost a sock and if the blanket was meant to do anything, it was too twisted and bunched between them to be effective. "I think a few minutes in the cooler air might be more help to both of you," she told him. "May I, Mr. Colton?" she asked, reaching for the baby.

"Call me Fox," he said, handing her the little boy.

Kelsey crooned to the child as she cradled him in the crook of her elbow. She blotted the tears from his chubby cheeks and let him suck on her knuckle when he turned his head. "Aww. Are you hungry, little man?"

The baby's cries eased, subsiding to a snuffle and smaller whimpers.

Fox's eyes were wide. "How'd you do that?"

"Practice." She laughed as he chomped on her finger. "He might be teething, too. What's his name?"

"He doesn't have one." Fox pushed a hand through his hair, the other holding tightly to the baby's blanket. He really did need someone to shape up that thick mass of hair. Was he growing the beard for winter, or too distracted to shave? "Well, he probably does, but whoever left him with me didn't share it."

She had no idea what he was talking about and she'd learned it was easier to keep a babysitting job when she didn't ask probing personal questions. "Do you have formula or any supplies?" She could tell by touch that a diaper change was in order once the baby cooled off a little.

"Yes, there was formula in the bag." He turned toward the open door. "It's upstairs."

"Do you think we might talk about the consulting position while he eats?"

"You'd do that?" The relief in his voice nearly made her laugh.

"You're not the first father I've rescued."

"I'm not the father at all," he said sharply.

Great, she'd offended him. "Pardon me, I—"

"No, no. I was out of line." He opened the front door and held it for her. "My brother's wife had a baby yesterday, no, the day before." He scratched his jawline. "I was up late with them. Then a full day of managing both his property and mine ended with finding this little guy on my doorstep. I'd like to say it's a long story, but it isn't. I was headed for bed and found him down here. I don't know why anyone would leave him with me. I'm… I, um, I haven't—"

"You don't need to explain anything." She didn't

want the gory details about his love life, or to hear why someone thought he should suddenly be on dad duty.

The baby had already dented the mystique of Fox Colton that she'd built up in her head. She'd turned him into the superhero of equine genetics and breeding. His reputation and success had been a big factor in how she'd planned her academic focus and mapped out her career.

She paused just inside the door in what appeared to be a cross between a lobby and a foyer. The floor was stained cement and a coat rack and bench to her left offered room to stow barn boots and coats. Just beyond the bench, a wide glass door was etched with the company logo at the center, artistically flanked by horses in various stages of a gallop. A stairwell bumped against the right wall to a landing before continuing up the longer back wall of the barn to loft that overlooked the foyer. There was another door up there.

"Everything he arrived with is upstairs in the house," Fox said, starting up the stairs. "This way."

"You live here, too?" She followed him upstairs, the baby still mouthing her knuckle. The reprieve wouldn't last much longer.

"It was the perfect place for the office," he said. "Easy access to the barns. I didn't want to build something new when everything I needed was right here. Just a little reconfiguring, some patience and more elbow grease." He looked around as if seeing it for the first time. "The house isn't huge, but I can't beat the commute."

"I guess not."

With the baby quieting down, she counted it a plus to make it into the house. Hurdle one, clear. She noted the gleam on the hardwood floors, a built-in shoe bench with cubbies above and below and hooks on one side. Had he built that himself?

"Do you want me to take off my shoes?" They were dusty from her long hike across his property.

He glanced down, frowned a little and shook his head. Was he that reluctant to hold the baby again?

As she followed him out of the foyer, she noticed the wall that stretched the width of the barn was actually lined with upper and lower cabinets and a narrow countertop in warm, golden granite. She barely had time to appreciate the use of space as his home simply opened up in front of her.

A full kitchen with more of that wonderful granite took up one wall, separated from the rest of the open living space by an island that could seat four people comfortably. She saw a dining table that might be an antique, or designed to look that way, and a seating area situated around a fireplace and a big-screen television.

The decor was streamlined and masculine without being stark. Homey, she thought as scents of leather and coffee drifted through the air. "Hungry, you said?"

On the kitchen counter near the sink, she saw a diaper bag, two bottles and a can of formula. Kelsey talked him through making a bottle while she changed the baby into a fresh diaper and clean clothes. To her, the infant didn't look much like Fox, so it was easy enough to believe his claim that the child wasn't his.

His personal life wasn't any of her business. All she wanted was the chance to work with him through the coming season, preferably longer.

"You have a beautiful home," she said, giving the baby his bottle. His eagerness made her smile.

"You're a miracle worker," Fox said with relief.

"It's only experience," she replied.

"Would that be easier if you sat down? Please, make yourself comfortable."

She chose one of the chairs near the fireplace and focused on the baby rather than the man. Something in the way he moved made her belly quiver with nerves that had nothing to do with the interview. She understood his approach and agreed with his philosophy of breeding sound and healthy animals, rather than for just speed. He didn't know her yet, so he couldn't know just how compatible they were professionally. It was the rest of him that caught her off guard. The tall stature, that weary gaze, those big, strong hands that stirred up a desire she'd let go dormant. She had to get control of herself before all of that longing flared to life in bright color on her face. The curse of her fair, freckled complexion.

"You said you had younger siblings?" he asked.

She pounced on the distraction. "Yes. I'm from a big family." She hoped this might be the start of an interview, as long as he didn't try to hire her as a nanny. "Caring for our younger siblings was expected."

"Did you resent it?" He sat down on a counter stool.

"Only once in a while," she replied. Before she'd discovered there was more to life, she'd been quite content to obey and cooperate and generally toe the family line.

He chuckled. "I understand. I was one of seven."

He must have come along too late in the birth order to learn much about infants. "Well, your unexpected guest here is growing fast. And possibly cutting his first tooth."

He groaned. "My little sister's baby is two years old now. She had a rough time when her teeth came in."

"Teething becomes a struggle for everyone," Kelsey agreed. Fortunately a couple of her last nanny posts were for preschoolers, so teething wasn't an issue. "If there was a nanny union, trust me, we'd negotiate for hazard pay."

"If it means avoiding more agonizing hours like this last one, I'd meet all of your demands." He sat forward. "Why did you miss the interview we had scheduled?"

She started to mention the email and voice mail she'd sent and stopped. Criticizing the boss wasn't the best way to get acquainted. "Car trouble. My apologies." The baby kicked and gurgled and she pulled the bottle out of his reach while he amused himself with the tassel on her jacket zipper.

"Shouldn't he finish?" Fox asked.

"He will," she assured him. Within a minute, the baby was reaching for the bottle again.

Fox cleared his throat. "I reviewed your résumé a few days ago. I know you're not here for a nanny position, but you can see I'm in a bind. Kids aren't…" He stopped cleared his throat. "I could use the help while I track down his real family. I'm not sure why he was left at my door, but I can't manage him alone."

So he was more afraid of the baby than of her. More likely he was afraid of what he didn't know about the baby. He wouldn't be the first dad she'd worked for who felt overwhelmed by the task.

"I made the trek out here to work with you, specifically on the genetics and bloodstock advising."

"And I'm looking forward to having you on board, in the lab and the barn," he replied.

Another surprise. She had arguments ready to convince him about what she could bring to his business. After missing the interview, she'd worried that wouldn't be enough. He needed an assistant and she needed a mental and professional challenge. The big sky and wide-open spaces where no one from her past could interfere with her plans and dreams were the perfect bonus. She lifted the baby to her shoulder and patted his back until he belched. They both laughed and the baby grinned. He was beyond cute when he wasn't screaming. Then again, most babies were. Fox's deep chuckle put a sparkle in his eye. It was improbable to think he loved the baby, but she could see he already cared.

"Your credentials in your field are remarkable, Miss Lauder."

"Call me Kelsey," she said as the baby took the bottle again.

"Kelsey, the job you came for is yours, whether or not you help with the baby. While he's only here temporarily, he will be around the house and the office. Foster care is a last resort."

Heat flooding her cheeks, she kept her head down, reeling from the way he said her name. This rush of awareness dancing through her system had never been so acute. She had a job—*the* job that could make her career—and she couldn't quite process the accomplishment because of her attraction to her new boss. Who was now off-limits.

"Baby John is only temporary," he repeated. "I'll find someone else if you'd rather not take on the nanny role."

"You said you didn't know his name," she said.

Fox's gaze rested on the infant, who was almost dozing now. "Baby John Doe." He shrugged. "Just until we find his parents."

The name made sense in a sad way. "How do you see the hours going? If I took on both roles," she clarified. She'd worked both live-in child care and hourly. Would he put her up in one of the bunkhouses on the ranch to be close? That would be a big financial perk. Or would she need to find an apartment and a reliable car in a hurry?

"To start, I'd want you to primarily be on baby detail and get acclimated with the ranch routine and business as time allows. I don't want to run you ragged."

"I've never been afraid of hard work," she assured him. Slowly, she drew the empty bottle from the baby's mouth and maneuvered him to get another small burp. He snuggled against her shoulder, his downy hair tickling her skin.

"That was immediately clear on your résumé. Not many people can be employed full-time and maintain the GPA you held in school.

"I'll pay you a competitive salary for each position."

She couldn't have heard him correctly. It took every ounce of her self-control to keep still for the baby.

"Once Baby John is settled with his family," Fox continued, "we'll cut that back to the consulting position. In the meantime, if you're comfortable with it, I'd like you to stay here. Consider the room and board a benefit in addition to your pay."

Maybe she was addled from walking and the stress of being late, but this offer had escalated quickly. She couldn't say no.

"Room and board and one salary is plenty," she began. "I—"

Fox sat up straight, his palms flat on strong thighs. "I need you to say yes. You'll be paid well for both positions," he reiterated. "It will make up for the fact that my house only has one bathroom."

He looked so sheepish about it, she wanted to laugh. "Then yes." In her wildest dreams she hadn't imagined the interview going this well. As the baby dozed on her shoulder, she shifted the conversation toward his breeding program and the number of foals he expected in the spring.

Her heart soared to be having an engaging, animated discussion with her professional idol even as she held someone else's infant in her arms.

"Is there a bed for him?" she asked. "It's better if he can sleep on his own, even for short naps." Better for both baby and caregiver.

"I'll give you the full tour." He motioned for her to follow him down a hallway and into a neat guest room. Bookshelves flanked the bed and a recliner upholstered in weathered leather had been tucked into the corner near the window. "This can be your room for the duration. Hang on."

She waited, then stepped aside as he returned with a bulky rectangular object.

"I used this for his bed." He settled the box into the corner by the closet and adjusted the quilt he'd used to pad it so it couldn't bunch up as the baby slept. "Unless you think it's unsafe."

"No, it's clever," she said, admiring his ingenuity. "I never would've thought to repurpose a hay bin for a crib." She settled Baby John Doe into the makeshift crib and breathed a sigh of relief when he didn't wake up.

"It's clean." He started forward and stopped himself. "And it rocks a little, too."

Kelsey obliged, rocking the hay bin, though the baby was out cold. "I bet he'll be a good sleeper," she murmured when they were back in the hall. "Do you have a baby monitor?" He shook his head, so she left the door cracked to be sure she heard the infant when he woke.

"Bathroom's right here." Fox reached into the open doorway and flipped the light switch.

She peeked in to see a well-designed bathroom space with all the necessities in upgraded finishes. "Two sinks? Smart."

"When I didn't add a second bathroom to the floorplan my sister, Sloane, insisted on two sinks."

"She lived with you?"

"No, but she harbors hope that eventually another woman will." He looked at her, his eyebrows drawing together. "I guess she was right."

Kelsey grinned, understanding sibling dynamics. "Since I'm only temporary, it's up to you how right she is."

His smile was slow with an ornery tilt and then it was gone. "Will it be a problem sharing a room with the baby?"

"Not at all." The baby would be a more congenial roommate than her last two had been. The guest room was a vast improvement over the cramped lab tech housing in the dorm she'd left behind. Sharing a bathroom with only one adult? This might be the best corporate housing ever.

"Thanks, Kelsey. I really appreciate this." When

they were back in the main room, he said, "Did you need to cancel a hotel reservation?"

"Oh, I hadn't found a motel." She laced her fingers together to keep her hands still.

"Perfect." He started for the door. "I'll help you bring in your things."

"Wait. My stuff is still in my car, which broke down. That's why I was late," she reminded him.

He glanced to the front door, though he couldn't see the driveway from here. "Oh. I assumed…"

"The car is a few miles east of town. I grabbed a ride part of the way and walked the rest."

His eyebrows shot up to his hairline. "You *walked*?"

"The rideshare app didn't have anyone available," she said, waving off his concern. "The car is safely on the shoulder. It's too dark to head out there now. It can wait until tomorrow."

"All right." He checked the windows and released a breath. "I guess we'd better find food for the two of us."

Her stomach growled, and his grin flashed again. It was amazing to feel both safe and valued. To be employed twice over. Though she'd learned to protect herself through the years, living under Fox's roof gave her an extra layer of security she appreciated right now.

Chapter 2

Hours later, after they'd demolished a couple of burgers and a salad, Fox watched as Kelsey sat on the floor in front of his fireplace. She changed the baby into a clean diaper and pajamas at light speed. It didn't seem to impede *her* progress when the baby kicked his legs or tried to roll one way or another.

Her sleek, strawberry-blond hair was still locked into a bun at the back of her head and he wondered how long it was when it was loose. She was a petite thing, with big hazel eyes in a pixie's face. He'd studied her résumé and read through the positive letters of reference from labs and stables alike. She exuded strength of character as well as physical confidence. Whatever had brought her to his door, he counted himself extremely lucky.

She bumped her nose to the baby's and then did

something with the last clean blanket that calmed Baby John instantly. When she lifted him to the crook of her arm he was wholly content.

"He looks like a baby burrito," Fox observed wryly.

She put the baby into his arms. "Swaddling is the technical term," she said, her voice as light and soft as a cloud. "But baby burrito works." She cleaned up everything and went to wash her hands. "Be right back."

He stared down into the baby's blue eyes. Was this one of his brother's children?

"I tossed in a load of his laundry so we have clean clothing for tomorrow," she said when she returned. "Want me to take him?"

Yes. No. Fox held on for the moment, more relaxed now that he had some help. He'd never known how soothing and right it felt to hold a happy infant. He didn't remember days like this with Sloane's daughter. His niece was like a hummingbird, always on the move or chattering. Often at a volume that made his ears cringe. "I looked up swaddling online. They make it look easy in the videos."

The baby yawned and scrunched up his mouth. Fox panicked, standing up and striding to Kelsey. "What does he need?"

"Probably this." Kelsey popped the pacifier into the little guy's mouth.

"Probably *you*," Fox said, handing the baby back into the arms of the expert.

He stared at her, openly in awe of her skills with the baby. She made child care look more like child's play. "How do you know what to do and when?"

He peered over her shoulder into the infant's drowsy

eyes. Baby John yawned again and then worked the pacifier.

"Years of practice," she said, rubbing the baby's back while she held him close.

"You don't look old enough to be Mary Poppins."

According to her résumé, she'd had two jobs as a nanny during her undergraduate years and occasional stints of child care between internships while she finished her master's degree.

"Brilliant *and* funny," she mused. "Good qualities in a boss."

He hadn't really been joking. According to her bio, she'd just turned thirty. Maybe dealing with babies had more to do with some innate female intuition than women wanted to admit. He wasn't about to say that out loud and have her walk out on him.

"I wish I knew how to find his family." He walked over and stared out the big windows that overlooked the nearby paddock. He could just make out the lights in the bunkhouse beyond the barn. "Someone has to be missing him."

"That doesn't mean someone wants him back," Kelsey murmured.

"I guess you're right." He hadn't thought of it that way. Should have. Hell, he hadn't had much time to *think* at all since taking the baby in. "I assumed the mother dropped him here, though I don't have any reason for that assumption other than the way he arrived." And now he had Deputy Bloom's concern in his head, as well. What if Baby John's mother was a victim of the Avalanche Killer?

"How was he dropped off?" Kelsey asked.

"He was bundled up in a car seat. The diaper bag

was stocked. He was clean." The baby had smelled like his niece just out of the tub. He hadn't made that connection until just now.

"So the basics of food, clothing and safety were met?"

"Yes. My first thought was that the baby was supposed to be dropped off at Wyatt's place."

"Why?"

"Because he's my brother. Deliveries frequently get messed up between his address and mine." He laughed. "And because his wife just delivered a baby boy. The day before this little guy showed up."

Kelsey smiled. "Logical."

He grinned down at her. They both knew it wasn't the least bit logical.

"He's out," she whispered. "I'll go put him to bed."

"He'll cry," Fox warned. Last night his heart had broken a little more every time the baby fussed. Although he'd napped quietly for a couple of hours while they'd eaten dinner and discussed horses. He and Kelsey had similar philosophies about breeding, and she was as familiar with his primary goal to breed a healthier quarter horse for ranchers as he was.

"We'll figure it out," she promised.

Her confidence balanced his lack thereof. She headed down the hall and he went to the kitchen for a beer. When she came back, only silence behind her, he shook his head.

"Miracle worker."

"I'm not," she insisted. "You just have a tired, content baby."

"Want a beer?"

"No thanks." She walked around him and poured

herself a glass of water instead. "Did you notify the authorities when he showed up?"

He was pleased she was already so at home in his house. "Yes." It helped to have someone to talk with, even if she was mostly a stranger. Except she felt like a friend after the time he'd spent reviewing her résumé. "I went straight to the sheriff's office. Fortunately or not, depending on your viewpoint, no one in the area has reported a missing baby."

"I'm surprised they didn't take him off your hands."

"They tried." Goose bumps rose on his arms and he rode out the chill that followed. "Sheriff Colton—he's a cousin—told me they'd call in child services to take care of him. But it felt wrong." He couldn't meet her gaze, unwilling to bare his soul completely. "Someone left him here, on the Crooked C. Everyone knows this is Colton property. I couldn't turn around and hand him over to strangers."

"I'm not judging you," she said so low he thought he'd imagined it. "I expect the sheriff was confident you could handle it."

Fox laughed. "Feel free to call and tell him the truth."

Her smile radiated equal parts amusement and acceptance. He hadn't seen that kind of look aimed his way since he was a kid.

"It's not considered news anymore, but my sister and I were adopted by Russ and Mara Colton when my parents died. Mara was my mom's older sister. She and Russ took us in rather than let us go into foster care."

"I'm sorry for your loss. The change must have been a relief as well as a challenge."

"Exactly both. They kept us with family and raised

us as if we were theirs from the start." There were inevitable differences between his parents and Mara and Russ, but he'd always felt awkward and ungrateful when he dwelled on them.

"And you wanted the same for Baby John."

"Family is important..." His voice trailed off as a wealth of painful old memories and newfound worries assailed him. His dad hadn't been the best example of patience and kindness. Fox couldn't help wondering if and when he might snap and do the wrong thing. "If he's a Colton we need to know. I'll start asking my brothers tomorrow."

"Asking is a good start, but why not run the DNA?" she queried.

"I should've thought of that." Proving he *wasn't* the father might light a fire under Trey to launch an investigation into the baby's real parents.

"Hard to see clearly when you're up to your eyeballs in a problem," Kelsey said.

"True." He smoothed a hand over his beard. "I'll get the ball rolling on the DNA testing first thing tomorrow." He'd have to call in a favor with the lab he used, but that wasn't much of a hurdle. "Unless one of my brothers owns up to this, I can strong-arm all three of them for a cheek swab."

"And a finger-stick," she said. "The blood test could rule someone out right away." Color stained her cheeks. "Not to imply your brothers would lie about the baby."

"No offense taken." He stood, pacing over to bank the fire for the night. "Going solely off his note-free arrival on my doorstep, it's a good guess the mother didn't tell the biological father about the baby."

Deputy Bloom's theory echoed in his head again.

There was a murderer on the loose in Roaring Springs. What if the mother had in fact been taken by the Avalanche Killer? Unnerving to think a killer might have been at his door. Then again, why would a cold-blooded murderer bother to spare a child?

He felt Kelsey's gaze on him as he moved about the room, but she didn't say a word. The quiet was such a relief. For Baby John as much as for him.

"I do like kids," he blurted.

"Good to know."

"I'm just better with them, more comfortable, when the parents are around."

"I understand that," she said with a soft chuckle. "Babies are demanding, even if the list is a short one."

"Thanks for giving me a pass." He wasn't sure he deserved it. But he didn't want her to think poorly of him, especially since he was going to be her boss.

"Thanks for giving me a job," she replied. "Two, really, along with great accommodations."

Her smile lit up the room, easing the exhaustion and burden of not knowing how to help the small human now resting peacefully in the hay-bin cradle in the other room.

"I know it's not what you came for," Fox began, "but would you help me unravel the DNA trail and find his father?"

"You want my help on that, too?"

He was asking too much. "It was your idea," he reminded her. "Not as fast as blood tests, but far more conclusive. Please?" he added. "With a certified nanny on board, the sheriff will give me more time before forcing the foster care issue." If Trey knew about his dad's lousy habits with kids, he'd be watching for Fox to screw up.

"Your lab downstairs can handle that kind of sampling?" she queried, her eyes bright with excitement.

"We can run preliminary tests at the office, but a full DNA panel would need to be sent out for a confident result."

"I see." The sparkle in her hazel eyes dimmed just a bit.

He felt ridiculous pressure to bring it back. "I'll get the samples and the blood tests of course." He'd need to talk with each of his brothers privately. "It's outside the scope of what brought you here—"

"Working alongside you is what brought me here, Fox. If finding the father is where you need my help in the lab, I'm game."

What star had he wished on to have this beautiful woman, so eager and assured, show up on his doorstep exactly when he needed an ally?

"We might be able to get help from the FBI lab," he said, thinking out loud. "I don't have any proof that the baby is tied to a major case, but they can't prove he's not."

"You don't mean the Avalanche Killer?" She curled into the corner of the couch, wrapping her arm around her legs.

"You've heard about the case?"

"Hard to avoid it," she said. "It's national news."

"And you walked around alone out here anyway?"

"I'm small but mighty." She raised an arm and flexed her biceps. The effect wasn't as impressive since any muscle on her trim frame was hidden by the chunky sweater she wore.

"Have to take your word for it," he said gruffly.

"You'll see. We didn't go over this yet, but will I be helping you with the horses directly?" she inquired.

What kind of a boss did she think he was? "Managing the baby and getting up to speed on the breeding program should keep you busy enough to start," he said. "We can take a full tour of the office and barns in the morning."

"I'm up for anything."

He could tell she meant it. If only he could promise her that anything didn't include looming family drama as they tracked down an unsuspecting father.

Careful not to break out into a happy dance, Kelsey took her glass to the kitchen. What a difference twenty-four hours made. Her feet and legs were achy from the long walk and she was running on fumes, but nothing could dim her bright inner glow as she prepared a bottle for the baby's next feeding.

She floated through the kitchen, moving baby laundry from the washer to the dryer on a cloud of accomplishment and pride. The great Fox Colton wanted *her*—unknown geneticist Kelsey Lauder—to assist his famous breeding program. This sort of collaboration would define her career.

Actually being hired was *better* than any of the positive-outcome scenarios she'd envisioned time and again on the long, solitary drive to Roaring Springs. Every step of the process between sending her introductory email to Fox to leaving her last assignment to standing on his doorstep had been worth it.

The baby had helped her cause, no doubt. While Fox wouldn't have invited her to stay in his wonderful house without the baby, deep down she was confident that he would have still hired her based solely on her academic merit. That realization eased the small sting of being a nanny yet again. Every time she found herself in the child care role she told herself it was the last time.

One of these days it *would* be true.

As much as she enjoyed children, babysitting jobs tweaked her old insecurities. Still, she reminded herself that her brain wouldn't shrivel, her knowledge wouldn't go unused simply because she kept this sweet baby happy and fed for a few days or weeks. Fox had given his word that caring for the little guy was temporary. She believed him. His heart was in the right place, taking in the child when he could've handed over the baby to an agency. That decision only reinforced her opinions of his character.

"You look ready to drop." Fox's deep, masculine voice snapped her out of her thoughts. "I guess that was rude," he added.

"I'm sure it's true." Even her hair felt weary. Shaking her head, she smiled. "I'm tired, yes, but more than thrilled to be here. I've admired your work for years and can't wait to get started."

He raised his beer in a toast. "Here's hoping reality isn't a crushing disappointment."

"Not a chance." She'd survived crushing disappointment and changed her entire life to overcome it. She didn't expect Fox to be a saint. If he'd been cruel to the animals in his breeding program, word would've gotten out by now.

"We'll do great work," she said.

"I've never shared the office with anyone." He

picked at the label on the bottle. "You'll have to speak up if I hover or mutter while I read or whatever."

"I can do that." She wasn't sure how to fix the sudden awkwardness rising between them. "Many siblings, remember? I know how to express myself and ask for what I need."

He lifted his head and nodded slowly. "I preferred to fly under the radar."

"Ah." She knew the type, had lived with brothers who went about their chores intentionally avoiding any praise or criticism. Just do the work and move on to the fun stuff. "Better to ask forgiveness than permission?"

"Something like that." His lips kicked up in one corner. "Don't feel like you have to stay up and entertain me."

"Okay."

"Okay." He rinsed out the beer bottle and dropped it into the recycling bin under the sink. "I'm up at dawn with the horses. I'll try not to wake you."

She smiled. "Same," she said. At his confusion, she added, "I'll try to let you sleep when the baby gets me up in the night."

"Thanks. Good night."

For a several minutes she just stood in the kitchen, reveling again in how things had turned around for her. Tonight she'd sleep in a comfy bed at the ranch rather than in a low-rent motel room with a questionable lock on the door. Baby duty or not, she could actually let down her guard and rest.

She wanted to do a back flip or let loose a victory shout. Tomorrow, she promised herself with a smile, turning out the lights on her way to the bedroom.

Fox stepped into the hallway from the bathroom

and nearly ran into her. She took a quick step back, stifling a startled cry.

"Sorry!" he whispered. "It just occurred to me you don't have your things. What do you need for tonight?"

"I can manage until we get my suitcase," she replied.

He arched an eyebrow in disbelief.

"Fine." No sense arguing, the man needed sleep as much as she did. "It would be great if you had a spare toothbrush."

When she'd first left home, she kept a small toiletry kit in her purse, just in case she had to run. She'd given up the habit about five years ago, once she was confident she could hold her own if her brothers or anyone they sent found her.

Fox turned back to the bathroom and opened the bottom drawer. After a moment, he stood up and handed her a toothbrush still in the dentist's packaging.

"Thanks."

"Make yourself at home," he said. "I mean that sincerely. You have no idea how much you're helping me. Good night." He disappeared into his room.

Kelsey brushed her teeth and then walked into bedroom she shared with the baby. The hay bin crib had been inspired and the soft baby snores were calming. The little guy was so content. "Your temporary daddy has that effect," she whispered to the child.

She'd seen Fox in interviews and every animal he met seemed to fall in love with him. People, too. More than once she'd watched a reporter take aim with a hard question, but Fox never failed to diffuse any angst or tension with a thoughtful answer and that self-deprecating smile.

He was smitten with the baby even if he was overwhelmed by all the things he didn't know about caring for a child. From what she'd learned by following his career, he took pride in doing things right.

A shadow blotted out the faint light from the hallway. Fox held out a T-shirt. "So you don't have to sleep in your clothes."

"Thanks." Here he was, seeing to the details. The shirt was soft and she could already smell the faint scent of him on the fabric.

He shuffled his feet, hooking his hands in his back pockets. "You should let me take the night shift," he said.

"Absolutely not. You hired me for baby care and I'll handle it."

"You just got here," he protested.

"There's a first day with every job." She smiled when he frowned. "You'll be the first to know if I need a hand."

He stared at her for a long, tension-fraught moment, as if weighing her sincerity. "I suppose that works."

She slipped into the bedroom and closed the door before he could find another argument. Tomorrow she'd have her suitcase and the fresh start she'd been after would be completely underway.

Undressing, she pulled the T-shirt on over her head. The hem fell to her knees, but it was the scent of the man, masculine and clean, lingering in the fabric that put a zing in her blood. She nipped that feeling in a hurry. She might have idolized Fox and his successful breeding program, might have fantasized about a relationship with an honorable man like him, but he was her boss now. She couldn't afford to let her hormones screw up her perfect job.

Oh, that had a nice ring to it. A real job. With pay and benefits and, for the duration of the nanny portion of the program, room and board, too. No more temporary situations that meant relocating in three to six months. She would give him two years, minimum. Take a break from the constant search for the next post.

Slipping into bed, Kelsey sighed with contentment. This might well be her best night ever. Definitely her best night in recent months.

She was well and truly safe. The Crooked C ranch had clear boundaries and if a couple of her brothers, strangers in this area, showed up asking questions, they'd be noticed and reported. Wouldn't that be fabulous?

Tonight was better than her first night in the college dorm. Back then, thanks to keycards and security officers, she'd known her brothers couldn't come in and make a scene or drag her back home. Walking through the campus had felt less secure, but daylight and crowds of people had been her buffer.

They'd tried to isolate her more than once during her college years. Only her quick thinking, her reputation and the self-defense classes she chose enabled her to follow her dreams. Lying here now, she realized every restless night, every uncertainty had been worth it.

She curled to her side. Still free. And staying that way. Smiling, she closed her eyes and tried to get some sleep before the baby woke up again.

Fox heard the baby crying and rolled out of bed, more awake than asleep. He padded over to where the makeshift crib had been under his window. The baby wasn't there. That's right, he had help now. He had a nanny.

So why was the baby still crying?

He padded out of his room, following the hiccupping cries, the hardwood floors cool under his bare feet. The bathroom light was on and the guest room door was open. In the dim light he found Kelsey on the floor, singing a lullaby as she changed the baby's diaper.

The words slowly filtered through his sleep-hazed brain and he recognized an old church hymn.

She had a sweet voice, even at a whisper. He didn't want to scare her, but he didn't want to interrupt, either. He leaned against the doorjamb and listened.

The baby was running out of steam and Kelsey cuddled him close as she rolled to her feet. Tucking the pacifier into his mouth, she swayed side to side, keeping his face out of the light as she sang another verse.

He could watch her for hours. Days maybe. Time slowed down, and Fox savored every precious moment until she had the baby nestled into the bed once more.

She came toward the door, and Fox stepped out of her way. She wore the T-shirt he'd loaned her over the jeans she'd arrived in. The fabric was thin enough that he could see she hadn't put on her bra, and he averted his gaze. She was his employee twice over and being half-asleep wasn't an excuse to ogle her.

He was suddenly aware he didn't have anything on but an old pair of flannel pants.

"Sorry we woke you," she whispered.

His body was more than willing to have her wake him anytime. He ignored the flash of heat. *Employee.* It became a chant in his head. "You look different."

She twirled her finger in the air as if turning him around. “Go back to sleep before you can’t.”

It was her hair. Her hair was down and flowing loose around her shoulders in glossy strawberry-blond waves. “You’re good with him.”

She smiled, then pressed her finger to her lips in a sign for silence. “Sleep now, employee evaluation in the morning.”

She turned out the bathroom light and disappeared into the darkness of what would be her bedroom while the baby was here.

Leaving Fox alone in the dark hallway. If he went back to bed, he’d dream of her, assuming he could get back to sleep at all. If he dreamed of her, it would be even more awkward between them in the morning.

He returned to his room, grabbed his reading glasses and the latest veterinary science magazine.

Chapter 3

A few hours later, Kelsey heard Fox leave to tend the horses and dozed off until the baby started stirring. If Fox meant to take care of the infant for some time, a baby monitor would be a good investment. It wasn't exactly her business, but DNA tests took time. Unless someone claimed the baby right away, he needed some proper baby gear just to make things run smoothly.

She rolled out of bed and pulled on her jeans. Today, once the baby was settled, she'd get to see the Colton breeding operation live and in person. Grabbing her bra, she darted down the hall to the bathroom, taking a few minutes for herself before the baby got wound up.

Perfect timing as Baby John was testing out sounds and degrees of fussiness when she returned to the bedroom. The moment he saw her he grinned, kicking his feet. He was such a cute little guy, all smiles in the morning, though he was surely hungry and in need of a clean diaper.

When he was all set, she carried him out to the kitchen and saw a note from Fox. *Morning chores. Back soon. Bottle ready in the fridge.*

"Well, isn't your temporary daddy the best ever?" she cooed to the baby. When the bottle was warmed up, she found a spot in the family room to feed Baby John.

Fox walked back in just as the infant finished eating. "Perfect timing," she said to the baby, making him giggle.

"You two are up early," Fox said.

"It's a baby thing," she said. "You understand."

"I do, actually. Baby horses and baby people keep crazy hours." He walked over and the tyke reached for him. Fox tickled his tummy and they both grinned. "I was going to start on breakfast," he said, his gaze still on the baby.

The man was charmed whether or not he'd admit it. "I can make breakfast," she offered. "You fixed dinner last night."

"Nah, let me. It serves as a nice mental transition from chores to office work."

With a thousand questions about the horses circling in her head, she let him go. She could ask about horses at the barn or the office. Right now, she needed to broach the subject that the baby needed some additional supplies if they were going to make this arrangement work.

"Did you get coffee?" he asked.

"Not yet," she replied. Holding Baby John to her shoulder, she went to the coffeepot to pour.

Again Fox had anticipated and poured her a cup. "Cream or sugar?"

"First cup of the day is always black," she said.

"The better to kick it into high gear?"

"Absolutely." She sat down at the island and situated the baby so he could slap the countertop, her coffee cup well out of danger. "Bliss," she said when she got the first sip in.

"Did he keep you up all night?"

"Just that one time." She breathed in that sweet baby smell, the better to get her mind off Fox, shirtless. He hadn't earned those lean, ropy muscles sitting behind a desk. "I think he'll adapt to your schedule easily. He's a good sleeper."

Fox put sausage patties into a hot pan and while they sizzled and snapped, he cracked eggs into a bowl. "Do you have food allergies or anything you can't stand to eat?"

"No allergies, and I'll eat whatever you set in front of me." Growing up being picky meant going hungry. Her mother hadn't entertained complaints at the dinner table. She caught the baby's tiny hands in one of hers and took another gulp of coffee. "Have you given any thought to baby gear?"

Fox looked to the other end of the counter, then back to her. "What do we need beyond formula and diapers?"

"Clothing?" She arched a brow. "Maybe a seat to make feeding him easier. The car seat is okay, but he'll start on cereal soon and an easy-to-clean seat that stayed here would be ideal."

For several long minutes, Fox worked on their breakfast without saying a word. He set a plate of fried eggs, toast and sausage in front of her along with a fork and napkin. She just managed to turn the baby aside before he caught the lip of the plate.

"An easy-to-clean seat?" he asked. "You mean a high chair?"

She caught the distaste in his voice as he glared at the open end of the island. Her stomach rumbling, Kelsey got up and spread out a blanket on the floor and put Baby John down to play so she could eat while the food was hot.

"He's temporary," Fox stated in a clipped tone. "If you think we need a high chair, I'll call my sister and borrow hers."

"How old is your niece?" Kelsey asked.

"Two."

She doubted his sister was ready to part with the high chair, but maybe she had other items they could borrow. "I understand," she replied. "We don't need a big bulky high chair with all the bells and whistles, but a few items would streamline his care, especially when I'm putting in hours at the office."

He frowned at his plate and sliced off a bite of sausage with a bit more force than necessary. "What items are you thinking of?"

"A portable crib could help," she began. "And a bathtub. The diapers and formula of course. He needs a bowl and a spoon." She stopped talking when he stopped eating.

"Make a list," he said. "We'll go into town after I show you around the office and barns."

She wolfed down a few bites of her breakfast and insisted on handling the dishes, taking care of the chore in record time. When she had the list in her phone and her shoes on, Fox picked up her coat and the baby's quilted jumper.

"Do we need the seat?" he asked.

"I can manage him." She was much stronger than she looked thanks to years of yoga and martial arts training.

They headed downstairs and straight into the office space. With the lights on, the etched glass popped even more than it had last night. The space was a bigger footprint than his home and it made her smile. He invested according to what mattered most. She respected that.

There was plenty of room here for both of them to work and ample floor space for a portable crib or a blanket for the baby. The space he'd turned into a lab was really designed for one person at a time, but it was hard to complain about that. "It's amazing."

It was immediately clear where he worked, the papers and notes sorted into piles across the wide desktop, surrounding a laptop waiting to come to life. She imagined him right there, reading through lab results or journals on horse health advancements.

The baby seemed as curious as she did, taking it all in with wide blue eyes. Having nothing to go on but appearance, she couldn't match the child's features to Fox's.

Fox walked over and used a remote to turn on a wall-mounted monitor. The grainy security-type video showed the interior of the barn and horses in their stalls. Another camera gave her a view of horses in the closest paddock.

"What a great idea." She could hardly wait to get out there and see it all.

"Helps primarily during foaling," Fox said.

"I'm sure it does." He'd be able to see which mares were getting restless as labor started.

Fox led her out of the office and once she'd put on her coat she zipped the baby into the quilted jumper, pulling the hood over his little head. "Have you introduced him to the horses yet?"

"No."

She trailed behind him out onto the porch, waiting impatiently as he locked the door. They followed the drive she'd walked up yesterday to a track that led to the closest barn. Adjusting the baby in her arms, she asked questions about the number of mares in foal and what sort of work she'd be doing, other than seeing to the baby.

"Let me take him." Fox plucked him out of her arms without breaking stride before she could argue.

She didn't want to argue. She wanted to skip or run or just hug herself. Hug *him*. The sun was shining over a crisp autumn day and the horses in the paddock were in perfect health. A bay mare trotted toward them, clearly in love with Fox. She had a scar along her flank, but she moved with grace and pride.

"This is Mags," Fox said. "Short for Magnificent. She was a rescue. Past her breeding age, but she's a good influence on the herd and she's always up for a trail ride."

Mags let Kelsey stroke her nose and neck, arching into the touch. She sniffed and blew at Kelsey's bun and sent the baby a curious glance when he gurgled.

Fox pointed out the other mares in the paddock that had been successfully bred. "These are due for pregnancy verification this week."

"I can do that," she volunteered. Hope fizzled when he shook his head.

"You'll get your chance, I promise." He smiled as they walked toward the barn. "Just take some time to settle in. We have months left before foaling and I have calls coming in each week for consultations."

Mentally, she did a fist pump. This was exactly where she needed to be. The baby should have been getting sleepy by now, but he was wide-awake and taking it all in. "He loves making friends," she observed.

"Is that a good thing?"

"It certainly isn't a bad thing," she replied.

The barn, in golden oak and dark brown trim, was framed by the beautiful backdrop of the ranch landscape. This might be the finest barn she'd seen. The sweet scent of hay teased her nose as she walked along with Fox through a wide center aisle flanked by roomy stalls on both sides. Long faces leaned out here and there, eager for Fox's greeting. The building and paddock were as thoughtfully designed as everything else he had shown her so far.

"You know how to plan."

"Better to do things right," he replied, smoothing a hand up and down the white star on the long face of a chestnut mare.

"She's a beauty," Kelsey said, stepping close enough to slide her hand under the golden mane. "This is the coloring you're known for."

"As you know, I'd rather be known for a durable quarter horse, but as my brother Wyatt pointed out more than once, a showstopper is great publicity."

"From what I've heard, you've accomplished both."

"Is that what brought you?"

She felt his gaze on her and kept hers on the horse. "In part." She'd lost count of the many things that had brought her here. After her last unhappy encounter with her brothers, she couldn't even put the list into order of importance. She wanted to learn from Fox and get into the daily and seasonal routines of producing stunning, healthy livestock. She needed to establish a base, some permanence. At thirty she'd grown tired of her nomadic career and home life. "My recent work in labs has shown me how much I like to get my hands dirty."

Fox laughed and the baby, nearly asleep on his shoulder, gave a start. He fussed a bit so Kelsey moved to take him. "He needs to be changed." She bounced him gently. "And he'll probably take a good nap after all this fresh air."

They'd walked a full circle and came up to his house from the far side. He had a brick patio outfitted with an ironwork table and chairs under a pergola and a big grill off to the side. She was surprised to see a playset in the grass nearby until she remembered his mention of a niece. So maybe he wasn't really afraid of children in general.

She held Baby John while he unlocked the back door, and they went upstairs. Having changed the baby's diaper, the little guy wasn't quite ready to sleep. Cradling him against her shoulder, she returned to the main room to find Fox staring out the window.

"If you want to go down to the office, I'll join you when he's asleep."

"You think he'll sleep in the truck?" he asked. "He's been quiet for two trips so far. We should go out and take care of your car, pick up your things and then the baby stuff, too."

"That would be fantastic if you're sure we have the time."

"We have the time." He picked up his jacket but didn't put it on.

They were locking up the front door when she realized her keys weren't in her pocket. Dang it. This oversight wouldn't help her prove herself as a competent and efficient caregiver and assistant. "I left my car keys upstairs."

"No problem." Fox reached out and took the baby. "Go on and grab them," he said. "I'll load him up."

On a quick apology, she dashed up the stairs and hurried back down again. Fox was walking along, talking to the baby boy in his arms about the sky and trees and the grass.

"Ready," she said.

Fox swiveled around and her breath caught. He and Baby John made a picture, the sunlight bathing both of them in a healthy glow. He was sinfully handsome with a sharp mind, a kind heart and gentle, capable hands.

She'd spent so much time focused on her independence she'd ruthlessly pruned all fantasies of domestic bliss from her imagination. But this? This vision could become her ideal. Not the specific pair in front of her—she wasn't foolish enough to set her sights on this particular man and the baby that wasn't his. She'd come here for a mentor. Better to keep things professional on that front. It had to be the generalities putting this unexpected flutter in her belly.

"We survived an entire minute without crying," Fox

said, a lopsided grin on his face. "I think he'd give you an A+ for teaching skills."

"As long as you're more comfortable with him, that's the real win." She shoved her hands into her pockets and wrapped her fingers around the car keys before walking over and opening the back door of the truck.

"I'll let you load him in." Fox handed her the baby and pulled the cotton blanket from his shoulder, revealing evidence of a productive baby burp. "Just let me grab a clean shirt."

She smiled to herself as he strode back inside the house.

Fox couldn't help noticing how effortlessly Kelsey managed everything the baby needed. It was hard not to resent her efficiency, even though that was exactly why he'd hired her. "You make it all look so easy," he said.

She glanced at him as he put the truck into gear and the flash of confusion in her hazel eyes quickly gave way to amusement. "Practice," she informed him. "That's all."

He liked her calm composure and her gentle, warm approach with the baby. And the horses. He wasn't looking for her to aim that generous spirit or those wide beautiful eyes at him personally. She was here to do a job. He couldn't trust himself with a baby, despite the assistance of the internet. It was highly unlikely, if he scared off Kelsey, that another capable nanny would wander up to the house.

Making a decision on the fly was a rare thing for him. He prided himself on thinking things through, exploring all the angles. But last night, he'd gone with his gut and it seemed to be the right call. Only time would tell if she held up to the breeding work, as well.

"Have you done any breeding?" he asked.

She sputtered and her pretty mouth dropped open and snapped closed again as she stared at him. "Beg pardon?"

He replayed the last few seconds in his mind and smothered a curse. "Horse breeding," he clarified, his face reddening. "Have you done any fieldwork with *horse* breeding?"

She toyed with the cuff of her jacket. "Only with the big animal veterinarians in college," she replied. "Most of my recent experience is in the lab, analyzing data, writing up reports."

"What about not-so-recent experience?"

She twisted in the seat to check on the baby, giving him a big, cheesy smile, but Fox sensed she was stalling. Then again, reading people wasn't his strong suit.

"I grew up on a working farm in a remote area north of here," she replied, facing forward again.

If only that narrowed it down. There were miles of remote areas north of the Crooked C ranch. He would've pressed, but it seemed rude, since clearly she wanted to drop the subject.

He followed her directions to her car and checked the odometer when they finally found it. "You walked nearly eight miles yesterday?" The Avalanche Killer was still out there doing heinous things.

"I caught a ride for most of the way," she said with casual ease. "Worth it since I'm working with the famous Fox Colton."

As a nanny. Which, having reviewed her background again this morning, was a position for which she was vastly overqualified. He'd make it up to her, starting with her car. He trailed behind her as she opened the trunk of a faded blue compact sedan that had seen better days. "We'll load up your things and then I'll—"

She slammed the trunk lid, frowned and leaned all her weight on it in a hard push until the latch caught. "Got it." She smiled. "It's finicky."

"Where's the rest?" He watched her sling a leather computer bag over her shoulder and roll a large wheeled hard-sided suitcase toward the back of his truck. He jumped into action, lowering the tailgate to load the suitcase into the truck bed. She wisely carried her computer to the cab and tucked it behind her seat.

"That's…everything?" She was thirty years old. Shouldn't there be boxes or books or gear of some kind?

"Yes. This is it." Her mouth pulled to the side. "Don't be so shocked. I've lived in dorms and guest quarters for several years now."

"But—" He'd been in college, worked a few internships along the way. Having stuff was counterintuitive to being comfortable in tight quarters. Still, he'd never traveled this lightly and he was a man.

"You'd be surprised how much I can fit into that suitcase. Less stuff makes it easier to move when I have to."

"Sure." Her situation prior to her employment with him was none of his business. "You're right." He backed away from her, resisting the strange urge to right some unseen wrong. He took pictures of her car and license plate and called the garage in town.

Once he'd arranged for the tow truck, he gave his

phone number and authorized the shop to charge the repairs to his account. He gave the car one more hard study before climbing back into the truck. Might be better to sell it for parts if Kelsey was willing. With what he intended to pay her, she could buy a vehicle better suited to the ranch and the rugged Colorado terrain.

He turned toward town, eager to put her car in the rearview until he remembered their next stop wasn't the office, but the baby store. "You can use one of the ranch trucks while they fix your car," he said.

"That's really generous," she replied. "I appreciate it."

"I gave the garage my phone number."

"Oh, I should have thought of that."

"It's not like you won't be within reach when they call." His palms itched at another poor choice of words. Admittedly, his new *assistant* and *nanny* had a sweet and wholesome beauty. Although they'd be working closely, she couldn't be within his literal reach. The wayward thoughts only proved he'd gone too long without a date. Forget the sex—the lack of dating let him fall out of the practice of having a casual, appropriate conversation with a woman.

"Did you bring the nursery list?" he asked. "I still can't believe I'm doing this."

"It's on my phone," she replied. "I promise to make it as painless as possible. With the right things on hand, it will be so much easier to care for Baby John. Do you have a budget in mind? Some things on my list are handy, not necessities."

"Whatever he needs," Fox said. "Whatever you want. Don't worry about the money."

"That's not the only factor."

He rolled his shoulders, but the tight muscles wouldn't loosen. Why would someone drop this kid at his door? "Like you said, I can pass on the gear to the real father when we find him."

"Mmm-hmm."

"What does that mean?" he demanded as he pulled into a parking space in front of the store. "I'm not good at this."

"Talking?" she queried.

"Yeah." It was at the top of the list of things he handled poorly.

Her auburn eyebrows, several shades darker than her hair, scrunched up when she frowned. It was pretty cute instead of intimidating. He should *not* be noticing those details and he absolutely shouldn't be charmed by them.

"You're great at talking. I've seen videos of your lectures."

"I can talk horses and genetics until people pass out from boredom. People themselves, small talk and all the rest of it, I'd rather avoid," he confessed.

"Wow." She blinked several times. "That's… Wow."

He decided he didn't want any clarification on the "wow." "I'm overtired and overwhelmed." He took a deep breath. "Like I said, don't worry about the budget. Let's just get in there, do what needs done and get back to the ranch."

She straightened her shoulders so abruptly he thought she might give him a salute. "Count on me."

He carried Baby John in the car seat, hoping that would make it easier for her to gather what she deemed necessary for baby care. He sure didn't know the difference between one type of bottle and another or the benefit of zipper pajamas over the ones with a thousand snaps.

The last time he'd been this close to baby gear was when his sister had been expecting. For Wyatt and Bailey, he'd shopped online and had the gift and a gift card delivered to their house. He'd never thought he'd be bringing baby gear into his home.

He followed Kelsey through the store section by section as she added items to the cart. This wasn't at all how he'd shop for a baby, given the choice. This wasn't how he'd do anything, actually. He preferred to research, skim consumer reviews and dig deep into product testing and results. After several minutes of watching her, he realized she wasn't just shopping according to her list. She seemed to be mentally going through her anticipation of Baby John's day. She chose more bottles, similar to what had been dropped off with him. She found diapers in his size and picked up a box of the next size up. They had a quick debate about the convenience and necessity of a changing table. He finally agreed because it looked like the shelves would be a good place to stow the baby's supplies.

Cruising through the bedding options, she turned to him. "I don't think you should invest in a real crib and he's too big for a cradle."

"You want to keep him in the hay bin?"

"No." She drew out the word and then her rosy lips pursed. "I'm thinking one of these things."

He belatedly realized they were standing in front of a display of portable cribs that boasted all sorts of features and colors. He wanted to cover his eyes or run away.

"It's safe, removes the hassle of assembling a real crib and we can take it to and from the office. Also saves you money and a potential fight later."

"Fight?" What the hell was she talking about?

"Well, the safe bet is that someday your wife will want to decorate a nursery without hand-me-downs."

"I'm not married." Wives typically expected children and he had no intention of taking that leap.

Kelsey cocked her head. "Not now. I just..."

He latched onto the more immediate concern of having the baby in the office. "Get two," he said brusquely. "One for the nursery and one for the office. We'll get tired of packing up that thing and hauling it up and down the stairs."

Her lips parted and closed. "Okay. Do you have a color preference?"

"Lady's choice."

"All right."

As she turned around to study the options, *he* studied the mass of glossy, rose-gold hair that was twisted into a bun and secured just above the column of her neck. Her skin reminded him of sweet cream. He yanked his gaze back to the chubby-cheeked baby.

Kelsey chose two sales tags from the display and moved on without another word. Surely they had enough by now. He was wrong. She paused in an aisle filled with bright colors and happy babies pictured in and around various bath seats. What fresh hell would he be asked about now?

To his immense relief, she made her choice without quizzing him. She selected towels and washcloths, soap and lotion. He saw a hooded towel with a goofy horse face and added it to the cart. She didn't notice.

"Do you have a rocking chair?" she asked as they walked by a row of over twenty rockers in various colors and fabrics and styles.

"If you count the one on the porch," he said. "I can clean it up for you."

"That works. Thanks."

He noticed the way her hand lovingly caressed a glider with simple curves in a clear, walnut stain. It reminded him of an antique bentwood rocker, despite the bold daisy-print cushions.

"Bailey obsessed about the rocker in her nursery," he said. He spotted a glossy white finish with a jungle-print fabric. "I think that's the one she chose."

Kelsey reached over and tucked the baby's pacifier back into his mouth. "Bailey?"

"My sister-in-law," Fox said. "She delivered their son two days ago. Hudson Earl Colton."

"A stately name." Kelsey smiled up at him.

He hadn't thought of it that way before. "It is. Earl is in honor of our grandfather."

She nodded, her gaze clouding over before she looked away. "Most moms spend hours in these."

"Not nannies?" he asked, trying to lighten the mood.

"Depends on the client," she said. "And the age of the child." She moved on, apparently unconcerned about rocking chairs now that she knew he had one.

Fox plucked the tag from the rocker she'd admired and followed in her wake. At last they seemed to be done, just as the baby started fussing.

"You've got this?" Kelsey asked, lifting the baby from the seat.

He nodded, and she carried the baby and the diaper bag away. He worked with the checkout clerk, somehow surviving the constant stream of happy chatter. "These too," he said, handing over the tags for the portable cribs, a changing table and the rocking chair.

"One for Grandma's house, right? That's smart."

He didn't bother to correct her. "Thanks." His parents were long dead and he'd never thought of Mara as grandma material, though she happily doted on the grandchildren she had.

His eyes nearly crossed when the register displayed the final total as he pulled the credit card from his wallet.

"The guys in the warehouse will pull the big items for you. What cushions did you want for the rocker?"

He stared at her, having no idea how to answer.

"It's included in the price."

"Right." He looked around, but Kelsey and the baby weren't in sight. "I guess something basic."

Clearly this wasn't her first time with an overwhelmed shopper. "Here." She smacked down a binder full of fabric swatches and flipped open the cover. "Basics are these."

None of the fabrics looked basic, but he found what he considered neutral in shades of brown with flecks of forest green. "This one is fine."

"You got it." She finished the sale and handed him his receipt. "Just pull around to the side of the building and they'll get those large pieces loaded for you."

"Thanks."

He took the cart out to the truck and stashed the bags next to Kelsey's solitary suitcase. She was only a couple years younger than him. His patience with dorms and short-term housing assignments had run out in his early twenties. How had she put up with the nomadic lifestyle for so long?

Of course he was able to buy acreage and had the space and support to build a business thanks to Wyatt. Fox knew he was lucky. Time and again he'd landed on his feet after one of life's ugly curveballs.

Locking the tailgate, he returned the cart to the corral in front of the store.

"Fox!" Kelsey stepped out, her arms full of the baby and her cheeks pink as she rushed across the parking lot. "I tried to hurry. Have you been waiting long?"

"Not at all," he said. Up close, he could see her eyes were damp, as if she was holding back tears. "You're upset. Did something happen?"

"No." She took a big breath and let it out in a rush. "No. I just—" Her smile wobbled. "I just got myself worked up. It wasn't my intention to keep you waiting. I know you have other things to do besides outfit a nursery."

"I really don't." She seemed to need the reassurance. "The breeding is done so it's just basic care and monitoring right now. The only thing I'd call pressing is finding this little guy's family." He took the baby from her arms and buckled him into the car seat. The process went smoother this time. Maybe there was hope for him after all.

When they were ready, he drove around to the loading dock. "Wait here," he said. He got out and double-checked the items as the warehouse team loaded the big items into the truck bed. He wondered what had set her off. They were hardly more than acquaintances and yet he couldn't leave it alone.

"Did you really think I'd leave you behind?" he asked when he settled behind the wheel again.

"You? No. Not really." She looked at everything except him. "This really is a nice town," she said. "You've lived here all your life?"

He ignored her attempt to distract him. "But it's happened," he pressed, unwilling to let this go.

She sighed. "It has. More than once," she confessed in a small whisper.

"Care to elaborate?"

"It's silly, but it turned into a silly fear."

Now he had to know. "Tell me yours and I'll tell you mine."

At last she turned his way. "Seriously?"

He nodded once. "As serious as a baby on a doorstep." The comeback made her giggle and relax into her seat. He felt like a conquering hero. "So tell me."

"I was probably seven or eight the first time. We'd gone to town for supplies and I wandered off, consumed by reading every label on every product. My mother says she called me back to the cart and I refused to obey."

Her parents had left her behind for being a kid? It was all he could do not to ask for names and addresses. Which was an outrageous response to an old hurt he couldn't fix. "You must have been terrified."

"Yes, I was. I still remember the colors and words first and then the fear. But in my family, disobedience was dealt with swiftly."

"Harshly, too?" he queried. His face heated, recalling the weight behind his father's strikes.

"On occasion, yes. My dad never struck me. He made Mom do it."

Fox swallowed. Not his place to judge her parents, and he had his own demons.

"In any event, I didn't lose track of my parents, or time, again."

"Then who else left you?"

"Once in high school a few of us missed our bus. At least I wasn't alone that time."

She was an adult, caring for a child in his protection. There was only one reason he could think of that she'd freak out this time. "You've had an employer leave you stranded."

"Yes."

He curled his fingers around the steering wheel, wishing there was a way to alleviate the pain haunting that single syllable. "I won't do that," he began. "Well, the odds are low anyway."

"What does that mean?"

"Not proud of it, but I actually did the stranding a time or two with my brothers. Got caught up in whatever puzzle was in my head and left them behind to go solve it."

She laughed and the carefree sound put an extra glow in the sunny day. "That's not the same thing at all."

"You'll never convince my brothers. I was the one with the vehicle both times."

"Well, consider me warned," she said. "I won't go out with you when you're in problem-solving mode."

Then they'd never go out at all. He wasn't great at turning off his mind. Of course she wasn't here to date him. She was here for the horses and the baby. And at the moment, the only puzzle that mattered was finding Baby John's father.

Once they got the nursery put together, he would have to go talk with his brothers. He'd rather walk over hot coals than ask if they had been out fathering children, but it had to be done. Baby John Doe could not stay with him indefinitely.

Chapter 4

Kelsey listened attentively as Fox pointed out various landmarks around Roaring Springs. Behind them, the baby babbled and gurgled happily in his car seat. Though she believed Fox's claim that he wasn't the father, she couldn't help noting how much he generally enjoyed the little guy.

They drove by the garage Fox had called to pick up her car and she was surprised to see it was already unloaded. How long had they been in the baby store? "Your friends work fast," she said. It was a tremendous relief that this time she wouldn't be worried about how to cover the repair costs. "The Colton name does indeed make a difference."

She'd never experienced that kind of attentiveness on reputation alone, primarily, because she'd done her best to blend in and fly under the radar after leaving home. Standing out was akin to posting a neon sign of her whereabouts to her brothers, and while she wanted to earn recognition in her field, ultimately she couldn't afford to take any unnecessary risks.

"Unfortunately, you're not wrong," Fox said, breaking into her thoughts.

"Why is your name unfortunate?" Fox Colton and the Crooked C Quarter Horses were legend in her mind. No one was perfect, but in her opinion, he came close.

He shifted a bit in his seat and when the baby squealed, he checked the mirror. She marveled at the smile that softened his expression. Did he realize Baby John had already won him over?

"I try not to abuse the influence. Not everyone is fond of the family, or the way the Colton businesses impacted the town and the area. My elders made some enemies along the way," he added. "Some days it still feels awkward."

She tried to retreat to the safe side of the line she'd crossed. "I can't imagine." When she'd left home, she hadn't changed her name, only her address. She stopped discussing the family she'd been born to and focused on making new friends and connections. For Fox it seemed like just the opposite.

"My sister had an easier adjustment at first. Our aunt had three boys already when we joined the family." He glanced at her as he stopped for the last traffic light in town. "Here I am, thirty-three years old and there are days I still miss my mom."

"I'm not sure anyone truly puts that kind of loss behind them." Good or bad, parental relationships affected so much. Kelsey missed her mother on occasion, usually when her brothers had done something stupid to try to take her back to the farm. She could hardly tell Fox all of that.

"What about him?" Fox aimed a thumb over his shoulder at the baby. "Will he adjust?"

"I doubt he'll have any recollection of anyone other than the family who raises him," she replied. "That family will have to choose how much they tell him about this time in his life."

Fox grunted. She didn't know him, but she'd bet her first fat paycheck his mind had moved back to the puzzle of the baby's paternity. She didn't envy him that task. Asking her siblings about the sudden appearance of a baby would make her edgy, too.

"I suppose that's good," he said as they made the turn to the ranch road. "Better to know a father and family wanted him than to dwell on the mother who didn't."

The bitterness in his voice sparked all kinds of questions in Kelsey's mind. Questions a new employee really shouldn't be asking the boss. He hadn't pressed the issue about her car or her lack of worldly possessions. And, in turn, she wouldn't press him on the issues of parents and abandonment.

It seemed like a fair trade.

A couple of hours later, Fox tightened the last screw on the changing table and set it upright. "How's that?" He wasn't exactly sure how he'd wound up with so much baby gear or how Kelsey had kept the little boy quiet and happy through it all.

At his query, she stopped folding freshly laundered clothing and crossed the room. Nudging the table and leaning on it a bit, she grinned. "Looks just like the picture," she said. "Well done."

He felt his lips curve in an answering grin. "Guess my skills go beyond analysis and microscopes." Lame. Handing out compliments wasn't in her job description.

Thankfully, his awkward comment didn't seem to faze her.

"Let's put it over here, under the window."

He moved the changing table into place and wondered what to do next. Kelsey had set up one portable crib after he moved the hay bin out. He supposed it was time to bring in the rocker. The hungry baby had made sure she hadn't seen it when he unloaded the truck. Would she give him one of those stunning smiles or that slightly baffled expression she had when he did the unexpected?

Gathering up the tools and trash, he lectured himself while he put things away. Her reactions shouldn't concern him one way or the other. And besides, the odds of him having a family of his own were slim to none. Kids were fine in small doses. But kids started as babies and those gave him trouble. Babies couldn't talk or communicate what they needed. He'd never felt entirely comfortable with his niece and she was already two. If he'd had any affinity for parenthood, it would've surfaced by now.

Of course Wyatt's newborn would give him another gauntlet to run in the months and years ahead. As long as no one asked him to babysit for more than a few hours, he could handle being the cool uncle. He would have the nerdy collections, know all of the fun trends and still breed the best horses in the state. Fox walked back into the temporary nursery and picked up the slipper chair his sister had suggested when he'd outfitted the guest room. For lack of a better solution, he put the chair in his bedroom. Once the cushions were in place, he carried the new rocking chair into the room and put it between the portable crib and the changing table.

Kelsey's hazel eyes rounded a moment before a frown marred her expression. "Why?"

"It's a good thing to have. You said so."

She stacked diapers onto the shelf under the changing table. "You told me you had a rocker you were bringing up from outside."

And that had been his plan until he'd seen the wistfulness on her face in the store. "This saves me cleanup time." He fidgeted while she stared him down. Escape was his best option. "I should go and interview my brothers. We need DNA samples to confirm he's a Colton." He cleared his throat. "You're good here?"

"We're good." She cast him a quick smile over her shoulder. The little guy was looking around and taking it all in from a hammock-like seat Kelsey called a bouncy chair. "It'll be easier for you to talk to your brothers without us around."

He didn't mean to make her feel unwanted. And he sure didn't mean for her to feel like she wasn't on equal footing with him. "I..." He lost his train of thought when she bent over to put something away on the bottom shelf of the changing table.

That never happened. His brothers often teased him that when he was focused a chorus line could dance by naked and he wouldn't notice. There was no way to not notice Kelsey. Yes, she had that petite frame, but she was curved in the right places. His fingers prickled, itching to touch her hair, to frame her waist...

What was wrong with him? She was the nanny and his new assistant. She had a right to work in both roles without being ogled by the boss. This was not a side effect he'd anticipated, but it was temporary. He just had to keep his eyes and hands to himself until they found the baby's father. Then Kelsey could move out of the house and he'd only see her in a work capacity. That would cure this burst of red-hot lust.

"Fox?"

"Hmm?"

"Did you want us to go with you?"

"What?" He shook his head. "No. No thanks. I just…" The sunlight streaming through the window brought out the gold highlights in her hair. Why couldn't he finish a sentence around her? "I'm just procrastinating," he said. "I'll call you when I'm on the way home…and you can tell me what to pick up for dinner."

When she smiled, the curve of her lips drew his full attention. Would that bottom lip taste as sweet as it looked? "I'm happy to cook."

"No." He'd said it too loudly, startling the baby. He waited for the wailing to start, but it didn't. The baby had barely cried since Kelsey's arrival. Clearly, she worked miracles. "I only meant you're doing more than enough already."

Her gaze drifted to the baby. "I'm sure it feels that way now, but it'll all balance out. I can't wait to learn from the best quarter horse breeder in the business."

He appreciated her graciousness about the whole mess she'd walked into but the heartfelt compliment made him uneasy. "Guess I've stalled too long," he muttered. He crouched down and took a picture of the baby with his phone. "Thanks again, Kelsey."

He made his escape, stopping at the office downstairs for supplies. Outside, he breathed in crisp air laced with pine and horses on his way to the truck. He had a momentary debate about leaving Kelsey and the baby without any transportation, but he couldn't go back in there. And really, after less than twenty-four hours, he couldn't imagine a baby crisis she couldn't manage.

He drove away from the ranch, taking the road up toward Wyatt's house. They were coming home from the hospital today and it would make sense to stop there first, except he'd had enough of tiny humans for the moment.

He'd start his interviews with his brother Decker. A year older than Fox, Decker had a head for business and currently served as director of operations for The Lodge. He called first, since his brother spent less time at work after his recent marriage. Finding Decker was still at work, on the drive up to Pine Peak Fox struggled with what he was about to do. How should he phrase his requests so he didn't offend his brothers?

Best to stick with his strengths and keep it academic. Clinical. A quick recap, a few questions, an easy-to-accommodate request. Then it would be rinse and repeat with his next two brothers until he was home again. With the baby and Kelsey.

The Lodge always struck him as masculine, clinging to the mountain, while The Chateau seemed more feminine, a beautiful asset to the valley. Both resorts boasted over-the-top luxury that drew in tourists looking for pampering and winter sport enthusiasts alike.

Entering the lobby, Fox headed for Decker's office. Fox wished he'd taken time to trade his Henley shirt, faded jeans and boots for something that didn't scream "rancher fresh from the barns."

Too late now. He knocked on Decker's open door.

"Fox!" Decker beamed, an expression that was relatively rare before he'd fallen in love with and married Kendall. "What brings you by?"

"I've got a situation," he began, "and I could use your help."

"Anything you need. Come on in."

Fox entered and closed the door behind him. He pressed his palms together and tried to state the matter as clearly as possible. "Two nights ago someone left a baby boy on my doorstep." He reached for his cell phone and pulled up the pictures.

"You? What? You can't be serious." Decker's dark eyebrows shot up toward his hairline. "Who'd you knock up?"

"I'm not the father," Fox said, tamping down his irritation. "Does the baby look familiar?"

Decker scrolled through the pictures. There were only three, but he went through them several times. A dopey smile brightened his face. Could his brother have fathered the child? "He's cute, even when he's mad. Congratulations."

"For what?"

"Looking at something besides a stud book or microscope."

"Ha. Shut up." Fox pushed at his hair. "The baby isn't mine." He managed not to mention the dry spell he was in. "I'm here to ask if he might be yours."

Decker reeled back as if Fox had punched him in

the jaw. "That's a hell of a suggestion." He pointed a finger between the two of them. "You really think the mother got the two of *us* mixed up?"

"Maybe the mother mixed up our addresses." Fox bristled. "I forget what a jerk you can be."

"Me?" Decker tapped his chest. "I'm a charmer and you know it."

Had he ever been grateful for the brothers he inherited through adoption? "Yeah, well, charm me and give me a cheek swab."

"Why?" He stared Fox down. "The kid isn't mine, either."

"Someone fathered him," Fox pointed out. "And someone thought that father was a Colton."

"Have you talked to Wyatt? He's the Colton who lives closest to your address."

"I'm working my way around. Is there a reason you don't want me to have your DNA?"

Decker spread his arms. "I'd rather not be cloned."

"No worries on that score." He pulled out a lancet for the blood typing test as well as a cheek swab. "I wouldn't put the world through two of you. Now, open up."

His brother laughed, but it died quickly. "If you aren't the father, why did the baby end up with you?" he asked before opening his mouth for Fox to swab his cheek. "And where is the baby now?"

"He's at the house with a new, um, nanny," Fox said. Carefully, he returned the sample to the tube and labeled it and the plastic bag with Decker's name.

"What about child services or whatever?"

Fox shook his head. "Couldn't do it. Call me a fool."

"Fool," Decker obliged. "You don't know the first thing about babies."

"I know they're small and loud." And as cute as a button when they were asleep. At least Baby John was, though he'd been too exhausted to appreciate the moment last night.

"My money's on Wyatt," Decker said.

That had been his theory as well, considering that the baby had been left on ranch property. "Well, the more samples I collect the better chance we have of finding his real father."

"If nothing else, this rules me out, right?"

"True." Fox stood up.

"Spoiler alert, you can stop looking at me like I'm a liar," Decker said.

"Maybe," Fox joked. "For what it's worth, I believe you might not know if you fathered a kid."

"Same goes, brother."

He deserved that. After all, the child had wound up at his door, not his brother's.

"What will you do if you can't find the father?"

"I'm not sure." He reached for the DNA collection kit. "It seems someone thinks he's family, but we all know I'm about the last person who should be a father."

Decker shook his head. "For a smart guy you can be so dumb."

"Excuse me?"

"You heard me." His brother shook his head. "Just because your dad was rough with you doesn't mean you'll be the same way."

Embarrassment and shame seized Fox's throat, made it hard to speak. "I didn't know you knew about that." It wasn't something he talked about. Why rehash what couldn't be changed? By the time he and Sloane had been orphaned, he was an expert at going unseen and he continued that habit while he sorted out the new family dynamics.

He shrugged. "Kids have super-powered hearing. Adults forget that. Mom and Dad mentioned it a time or two."

"Too bad the little guy at my place doesn't have super-powered communication skills. I'd love to know where his mother is."

"Good luck," Decker said, walking Fox to the door.

"I appreciate the assist. If you hear anything helpful, let me know."

"You got it." He pulled Fox in close and slapped him on the shoulder.

Back in the truck, breathing easier, Fox sent Kelsey a text message to check in. She replied immediately and included a picture of the baby sound asleep in the new portable crib.

Show off, he texted back.

With the phone on mute and a smile on his face, he drove down the mountain toward the new house his brother Blaine had built for his family.

Fox really didn't want to upset his brother's newfound happiness. He parked, cut the engine and checked his phone.

It's all in the sway.

The text message from Kelsey made him feel as if he had someone to share a secret with, even though he usually preferred his solitude.

He was still smiling when he knocked on Blaine's

door. The conversation went much the same as it had with Decker. There had been zero familiarity when he looked at the pictures and general denial that he could have somehow fathered a child this age. With Blaine's background, Fox had to take his word that he wasn't even in the States when the baby had likely been conceived. Still, he was willing to give a DNA sample to further Fox's search.

"Have you considered that whoever left the baby with you knew you'd take him in?" Blaine asked. "Your adoption isn't a secret."

Fox labeled the sample, irritated when his hand shook. With the blood test and the cheek swab in the kit, he closed it up. "It was too cold to leave him outside," he said.

"Stop." Blaine didn't show his serious side often, but Fox had never been comfortable on the receiving end of all that intensity. "You think the baby is a Colton."

"I think someone believes that, yes."

"Fox, you don't have to take this on. 'Someone—'" he used air quotes "—is mistaken."

"Time and DNA will tell," he said. How did his brothers read him so well? They'd never been particularly close as kids and years of college and careers had separated them further.

"You don't owe the universe or anyone a debt for being adopted," Blaine said. "Dad and Mom would tell you the same thing."

Russ maybe. Mara, well, he wouldn't be surprised if she kept a tab in the back of her mind with Fox's name on it.

"That's not what this is," he denied. "A baby showed

up at my door. A baby can't fend for himself. He needs his family and I'm trying to find them."

"So taking in a random baby has nothing to do with us taking in you and Sloane when your parents died?"

Fox shook his head, not trusting his voice. His stomach churned at the thought that the baby had been left at his door because his family was dead.

"Fox, come on. It's me. You should talk about it."

"Nothing to say," he managed through gritted teeth. "The kid showed up and I'm stepping up until we find his family."

Blaine nodded to the picture on Fox's phone. "Looks a little small to put to work."

"He'll grow," Fox replied, appreciating the joke. "Thanks for the assist."

He made a quick exit, checking in with Kelsey before he pulled out of the driveway. This time Kelsey sent him a picture of a casserole dish in the oven and a note that he had forty minutes until it was done.

His stomach growled. She shouldn't have cooked, but he couldn't deny that whatever it was looked delicious, even half-baked. What was this strange connection he felt with her? She put him at ease and he willingly let down his guard. Maybe whatever magic she used with the baby worked on him, too.

By rights he probably should have notified the sheriff before hiring a nanny for a child that wasn't even his. Too late. He wasn't turning over the baby to the foster system until he had more information. Who would even complain about it except the baby's actual family?

One brother left. Driving back to the Crooked C, he took the fork toward Wyatt's side of the Crooked C.

When he reached his brother's sprawling ranch house, he parked and texted One more stop to Kelsey.

Last week, he would have rung the bell without thinking. But after only one restless night with the baby, he knew better. They couldn't have been home for long and he didn't want to upset or wake the newborn. He rapped lightly on the door, prepared to send Wyatt a text that he was outside.

His big brother came to the door, looking a bit worn out, but as happy as Fox had ever seen him. "Hey, are you the welcome home committee?"

Fox regretted not bringing over anything helpful like a meal, a box of diapers or beer and cigars. "I'm empty-handed tonight," he admitted. "I won't be next time."

"Not a big deal, we're set at the moment." He invited Fox into the house. "Mom brought over soup, lasagna and a pan of brownies."

In the background, Fox heard the thin cry of Wyatt's new son. "I only need a minute," he said, his palms going damp. After having this conversation twice now, he should be a pro. "It's a private matter."

Wyatt cocked his head. "Let me make sure she's set."

"Of course."

"Grab a beer from the fridge if you want one."

Fox cooled his heels in the kitchen. He didn't want a beer, just the DNA. And if Mara had brought the beer too, he wouldn't feel right about drinking it. Unlike his sister, who she folded right into the family, his aunt had never been as warm toward Fox. He couldn't imagine how stuck she'd felt, coping with her own grief while trying to care for her sister's children, but he still had no clue what had caused the rift between him and Mara. Perhaps he had hurt her feelings or pushed her away when she'd been trying to help fill the void left by his mother's death.

Water under the bridge now. Kids and parents were people and not all people got along equally. Fox accepted that, understood it was okay that he'd never feel that soul-deep sense of belonging with anyone other than Sloane or in his own home. Wyatt dashed back in and out again with a glass of water for Bailey. When he returned he slid into the chair at the kitchen table. "What's the deal?"

"A baby showed up on my doorstep," Fox said. "The night after Hudson was born, in fact."

"A babe? It's not nice to brag."

Fox would've smacked him, but Wyatt's exhaustion could be forgiven. "Not bragging. It was an *infant*—not a woman." He sighed. "He's about six months old, based on the internet search I did."

Wyatt rubbed at his eyes. "You would do an internet search."

"It's not like his mother or whoever left me his birth certificate and medical records." If anyone deserved a pass it was Wyatt, and yet Fox felt judged.

"The baby was clearly left with me by mistake."

"You're sure?"

"I do remember how babies are made."

"And you haven't…?" He wiggled his eyebrows.

Fox rolled his eyes. "I haven't." In far too long. That had to be a factor in his instant attraction to having Kelsey living with him.

"Why would someone leave a baby on your doorstep if you haven't…y'know." Again with the eyebrows.

For the first time in his life, Fox actually hoped to hear a baby cry. Anything to put a twist in this particular conversation. "My first thought was someone must have been looking for *your* doorstep, not mine."

The expressions that rippled over his brother's face were worth the wait. Indignation, bafflement, denial and then flat-out anger. "No. Not a chance." He looked around furtively, as if he expected Bailey to pop out of a doorway and smack him on the head. "The only baby I've fathered is in there with his beautiful mother."

"That you know of," Fox said. Taking pity on Wyatt, he held up his hands in surrender. "I believe you, I do. But it's logical to assume the baby's mom or whoever was looking for a Colton."

"Decker," Wyatt said, his gaze menacing.

"Already talked with him. He denies it."

Wyatt didn't look convinced. "So let protective services sort it out, Fox. You aren't prepared to deal with an infant."

Direct hit and the truth hurt. "I hired someone to help," he said. "A nanny." Fox pulled the pictures up on his phone and handed the device to Wyatt. "Does he remind you of anyone?"

"Are you kidding?" Wyatt studied the pictures. "He's a cute kid, but I barely recognize *you* after a couple of days in the maternity ward with Bailey and my son."

"And you didn't even do the hard part," Fox joked. He'd sat with enough mares through foaling to know he wasn't cut out to support a wife in labor.

"Don't talk to me about any of it until you've done it yourself," Wyatt grumbled.

"It wasn't an insult," he said. Though it had clearly come across that way. "Can you please give me a DNA sample to run against the baby's? I'm trying to figure out which Colton he is supposed to be with."

"It wasn't me," Wyatt insisted.

"I believe you." Fox believed all three of his brothers. He definitely didn't want to think any of them would lie about having a son if they'd known. "Still, a sample helps me narrow down who could be the father."

"Fine." Wyatt opened his mouth.

Fox swabbed Wyatt's cheek and labeled the sample. "Thanks."

"How long before you know anything?"

"DNA tests can take some time," he admitted. "With luck and a favor or two, we can get it expedited. I was going to reach out to Agent Stefan Roberts in the morning." After Deputy Bloom's comments, Fox thought the FBI would be interested in helping, if only to separate the baby's appearance from the Avalanche Killer case.

"Perks of being a Colton," Wyatt quipped.

Fox heard the baby fussing and with another congrats, he let his brother go enjoy his first night of fatherhood at home. Before he left, Fox couldn't resist one more text to Kelsey.

OMW. Need anything?

He waited, but she didn't reply immediately. Had something happened? Having no real cause to panic did nothing to slow his racing heart. He turned the truck for his place a bit faster than he should have on roads that were cloaked in darkness. When his phone chimed with a text message alert, he used the app that read the text aloud.

All good here. Turns out your Baby John Doe likes bath time.

Fox pulled over and took a deep breath. It also gave him a chance to view the picture and the video she'd added to the message. While his heart rate returned to normal, he stared at a stranger's son having a grand time in the baby bathtub. The little guy was all grins, his hands splashing in the water. The video was less than twenty seconds long. He hit Replay a time or two, maybe three. The kid was adorable and Kelsey's voice in the background was warm and competent. Soothing.

He needed to get a grip.

There was a hot meal waiting for him, prepared by a pretty and intelligent woman he found immensely appealing. Unfortunately, due to the circumstances, she was off-limits. It would benefit both of them if he could remember that for more than a minute at a time.

Kelsey had taken a chance making dinner. It was entirely possible her new boss wouldn't appreciate her rooting through his pantry and cabinets to find ingredients.

Although cooking was a common sense thing to do, she'd worked with some quirky people through the years. Sometimes her access to public areas of the home was restricted to a single shelf or maybe a portion of the refrigerator. In one home, she'd had a mini-fridge and microwave in her room and general kitchen access was off-limits unless she was preparing or sharing a meal with the children in her care.

Oddities aside, it was still a big improvement over the way life would be if she'd stayed with her family.

She caught the faint rumble of the truck engine as Fox returned and her heart gave a happy, if inappropriate, spin in her chest. None of his texts had given her a hint about the meetings with his brothers. Of course, that wasn't her business and she reminded herself to push the mute button on her natural curiosity.

She'd given the baby a bath and a bottle and rocked him to sleep. Last night he'd gone almost five full hours before waking up. Over the next few days, she could get the little guy on a schedule that would mesh better with Fox—and her—in the long run.

DNA results could take weeks and he didn't seem inclined to hand over the baby to anyone else in the meantime. Maybe it really was his child and she was allowing her professional fascination with him to cloud her judgment.

Fox was like a force of nature. At least to her lonely and long underused feminine senses. Not stormy, but steady as a sunrise. The calming voice, intelligent eyes and the flashes of humor twisted her up in unexpected ways. She'd barely been here twenty-four hours and she found herself blushing and wishing for things she didn't have a right to want from him.

The timer went off for the casserole and she pulled it out of the oven just as Fox entered the kitchen. "That smells fantastic."

Thankfully the oven was a convenient excuse for the fresh burst of color she felt rising in her face. "Just in time." She set the oven mitts aside and turned, nearly plowing into him.

She'd already found her balance by the time he caught her elbows, but the brief contact of his fingers against her bare skin sent a ripple of anticipation through her.

The man could move quietly when it suited him.

He'd come up behind her to check out the casserole. "What is it?"

She'd taken a chance, building from what appeared to be staples he had on hand. "I wasn't sure what you liked, so..."

"I'm sure I'll love it. Never been a picky eater." He moved toward a cabinet and pulled down plates for the both of them. Then he did a double take, pointing to the now-empty stretch of counter. "What happened to the baby's stuff?"

Crap. She should've asked his permission to make any changes. This was his home and though she'd been invited to stay, her title was nanny—in the house at least. "I can put those things back. I overstepped." She clamped her mouth shut before the babbling got out of control. "I moved those things as part of finishing the nursery."

"Temporary nursery."

"Right." She gave him a wide berth as she moved to a different cabinet. "I have a tendency to organize and I didn't think you'd want Baby John's things scattered all over indefinitely. I apologize if I was out of line."

"You weren't." He seemed distinctly uncomfortable. "You don't need to walk on eggshells around here, Kelsey. I'm grateful for your help with the baby and since you're living here, you should feel at home. I'll get used to it."

"Great, thanks."

He held out plates and she served up the casserole she'd pulled together with rice, chicken, salsa, cheese and a crumbled tortilla chip topping. He carried the plates to the island and she poured water for herself.

She'd noticed a jug of tea in the fridge. "Would you like tea? Something stronger?"

"Just water. I had a beer over at Wyatt's."

"He's the brother who just had a baby?"

"Yes. Good memory." Fox dug into the food when she sat down. Closing his eyes, his entire body relaxed over the first bite. "You did this with the leftovers in my pantry?"

She nodded. "Making something out of what looks like nothing is one of my strengths."

"I'll say. Did your mom teach you to cook?"

He was fishing for details in her past that her résumé glossed over. She'd honed her skills in this area as well, finding ways to open up without exposing too much. "Yes. Mom kept us all engaged with kitchen tasks. Part and parcel of a big family."

"Well, tell your mom I'm grateful next time you talk."

Kelsey shoved a big bite into her mouth so she couldn't answer. At the moment, she was belatedly grateful to the employers who hadn't cared to know anything other than how good she was with children.

"Did I say something wrong?" Fox asked quietly.

"Oh, not at all," she replied.

"Your face is turning red."

"Spices do that," she told him. "And sunlight. Sometimes wine." She shrugged. "Curse of the fair skinned."

"Okay. If I do say something wrong or screw up, especially with the baby, tell me."

"All right." He was the strangest boss she'd ever had. If only she knew if it was because of her infatuation or reality. "I'm really excited about working with you and the horses. I'm excited about the baby, too," she added when he frowned.

"That makes one of us." He chased a few grains of rice around his plate. "He really likes baths?"

"He sure did tonight."

"I probably should've done that last night. My sister would've known what to do."

She studied him as unobtrusively as possible with him sitting so close. "You did great, I'm sure." He seemed inordinately uptight about caring for a child. "Kids and horses aren't that much different in the early days. They eat, poop, play and sleep."

He stared at her, then burst out laughing. The sound filled her with a glow of pride as big and happy as the day she'd won her first science fair. Better actually. She didn't have to take his laughter home and have her father rip her heart out by tossing that beautiful sound in the trash.

She sipped her water and finished her dinner, pleased when Fox filled his plate again and devoured the second helping. "I didn't have time to make anything for dessert."

"I don't expect you to do the cooking."

"You didn't seem all that happy about tracking down your brothers. I wanted to do something nice. And there was all this time between loads of laundry."

His brow furrowed. "I didn't find a single extra minute when I was on my own with him."

"You will." She sipped her water again. "What time do you usually get started in the office?"

"Normally, I'll do the morning rounds with the horses, come back and clean up, eat breakfast and then head to the office around eight. Wyatt and I share a few ranch hands. They'll come and go through the day. Now that Hudson's here, they'll be handling more of the work on his operation."

She let a thousand questions flit through her mind, all of them too nosy. "You're sure you want that second portable crib in the office? We have the baby monitor now. The signal will reach downstairs."

"Absolutely. I don't want to run you ragged."

His voice was a smooth tenor, and when he'd talked to the horses this morning on the tour, every single one of them had been tuned to his voice.

When it seemed he was done, she reached for his plate. He caught her hand. "What are you doing?"

She snatched her fingers from his light grasp, but the heat and tingle lingered. "I didn't mean to rush you."

"You aren't rushing me." He aimed a curious gaze at her.

"Okay." She didn't need a man of his intellect getting curious. "Then can I clear your plate?"

"No. You cooked in addition to the nanny responsibilities. Cleanup is on me."

Resistance was a slippery coil in her belly and it irritated her. She'd left home fifteen years ago and still, the old habits cropped up. Girls did the cooking and the dishes. She might be back on a ranch, but Fox wasn't of the same antiquated mind-set as her father or brothers.

"Cool," she managed. "Thanks."

He shot her another quizzical glance as he carried plates to the sink. Thankfully, the baby monitor lit up and Baby John's first whimper filled the awkward space.

"So much for giving you a break," Fox muttered. "You want dishes or baby?"

Did he really mean to make it sound like they were a team? The idea of it fizzed through her. Delightful, intriguing and generally wonderful. "I'll take the baby. He might get himself back to sleep."

Fox held up crossed fingers. "Does that happen?"

She smiled. "Do you wake up in the night crying?"

"Only once or twice a year," he replied with a wink. "And you're right. I get myself back to sleep."

"See? We all grow up. Sleeping is a skill," she added as she dialed down the volume on the monitor. Baby John had worked himself into full cry and needed attention. Glancing at Fox's bewildered expression, he was better off with the dishes. "He'll get the hang of it soon."

She went to tend the baby, while her mind lingered over the man she'd left in the kitchen. He'd made it sound like a joke, but what if he'd been serious? Babies scared him, that much was obvious. She chalked that up to a lack of experience. Easily remedied, despite his doubts. But what sort of pain or fears would make a man like Fox Colton wake up crying in the night?

It wasn't her place to ask.

Chapter 5

Fox had learned to recognize treasure when he saw it in horses and in people. Kelsey was pure gold with a little magic thrown in. In a breeding program he'd call it the X-factor, an intangible no amount of genetic testing or analysis could account for.

Within days, she'd managed to get the baby on a schedule that let all three of them sleep through most of the night. He didn't wake up anymore and unlike his brother and sister-in-law, Kelsey never appeared exhausted or bleary-eyed in the mornings.

She picked up on the routine he preferred in the office and around the ranch. With her overseeing the pregnancy verifications he had the herd ready for winter in record time. Once he was sure she could handle herself on a horse, he encouraged her to go and ride the property while the baby napped in the office.

Baby John loved the horses, gurgling in delight and reaching for them whenever they took him around the barn or out to one of the yards. Fox occasionally interrupted his day with research for a pack or sling that would allow the baby to ride with them, but he closed the window before making the purchase. Baby John was only a temporary resident. There would be time for Fox to ride out with Kelsey once the baby was back where he belonged.

The blood typing had been inconclusive. Soon, thanks to Agent Roberts's request for a rush order, the FBI lab would send them the results of the DNA tests.

Fox glanced across the office where Kelsey leaned back against her desk, her legs stretched out and a research paper in hand. Beside her, the baby scooted around on a blanket making happy noises. They couldn't keep this up indefinitely, but it worked for now.

These everyday moments reminded Fox of his mother and the early years when his life had felt perfect. *Almost* perfect. How different would his life be if his parents had lived?

Kelsey, engrossed in the reading material, caught a squishy ring with various textures when the baby flung it aside. She returned it to him, over and over again. Why had they purchased that item? Teething, grasping and cognitive development, he recalled.

He was sure things hadn't been so well researched and labeled when he was a baby. He turned out okay. Mostly. "I can't remember when my dad started hitting me." Surely his father wouldn't have struck an infant. He thought of his new nephew and his older niece.

Had he been a toddler the first time his dad delivered a painful blow?

That image seemed too early. His mom would've kept him out of range if she'd known his dad was violent.

"Fox?"

The horror in her voice, on her face, snapped him out of his reverie. "Sorry. I look at him and can't imagine causing him pain but..."

Her initial shock was already fading to comprehension. "You wonder when you'll snap and turn into an abuser."

He pushed his reading glasses to the top of his head and rubbed the bridge of his nose. It sounded ridiculous when she said it.

"My money's on never." She returned her attention to the baby and whatever she was reading.

"You're awfully certain." He walked over, suddenly afraid to touch the baby.

She gazed up at him. "You're a scientist, you know better."

Maybe on a logical level, but having the baby around triggered all the old worries.

"Picasso had four children," she stated. Her lips slanted into a frown. "None of them turned out to be phenomenal painters."

"I'll have to take your word on it."

"They each had their own skills and talents, separate from their genetic history. None of us are merely the sum of our parents."

"I've disappointed you," he said. Her confidence in him eased the worst of his fears. "Forgive me for being human."

"Done." She turned a radiant smile on the baby. "Becoming our parents is a universal fear."

"Worse when your parent sets a lousy example."

"True," she allowed. "But come on. A person capable of beating up a kid wouldn't have taken in a child the way you did." She stood, putting the baby into his arms before he could protest.

"I didn't have the best examples, either." She folded the blanket, draped it over the side of the portable crib.

The baby found a button on his shirt, his tiny fingers already working to explore it. "I know I'm being dumb about it."

"You're not. It's natural, as I said." She held out her arms and Fox wanted to walk into the embrace she clearly intended for the child. "I worked as a nanny one summer for a family expecting their third child. They had two little boys and this time it was a girl. The mother was terrified."

"Why?"

"Because her mother and grandmother were obsessed with body image. All her adult life she struggled to be healthy, to break those negative messages and cycles. The baby wasn't even born yet and she was brainstorming protective solutions."

"Those are behavior patterns, not genetics." He understood the point she was trying to make, but there was another facet to his trouble.

In his memories, his mother had been perfect and Aunt Mara a poor substitute. He was grateful his aunt had opened her home to Fox and Sloane, but somehow Fox always irritated her, so he stayed out of her way. It was sad and lonely, but he had Sloane to help him get through it.

"My mom was amazing. It baffled me for years, when I learned not all dads were like mine, why she married an abusive person."

"Ah."

The baby rubbed his face against Fox's shirt. "Care to elaborate?" he prompted when Kelsey moved to fix a bottle.

"You really are worried you'll change from Dr. Jekyll to Mr. Hyde with a child around."

"I am." He sat down in his chair, rocking a bit for the baby's sake. If there was a switch in the DNA, a recessive gene or a chemical imbalance that occurred at a certain age, he might not be safe around Baby John or any other child.

"Do you just need to vent or are you looking for an opinion?" she asked.

He appreciated having the option. "You're a geneticist. Opine."

She handed him the bottle and the baby latched on and started suckling enthusiastically. "I'm one of twelve kids in my family and all the neighbors had big families, too."

She'd told him she had several siblings, but one of *twelve*? Just thinking about the noise and chaos overwhelmed him. "What planet are you from?"

"I'm not allowed to say."

He liked the way her eyes sparkled when she was amused.

"I worked my way through college taking care of children, which put me around plenty of parents. No one is perfect. Mental illness can play a part in abusive situations of all kinds."

"The brain is a great and terrible thing," he said, echoing a professor from school.

"It is. In my professional opinion, you were too young to accurately understand your parents' marriage. What your mom did or didn't know about your father is irrelevant."

"How can you say that?" He pushed to his feet, restless with nowhere to go and a baby in his arms. He didn't want to hear her answer, yet it was pure cowardice to leave. He'd invited this—he should hear her out.

"Because you aren't him, Fox." She took the baby from him without interrupting the feeding. "You share some DNA, but you're *you.* You choose how to act, how to express your disappointment or anger. You *choose* self-control or destruction."

She was right. He knew it in his head; it was the rest of him that struggled to keep up and accept that basic truth. The baby fussed and she shifted him to pat the air out of his tummy.

Fox went to the crib and set it up for Baby John's naptime, while she let him finish the bottle. A few minutes later the little guy was dozing on her shoulder.

"Were you often a therapist for your family clients?" he asked.

"Only the smart ones," she replied.

The sassy smile on her lips tempted him like nothing else. His palm was on her arm and he was leaning in before he caught himself. At the last minute, he brushed a kiss on the baby's head and retreated to his desk.

He was too comfortable around her. It was as if he'd been caught in a happy-family web that grew stronger with every passing day. With any luck, she had no idea where his thoughts had led or how desperately he was trying to tamp down his desire for her.

They were employer and employee. Colleagues. She was already an asset to the business and that would only be more valuable with time. He couldn't screw that up, or risk everything he'd worked for to explore this physical attraction.

Kelsey rubbed Baby John's back until he pulled his knees up under his chest and pushed his butt into the air. The pose was his preferred position for napping, and soothing him gave her an excellent distraction from her whirling thoughts.

Fox had nearly kissed her. She'd wanted that kiss. His breath had fanned her cheek and his scent clung to her clothing. Of course it did. She was living in his house, working in his office. She pressed her lips together. Kissing him would have been incredible. And wildly inappropriate.

He was her boss and they were just learning how she could best support his business. Requests for his insights into breeding programs were frequent, as well as queries about supporting the health of broodmares.

This wasn't the place for kisses, no matter the potential.

"Do you think he'll adjust?" Fox asked when she settled behind her desk once more.

They'd had this conversation before. She kept her gaze lowered as she marked the place where she'd left off in the research paper on holistic methods for controlling symptoms for in-season mares. "He's the tiny king of adjusting," she said.

He looked at her over his reading glasses and her pulse raced. Why was that so sexy?

"I mean to his real family," Fox said. "They'll do things differently than we do. I remember struggling to keep up with the differences when we were jumbled up with Russ and Mara's boys."

"You were grieving. He's just a baby, too young to know what he's lost."

"Maybe." Fox turned back to whatever he was reading.

Kelsey set aside the research in favor of working on the query Fox had assigned to her. She needed to persuade another breeder to share some data that they could analyze and possibly incorporate into his current system.

"I appreciate your help. I couldn't have let him go to strangers."

Though his voice was quiet, the intensity hit her like a sucker punch, stealing her breath. "You made a good choice," she replied softly. "Family should step up. I'm sure his father will appreciate everything you did when we find him."

"It bugs me that the father hasn't knocked on my door." He stood up and started pacing in front of the glass doors. "It's not like we're living in New York City," he was saying. "Word travels fast around here."

Kelsey sat back and gave Fox her full attention. That backfired as she was mesmerized by the way he moved and gestured when he spoke. She had to work to keep her mind on his words rather than his big hands or those long, muscular legs.

"Maybe everyone is more comfortable believing you are the father."

He rolled his eyes. "You're probably right. Regardless, when we get the DNA results back, I'm not wasting any time handing him off. He needs to be with his real family. Hopefully they can tell me why he landed on my doorstep."

She agreed with the sentiment behind the declaration, but in her experience, family of origin was rarely perfect. "Do you intend to stay in his life?"

His mouth fell open. "I hadn't thought of that. Guess that's a done deal if he's a nephew."

"Good."

"Why?"

"Because you're attached," she began. "And because extended family is important. My aunt helped me..." She nearly said *escape*, but said, "Prep for college," instead. "I spent as much time as possible with her." Every day from her escape from home until she boarded the bus for freshman orientation. She credited everything she was right now to her aunt's courage and example.

"She inspired you," Fox observed, dropping back into his desk chair.

"Yes, she did. What was the biggest adjustment for you after your parents died?"

"Going from one little sister to having three brothers." He chuckled. "But I'll always be grateful they didn't leave us to the foster system."

"Sounds like you have a good family and a strong support network."

"That's true. They're good people. I'm still closest to Sloane. Some days I feel like she was cheated since she only remembers Mara as a mom."

"But you've said Mara doted on her."

"She did until the twins, Skye and Phoebe, came along. Something about me always rubbed her the wrong way, but we managed."

Managed? Kelsey didn't like the way he said that.

"Russ took me under his wing, taught me there were options and choices. Maybe Mara resented his making time for me, when he often wouldn't for his own boys. When I left for college, it was for a business degree to follow him into the Colton Empire."

"Seriously?" She couldn't quell the shock. Fox in a suit would make her hormones sit up and beg. As if they weren't doing that already. "Hard to envision you in an office." This was where he belonged.

He looked at her over his glasses and arched an eyebrow. Drooling was a valid concern.

"Fine, this is an office." She rolled her eyes. "You know what I mean. I can't see you in a high-rise, schmoozing with uppity clients."

He laughed, dropping his glasses to the desktop. "Only Russ ever saw that life for me," he admitted. "I wanted it, right up until I got to college and discovered biology and chemistry made more sense to me than profit and loss statements."

"Lucky me." She grinned at him, but his gaze had shifted to his monitor.

They worked a bit longer in a companionable silence as she switched gears, reviewing a decades-old study on breeding quarter horses for more speed in the rodeo ring. It wasn't Fox's goal at all, but the way they'd matched sires and mares had been of particular interest. The report had several pictures of foals and made her think again about Baby John Doe's early months.

"Do you have any baby pictures?" she asked as she worked.

"Probably stored away in a box somewhere," he replied after a minute. "My mom—Dana, I mean—enjoyed making scrapbook pages when I was little."

She could hardly picture him little. He was bigger than life to her, and not only by reputation after the recent days as his nanny and assistant. His heart was bigger still, full of his ideas for his own ranch and the breeding programs he worked up for clients. And still he had room to care for a stranger's child.

"You want to compare me to Baby John Doe?"

"No. You said he isn't your son." Her history, as much as she tried to forget it, was gone. At least he had that little piece of his parents. "I was just curious. Maybe we should be taking pictures of him. For him to have later."

"It's not a bad idea." He traded his glasses for his cell phone and quietly snapped a few pictures of the baby asleep.

His response, the instant action, made her feel as if someone had stirred sweet, melted caramel into her soul. She didn't have anything from her first fifteen years. Assuming her siblings and mother had followed the usual directive when someone left the community, all evidence of her had been stored away—likely destroyed—to reframe a family she'd never been part of.

"I think guys are different than girls," he said when he returned to his desk.

"If you're just now thinking that, I'm not surprised you aren't the father," she joked. "Do we need to have the talk?"

"Ha-ha." He set his glasses back on his nose, then leaned back in his chair and stared up at the ceiling. "I think men and women look at their history differently. Through different lenses. And of course, girls have the power to give birth."

"Some girls want more than motherhood," she muttered.

"As they should," Fox said.

He was oblivious to her inner turmoil, his mind clearly busy formulating a separate point, but she was nevertheless intrigued by what he had to say on the subject of gender roles and relationships.

"I'm not articulating it well," he admitted. "Girls look at the people of a family, the faces and the feelings, and guys look at a family like a legacy."

"Are you saying girls are shallow?" She wasn't truly mad or offended. His mind was an interesting place and she had a feeling he was working his way through something far more personal. It was her problem if something stomped on the old nerves that were still raw.

"Stop putting words in my mouth," he replied with a sheepish smile. "It's not hardwired the same in each person, male or female, I know that. We all have our own balance point."

"You're wondering if—in general—boys grow up with an inclination or pressure to provide because they saw their dads providing?"

"Yes, exactly. It's not all genetics or all learned behavior, as you said earlier. The women in my life can pore over baby books for days, but I can't imagine my brothers want to look back on their baby pictures any more than I do."

"Huh." Was her craving for a bit of that a result of feeling rootless after her escape?

"Work with me, Kelsey," he said. "Did the women of your family pore over baby books?"

"Yes." She tried not to squirm while he stared at her. "And, yes, as a general rule, the boys only showed up to make fun of siblings and cousins."

"Not you, though. No doubt you were too adorable," he said.

She laughed, though she felt a blush rising into her face. "They loved to make fun of me. I was a pale tomato."

He laughed. "That's a baby picture I want to see."

"Good luck with that. Baby pictures weren't on my mind when I left home." Sneaking out with only a backpack stuffed with clothing and her math and science notebooks, her focus had been on making it past the gate without getting caught.

"When was the last time you visited?"

"I don't visit." She shifted her attention to another thick stack of papers she needed to wade through. "Leaving home was a permanent thing for me." Final answer, one-way trip. Unfortunately, her brothers were rather persistent in their demands for her to come home and do her duty for the family.

Not gonna happen, guys.

"You don't have *any* contact with your family?"

She didn't need to look at him, the disbelief was clear enough in his voice.

"I'm not judging," he added.

His chair squeaked and she heard each of his footsteps as he crossed the room.

"No, you wouldn't," she murmured, still not looking at him. It wouldn't occur to Fox to judge someone, harshly or otherwise. He might be the best person she'd ever met.

"Kelsey?"

She steeled herself for his reaction. "My family isn't what you'd call forgiving. And it's a subject I avoid. The reasons I left..." She looked toward the playpen where Baby John was napping. No helpful distraction from that quarter. "Well, there were several." Hooray for that kernel of honesty.

The brief rally in her head was cut short when she glanced up and caught him watching her with a mixture of curiosity and pity. Ick. She wanted to be seen as an equal, not a project. No family was perfect.

"I'm here now," she said. With luck, her brothers wouldn't find a way to wreck this ideal job for her. They'd caught up with her at one overnight on her drive to Colorado, but her years of practice in evasion enabled her to leave them in the dust. She hadn't seen them since and she hadn't told anyone about her destination. "I left home a long time ago and I've made it a habit to live in the present."

"But you went to college, planned a career."

"True." What was he getting at?

He tapped his reading glasses against his palm. "That indicates you had an eye for the future, living beyond the moment."

Without a degree, her only career path would be nanny, which was hardly any different than staying home would have been. "One primary reason I left was because my parents wouldn't have let me go to college."

His gaze narrowed. "You're joking."

"I'm not." Her cheeks were hot and her fingertips were tingling. "I wanted to keep learning."

"Kelsey, that's..." His gaze darted around the office as if he could find the right words tacked up on the walls.

"Archaic? Backward?" she supplied.

"No." He shook his head. "Well, yes." His sky blue gaze sliced right through her defenses. "Cruel," he declared. "With your mind, that's just cruel."

If anyone had given her a higher compliment, she couldn't remember it. Not when he stared at her as if she could answers life's biggest questions. "My family has a strict and firm value structure," she said. "Me going to college would have rocked their values."

"More than losing you entirely?" He uttered the words as if she were invaluable. Her heart couldn't take much more. "Can we set it aside? Please?"

"Just one more question."

She nodded. He was her boss twice over and she was caring for an infant he'd taken under his protection. She owed him answers to any questions or concerns.

"Do you regret leaving?"

She'd been prepared to answer a much different question and it took a moment for her to regroup. "No. It was the right thing for me." Life with her family would've stifled her mind and crushed her spirit. Better to live alone than merely exist as a cog in the wheel. If only her brothers would accept that she'd never go back.

"Do you miss them?"

"I don't miss fighting for the last roll at dinner," she admitted wryly. "And that's a second question," she joked.

"I have many...but I won't press."

"I appreciate that," she said sincerely. Dwelling on her family always made her feel as if she'd been caught at the edge of a quicksand pit and the wrong thought or move would suck her in forever. "Do you mind if I step out for some fresh air?"

"Go ahead," he replied, starting back to his desk.

Outside, she filled her lungs with the clear mountain air, exhaled slowly. Walking out to the nearest patch of grass, she stretched her arms overhead and repeated the cleansing breaths until she felt steadier, calmer.

Questions or not, she was safe here as an employee and a woman. Fox needed her for the baby as well as the breeding work he was so passionate about. He wouldn't hold her family antics against her, though she wouldn't want her brothers to test his patience.

She moved slowly through a series of movements she'd compiled through years of self-defense, yoga and martial arts classes. It was her own blend, one she practiced regularly to keep herself limber and strong. Even a short break could make a big difference.

A few minutes later, her body and mind quiet, eyes closed and palms pressed together in front of her heart, she heard the hum of a car engine. She opened her eyes in time to see a dark sedan roll smoothly away and disappear into the trees.

Fox couldn't help keeping an eye on Kelsey. She'd stopped in perfect view of the only window on this side of the office anyway. She moved fluidly and slowly through yoga poses he recognized from the internet and other forms he'd never seen. It was beautiful and mesmerizing.

And he really shouldn't intrude, even from this side of the window. He'd done that enough, though he hadn't meant to upset her. He merely wanted to get to know her better. She was inquisitive and upbeat and generally a burst of pure sunshine any time of the day or night. She made it easy for him to open up and, remarkably, she understood when he was lost in thought and she didn't hold it against him.

He forced his mind away from Kelsey and studied the breeding plan and proposal they'd been developing for a new client. She came back in and settled back to work without a word.

When the baby woke, Fox waved her off and dealt with the little guy himself. He needed the movement while some ideas percolated in the back of his mind. It still surprised him that the baby smiled whenever Fox walked into view. He kept checking to see if anyone was behind him.

Kelsey had made that possible. She'd managed to smooth out the rough edges and mute his insecurities. He'd learned from watching her, and gained significant baby-care confidence in record time. He had the baby changed and was warming up a bottle when she walked over.

"I think I have the breeding recommendations pinned down," she said. "I put them on your desk for review."

He was sure her plan was solid, but he'd review it and put her mind at ease. At the end of the day, it was his name and his company's reputation on the line.

"Do you want me to take him?" she asked, tickling the baby's foot.

"I'm good, thanks to you." He carried the baby, the bottle and a burp cloth back to his desk.

Fox felt an affinity for the way Baby John watched everything, soaking up details. It was silly to think the little guy might've picked up anything from him in such a short amount of time and at such a young age, but he couldn't deny that sense of connection.

He split his attention between reviewing Kelsey's plan and feeding the baby. From the corner of his eye, he caught Kelsey checking on him a time or two, but he managed to avoid any catastrophes.

"The plan looks good," he said. Baby John, wide-awake and tummy full, was ready to play. "What do you say we head to the barn?"

"I'll get his coat."

He slipped on his barn jacket while she bundled up the baby and covered his head against the crisp October breeze that kicked up more frequently as winter edged closer. With the baby in the stroller, they walked out to the barn.

Every step struck Fox like something out of a Norman Rockwell painting. Cozy, domestic and not at all the way he'd pictured his life at this stage. They strolled along, the two of them engrossed in his favorite topic of building a better quarter horse. Occasionally, the baby chimed in with a squawk or gurgle, and one of them would answer as if he'd actually said something intelligible.

Outside again, they paused at the fence to watch the horses in the paddock. Only one or two of the mares were starting to show, but he was already excited about the foals they'd meet in the spring. He loved working the herd, managing the ranch and seeing smart breeding plans come to fruition.

Further out in another pasture, the yearlings were enjoying the crisp autumn weather. Their personalities had started to show within a few months and some of them had clearly picked up habits or quirks from their mothers.

"How much do kids internalize from watching their elders?" Fox mused.

It was a topic he'd pondered long before the baby appeared on his doorstep. Now, with a baby and nanny around 24/7, he was second-guessing his purposeful avoidance of having a wife and family. He certainly hadn't had the best examples to emulate. His father struck fast and hard and seemingly out of the blue. Fox had done his best to go unseen and be obedient, though it had rarely mattered. His mother had doted on him, possibly to make up for his dad's malice, yet her love and support always felt sincere.

"Behavior, or emotion?" Kelsey asked.

"Either, I suppose. The adults in the herd teach and guide the foals every season. When new horses come in they have to adjust to the new dynamic."

"Are you trying to compare foals and human babies?"

His lips tilted in a self-deprecating grin. "Maybe a little. A horse is a family animal."

"Herding animal," she corrected. "I do see your point, though. Horses run on instinct. People have the benefit of reason."

"When they use it," Fox said.

"True."

"My mom never made excuses for my dad," he said,

thinking out loud. “You see that on television or in the movies. A nurturing parent will take the blame or overcompensate for the abusive one. She didn’t. Or maybe she would have if she’d lived longer.”

His parents were gone and until Baby John, he would’ve said he’d coped with the loss and adjusted to the new family. Though Russ had worked constantly on building the business, when he was around he’d only touched Fox, or the other kids, with affection. He gave out hugs and high fives, a firm pat on the back and encouraging words. Mara had found fault with Fox no matter what he did. So once again, he sought ways to go unnoticed in the place he called home.

It was irresponsible not to examine what he’d internalized from those conflicting examples.

Fox looked down into Baby John’s sweet face. “You’ve been around babies more than me. Is it some infant survival instinct that he seems to fall in love with every person he meets?”

She chuckled. “I think that’s just his nature. Some babies have colic, others don’t. Some get ear infections when the wind blows wrong. Some babies are naturally happier than others.”

“Due to genetics or environment?”

She rolled her eyes. “A child care expert might tell you Baby John is happy and outgoing because he feels loved and secure.”

The expert would be wrong. Fox could provide security in the interim, but he couldn’t love the baby. Eventually the DNA findings would lead them to the real father who, hopefully, would love this little guy. “Then I’d tell that expert security trumps love at this age.” She pinned him with an arch of one eyebrow. “I care about him, but I'd be a fool to fall in love with him when he needs a real family."

"Did you feel loved and secure when your aunt and uncle adopted you?"

"That's different," he replied. "I was their actual nephew."

"The blood typing showed this guy could very well be *your* nephew."

An excellent reason to wait for the DNA results from the FBI lab. He couldn't bring himself to answer the question of what he'd do if one of his brothers didn't step up and take in Baby John. One of the mares wandered up for some sweet talk and affection and he and Kelsey obliged to the baby's delight.

"Do you want children of your own?" Her hesitation was answer enough. "You don't."

"I'm not sure. Coming from a big family, babies and toddlers were always around. It seemed inevitable. College was a wonderful break from that, except when I took nanny jobs to pay the bills. You'd think being out on my own for the past eight years would've helped me sort out if I want my own children, but I'm not sure it's been long enough."

And he'd pulled her right back into the job cycle she'd been avoiding. There was a pinch between his shoulder blades. Not overworked muscles, but pure guilt. "Maybe you should help me hire a nanny," he suggested.

"Stop worrying," she said. "I took this job, both of them, with my eyes wide-open. I don't regret it and I won't renege on our agreement."

"Thanks. You have no idea how grateful I am."

"I do." She snorted. "You and the baby were a mess when I showed up."

Fox turned away from the horses in the paddock to watch Baby John fighting off a nap in the stroller. "Why would his mother give him up?"

"Why did you take him in?" she countered.

He shrugged. "It was the right thing to do."

"She probably felt the same way."

Kelsey made a valid point. But it would be easier to accept that as truth if the mother had put the baby on the correct porch or provided more information about his origins.

"What will you do if the father doesn't want to do the right thing?" she asked.

"I guess the sheriff and child services will step in." Though it would upset the family, he couldn't imagine his brothers—assuming one of them was the father—would shirk the responsibility.

"You wouldn't consider adopting him yourself?"

There went that pinch between his shoulder blades again. "Would you, in my place?"

She sighed, her gaze on the horses cantering with the breeze that stirred the grass. "A man with a baby? It's been known to draw in the ladies."

The reply was so un-Kelsey he laughed. "Sweetheart, I'm a cowboy. All I need to do is polish the boots, put on the white hat and ride into town on my horse."

She stared at him, her lips twitching, until she lost control and laughed along with him. The sound lightened his load, eased the tension in his shoulders and drew him in close. She had such a kissable mouth. The color reminded him of the rosy glow on a summer peach. Would her lips be as soft and tender?

He really shouldn't be noticing details like her lips. She was the nanny/his new assistant and wanting her was highly inappropriate. She was off-limits.

He dragged his gaze to the horses, but it wouldn't stay there.

Watching her—covertly—had become his new favorite hobby. Her teeth would sink into that center swell of her lower lip when she was puzzling something out. Her nose wrinkled when she laughed at the baby's antics. And whenever she'd read too long, she closed her eyes and massaged her forehead.

He shouldn't know any of these things, yet it was a proximity issue and the result of talking about families past and future. Not to mention a hazard of the job. How could anyone care for a baby as cute and cooperative as Baby John and not get sentimental about family?

Just because she currently lived with him and they tag-teamed daily responsibilities didn't make them a family, he reminded himself sternly. She was living with him for the sole purpose of caring for the baby. If she were just his assistant, he would've expected her to find an apartment in town.

Kelsey living in town wouldn't work for him. His stomach twisted at the idea of not having her around for dinner or breakfast. After these days with her so thoroughly in his life, waiting for her to arrive in the morning or watching her drive off the ranch each night would be torture.

Fox sighed. The best cure for his runaway thoughts was work. "We'd best get back to the office."

Smiling, she turned the stroller around. "In case I haven't said it, this really is my dream job, Fox. Thanks again for the opportunity."

On second thought, the best cure might be to put some distance between the two of them. He paused at the barn. “If you’re good for the next hour or so, I need to ride over and check in with Wyatt.” It was a lie, but one that was best for everyone.

“Take your time.” She gave him a little wave. “We’re all set here.”

Chapter 6

In the days following their conversation at the paddock, Fox retreated into himself. Kelsey didn't try to draw him out. He was clearly wrestling with issues only he could sort through. It wasn't her place to point it out, but she thought he'd been lucky to escape an abusive father. Hopefully, when the DNA results came in, he would find some peace about all of it.

She got the baby onto a schedule that gave them both time in the office and out with the herd, and she reveled in this wonderful new turn her life had taken. Living with Fox posed challenges as she worked a little harder each day to mute her growing attraction to him. Their conversations made it worth the effort. He had a brilliant mind and discussions with him were fast, enlightening and entertaining as well as informative.

And with Baby John keeping the issue of fatherhood front and center, those conversations frequently cycled back to hereditary traits. Their respective areas of study forced them to ask if genetics or environment weighed more in an animal's development. Extending that thought process to people and family was natural.

Children were tiny mirrors of what they saw. It was the first method of learning and figuring out their place in the world. Living by example was a real thing, though children weren't destined to simply replicate every action into adulthood.

It was clear to her that Fox worried about becoming like his biological father. But she couldn't see him turning abusive and she didn't believe in a trait like that suddenly turned on like a light switch. His temperament was the polar opposite of cruelty. Fox had an innate kindness and a wry sense of humor. Even in that moment when she'd knocked on his door, when he'd been up to his eyeballs in wailing, miserable baby, his instinct had been to care and gather the child close, not push him away. Maybe that should be her personal goal within her professional role here. Given some time, she could help him see that he had excellent potential to be the best kind of dad.

After his morning nap, she tucked Baby John into the stroller and headed for their daily tour of the barn. She could be happy dealing with horses and foals for the rest of her days. As much as she enjoyed this particular baby, she still couldn't see herself raising children of her own. Definitely not with a man who, like her father, considered child-rearing beneath him.

She gave a start at the sound of an engine coming to life. Turning, she saw one of the Crooked C trucks rumbling down the road to the bunkhouse. The driver, a cheerful man named Luis, waved at her and the baby and she waved back, returning his smile.

She scolded herself for being jumpy. A working ranch meant people coming and going as they tended to the needs of the animals, people and land. However, that didn't explain away the car she thought had followed her into town when she'd made a grocery run a few days back. Fortunately, the car hadn't followed her into the parking lot. But the entire time she'd been in the store, she'd half expected her brothers to ambush her between the potatoes and greens.

"I don't usually get such a long break from them," she told the baby. Her brothers had serious skills when it came to finding her. No matter what they thought, she wouldn't change her mind and go back to that life. "You'd think fifteen years of saying no would be enough." She cuddled Baby John on her hip as they entered the barn. "Let's go see the horses."

The baby's eyes were wide, taking it all in as she talked to him about the horses and the other things in view. He might not grow up here with Fox, but it was never too early to plant those animal-loving seeds in his heart.

Pepper, one of the gentlest mares on the ranch, stuck her nose out of her stall when she heard Kelsey's voice. Walking over, she pulled a chunk of carrot from her pocket and opened her hand, offering the treat. Delighted, the baby squealed, kicking his legs as the carrot disappeared from Kelsey's flat palm.

Kelsey pampered the mare, rubbing her ears and neck. The horse and baby seemed to understand each other, the mare giving the occasional snort when Baby John's babbling paused. A trip out here never failed to put her at ease. Fox had good stock and he invested the time and care and money to make sure everyone thrived, from the animals all the way up to the people caring for them.

Done at the barn, Kelsey settled the baby back into his stroller for the walk back. She'd give him his next bottle outside on the back porch. A day as clear and warm as this one should be enjoyed.

"What will you think of snow, little guy?" She'd talk with Fox about picking up warmer outerwear for the baby for winter. The first frost would arrive any day now and the snow wouldn't be far behind.

Bottle in hand, she carried Baby John around back and found a good spot to soak up the sun. While the baby ate, she watched the wind move through the trees, thoroughly content. It was nice to feel useful in her field during this last stint as a nanny. Her top two skill sets had rarely aligned while she'd put herself through school and it had left her feeling unfulfilled. This time, having the balance of the engaging work with Fox made her enjoy both tasks more.

Her enticing hunk of a boss was certainly a big factor in how much she enjoyed both jobs. She smiled, thinking of Fox, and Baby John smiled back, formula dribbling from the corner of his mouth.

"You're the sweetest goofball," she said, blotting away the mess.

A burst of light flared across the baby's cheek, startling her. The glare had been as intense as a camera flash in a dark room. The sun must have reflected off something nearby. "Too jumpy," she muttered. "There's nothing out here but the two of us."

The flash occurred again and this time she stood up,

angling away from the source. A few minutes later the flash lit up a patch of the house. She'd bet her first paycheck that someone was watching her from the trees and the sun was bouncing off binoculars.

The familiar urge to bolt pulsed through her system. She waited until it subsided. If her brothers were behind those lenses and she moved too soon, they'd only get sneakier. She wouldn't give them the satisfaction or the advantage.

Keeping an eye on the trees, she put the baby to her shoulder to burp him. When he was ready for the rest of his bottle, she headed inside to the office. The last thing Fox needed was the theatrics of her brothers, but as his nanny, he needed to know the risks.

As she rounded the corner of the barn, Fox walked up from the opposite direction. His hair mussed by the wind and that just-shy-of-perfect smile curving his lips scrambled her thoughts.

"There you are," he said, pushing his hair back. "I thought you two were still in the barn."

The baby twisted away from her, seeking Fox's attention. He indulged the little guy, letting the baby catch and hold his finger.

"No. I—" She took a deep breath. "We were soaking up the sunshine around back."

"Great day for it." He opened the door and urged her to go in.

When they were in the office, she forced the words out in a rush. "I think someone is up there in the trees behind the house. Possibly watching the ranch," she added when Fox's shoulders went stiff. "I could be way off base."

He took the baby and gave him the bottle, but his

gaze rested on her. "Start at the beginning," he suggested.

"I'm probably overreacting," she began. "As I was feeding him, a light flashed over his cheek, like a reflection. When it happened again—"

"How many times?"

"Three that I noticed near us," she answered. "The last time, the reflection hit the siding. Oval, too perfect to be sunlight bouncing off something natural." She fidgeted with the burp cloth. "Do you think someone is checking up on the baby?" She preferred that scenario over the possibility of her brothers finding her out here. "Whoever was watching was a ways out, and they would have needed binoculars."

"Which can reflect light," Fox said.

Voice stern and eyes cool, she knew he'd handle it and she didn't have to embarrass herself or risk the best job ever by bringing up her annoying brothers and their issues. If her brothers trespassed on Colton land, she'd deal with it.

"I should take this to Deputy Bloom or the sheriff," Fox said. "Have you seen anything else out of the ordinary?"

His comment served as a reminder about the Avalanche Killer and the threat he posed to young women in the area. That explained Fox's sudden concern for her. She felt selfish for worrying it was her brothers out there. "There's been a car I don't recognize in the area a time or two. A black sedan."

"Up behind the house? When?"

"No, not so close," she said. The baby grew restless, reacting to Fox's distress, and she took him back, settling into her desk chair. "I noticed it a few days ago.

It's a new car, in good condition." And her brothers wouldn't drive a car that expensive. "It didn't have a Crooked C logo like the other cars and trucks that are usually around."

"Maybe the mother is having second thoughts." Fox skimmed his fingers over the baby's head. "Or the real father found out where his son landed. I know I wouldn't stop searching if he was mine." He stepped back and pulled his phone from his pocket.

Relieved, her pulse that had been racing minutes ago throttled back to normal. "Some coolheaded nanny you've got here." She spread a blanket on the floor and turned the baby's attention to a cloth book with bold contrasting patterns.

"I'll say."

She shot him a look but he was distracted with his phone. "What's that mean?"

"It means you're remarkable. You might feel rattled, but the baby has no idea. That's an impressive skill."

Skill? It was life. Survival. In her family, upsetting the new baby was never worth the hassle. Whatever was going on, be it worry, an argument, or even homework, it was better to keep anything distressing away from the newborn.

"You've given him all he needs," she said. "A full tummy and plenty of happy attention."

"Somehow I think his contentment is more about you than the formula or a cloth book." He held up his phone. "I'm calling my cousin Trey to come look around."

His compliment wrapped around her heart, as comforting as a hug. Kelsey let her imagination run wild. As safe as she felt on the property, it would be absolutely amazing to rest her head on his strong shoulder and feel his arms come around her.

Not exactly the wisest train of thought for a woman crushing on her boss, but she enjoyed the diversion while he spoke with the sheriff.

Fox could see Kelsey was spooked, no matter how cheerful she was with the baby. The signs were there, in the way her mouth pinched and her brow flexed. He also noticed that she'd positioned herself between the baby and the front doors.

"Sheriff is on his way," he said after he ended the call. "Want me to take the little guy?"

"We're good." She kept her head down, tickling Baby John's tummy. "He's always happy when you join us."

"I'm always happy to join," he murmured, realizing it was true. He'd come a long way on the baby interaction scale since Kelsey had arrived. Every day seemed more intriguing and less terrifying. "With you around, it's easy to forget how much baby care frightens me."

"He's a good training-wheel baby," she said. At last she looked at him, but she was frowning a little. "Actually, that might be wrong."

"How so?"

"Your mystery boy here is sweet as can be and easy to please. When you do have your own kids, you might be in for a rude awakening."

"Like Wyatt and Bailey?" So far their newborn had zero interest in sleeping for more than a few minutes at a time. Each time he visited, Wyatt looked strung out, though his brother was happier than Fox had ever seen him.

"Some newborns are sleep resistant at first. They'll figure him out." Kelsey gave a little laugh. "One of my little brothers refused to sleep in the cradle. He had to be held, preferably by Mom. Eventually, we swaddled him in one of her sweaters and discovered all of us rested easier."

"Have you mentioned that trick to Bailey?"

Her lips kicked up on one side. "You could," she said. "You'd be her hero."

"Please. They'd know the idea came from you."

The baby rolled to his back, the cloth book caught in one tiny fist. He shook it and giggled, his legs kicking into the air.

"Is it normal to feel like I can see him grow from one day to the next?" Fox asked.

"It is," she replied. A dreamy look transformed her face, her mind clearly in the past. "Especially for someone like you with excellent observation skills."

She had top-notch observation skills, as well. Fox started to ask how many siblings she remembered growing day by day when he heard a car door slam out front. He tickled the baby's wriggling foot before he popped up to answer the door and show his cousin into the office.

"Thanks for coming, Trey," he said after he'd introduced Kelsey.

"How's your little John Doe?" The sheriff smiled down at the as-of-yet unclaimed baby. "He looks happy enough."

"The three of us are getting on just fine," Fox replied. "Thanks in large part to Kelsey."

The baby gave the sheriff a wide smile, flapping his hands in the air.

"Looks that way." Trey grinned. "Any progress on the parent search?"

"Not yet," Fox said. "All of the ranch hands denied any connection. Agent Roberts fast-tracked the DNA for us, so we're hopeful the results will be in soon."

"If you're content, then I suppose this is still the best place for him."

"His mother thought so," Fox said.

The sheriff raised an eyebrow. "Assuming his mother is actually the person who put him on your doorstep."

His cousin had a valid point, one that struck a little deeper after what Kelsey had seen. "We called because Kelsey has seen an unfamiliar car in the area lately along with a strange reflection from the road up behind the house."

"What kind of reflection?"

"I think it was sunlight bouncing off glass," Kelsey said. "From the angle, it seemed like someone might have been watching the house."

"Show me," Trey said. "Talk me through it."

Fox carried the baby as they all traipsed outside and around to the back patio. Kelsey pointed out the landmarks as she explained what she'd seen as Trey took notes.

When they came back in, the sheriff tucked his notebook away. "It's probably nothing, as you said, Miss Lauder. Still, we have a serial killer on the loose and I don't like that Fox hasn't seen any of this trouble for himself."

Fox bristled. "You're questioning her story?"

"Take it easy." Trey rested his hands on his hips. "First, it's my job to play the skeptic until we have hard evidence. Second, *you* aren't exactly the Avalanche Killer's type. She is."

Immediately contrite, he subsided. "Hadn't looked at it like that." Although he was glad Trey probably believed Kelsey, the comments didn't ease his mind at all.

"Why don't I go on up and look around? Deputy Bloom is headed this way. We'll see if we can find anything helpful. I'll stop back when we're done."

"Thank you, Sheriff," Kelsey said.

Handing her the baby, Fox walked his cousin to his car. "You think the killer's snooping around the ranch?"

"I think there are plenty of variables," Trey hedged. "You were smart to call. Trust me, we're not leaving any stone unturned." He hesitated. "What do you know about your nanny?"

"She's an expert on babies, all of her references agreed on that. She's unflappable, has an endless well of patience, and I'd be lost without her." She was already his best asset, in or out of the office, though he didn't share that information with his cousin.

"What you're doing is admirable," Trey said, "but don't hesitate to ask if you need child services."

Inexplicably annoyed by what had surely been a supportive comment, Fox headed back to the office after his cousin went about his business. He found Kelsey reading to the baby.

This time she met his gaze right away, her eyes sparkling. "Thanks for making the call," she said.

"They might not find anything," Fox warned.

She shrugged. "It helps to know someone is trying. You, the sheriff..." Her voice trailed off and the baby squirmed on her lap. "Well, it helps."

Who in her past hadn't made the effort when she

needed help? He crouched down, his gaze locked with hers. "I won't let anything hurt you out here." The promise was out there, a vow humming between them.

Her eyes shimmered with a rush of emotion. He didn't press and he didn't downplay his words. She was on his property, working for him in a dual capacity. He felt a similar responsibility to keep all of his employees safe.

"I *can* take care of myself," she assured him. "And I won't let anything happen to John."

He believed she meant every word. Although he'd seen her strength with the horses and in her daily yoga habit, it was hard not to have doubts based on her petite frame and gentleness with the baby. "The sheriff's right," he said. "With everything going on around here, we need to stay vigilant."

The baby fussed, and Kelsey went to change him while Fox stepped outside, trying to get a glimpse of Trey or Deputy Bloom searching for clues or evidence up on the road. He couldn't think of any good reason for someone to sit up there and watch his office.

His home.

Anyone spying on the breeding operation would have more success by searching the barn or cracking his computer records. Fox didn't have any idea how a serial killer's mind worked. Didn't *want* to know. He wasn't sure which was worse, thinking that a killer might be hunting Kelsey or thinking that someone was interested in taking the baby.

Both options gave him chills.

More than once she'd gently pointed out how attached he was to the baby. Could she also see he was becoming more attached to her every day? It wasn't practical, but he hadn't figured out how to stop it.

She'd transformed his house into a home practically overnight. Her laughter was contagious and her conversation captivated him. Each time they sat down to dinner or one handed off the baby to the other he fought the urge to touch her cheek or hair or kiss her. She was invading his dreams and he didn't mind at all. Since moving in and starting his business, he'd enjoyed the solitude of living alone, yet having Kelsey near made him reconsider how a family could look in this same space.

It was a damned appealing concept.

Trey returned, his steps heavy as he crossed the drive. "We didn't find anything specific," he said. "What I wouldn't give for a boot print or clear tire tread about now." He glowered at the horizon.

"Thanks for coming out." Fox shook his cousin's hand. "It puts my mind at ease."

"It shouldn't," the sheriff said. "Not until we have the killer in custody. Stay on guard."

"We will," he promised.

"And keep me in the loop about the baby," Trey added, striding out to his car.

Fox agreed to that, as well. Staring up at the rarely used access road, he tried again to think of a motive for anyone to spy on him. Unsuccessful, he returned to the office and applied himself to the evaluation of the failed pregnancies last season.

It wasn't quite enough to keep his mind from searching for how to best protect the woman and child living under his roof.

* * *

His blood rushed in his ears as he watched the sheriff and deputy search the area behind Fox's house. Let them search. They wouldn't find anything—he was too careful. Too good.

He breathed deep, the crisp, pine-laced air stinging his lungs, affirming his life. The adrenaline, the anticipation was almost as addictive as the moment he put his plans into action.

The only thing better than watching the life drain out of a pretty face was the abject fear that came first. He had his system down now, knew what he would feel in every step of the process. The confusion would rev him up. The begging and pleading would confirm his power. After that, the loss of hope and resignation when his victims knew he would prevail gave him a sweet, confident calm.

And when it was over, a new facet of the game began as he outsmarted everyone trying to stop him.

Chapter 7

Kelsey was on edge after a night plagued with dreams of her brothers chasing her away from her new position with Fox. She much preferred the restlessness that followed her dreams of sharing sizzling-hot kisses with her boss. She gave in and hauled herself out of bed early, just to clear her mind.

Uneasy about being watched yesterday, she only went as far as the front porch when it was time for Baby John's midmorning bottle. Here, they couldn't be seen from the access road on this side of the barn Fox called home. Yes, she needed to be vigilant, but today she concluded she was better off not knowing if she was being watched.

This location also gave her an excellent view of the handsome rancher riding back to the barn after his morning visit to Wyatt's acreage, sitting tall in the saddle, his hat shading his eyes and his hands easy on the reins. Her mouth watered. She wasn't some innocent girl and yet her heart fluttered just watching him move. Her every nerve danced with increasing awareness and appreciation of his masculine form and roughhewn sensuality.

With a slow smile and a tap to his hat, he turned toward the barn while she dragged her heart rate back to normal. It was *not* appropriate to drool over her boss in the office or while she lived in as his nanny.

The baby patted her hand. It wouldn't be too much longer before he was ready to hold his own bottle. He grinned and milk dribbled down his chin. She had to chuckle. The little guy was a cutie, and such a flirt. She dried his chin and held the bottle out of his reach when he noticed Fox and started babbling.

It sounded like *da-da*, though Baby John probably was still a little young for making real, meaningful words. "Look at you growing on schedule," she crooned. "Such a big boy."

A few minutes later, the baby was nearly done with his bottle when Fox came into view. He paused at the top step, leaning a shoulder against the post. "It's a gorgeous day."

"We agree," she said. "How are things with Wyatt?"

"The cattle are fine." His lips kicked up to the side. "Wyatt's showing serious envy whenever I mention the perfect schedule you have for Baby John."

The baby started chattering and she turned him so he could see Fox better. He suddenly let out a loud burp, making Kelsey and Fox laugh.

"Something else is on your mind," she said.

He tapped his cell phone against his open palm.

"The DNA results just came in." His gaze locked onto the baby and his straight dark eyebrows drew close.

"Already?" Kelsey was impressed by the quick turnaround. The Colton influence hadn't been exaggerated. "Your Agent Roberts really came through."

"I'll say."

For a man who wanted to be done with child care he didn't appear to be in a hurry about getting into review the findings. "Would you like to go in and get started?"

He turned toward the mountains, the peaks glowing in the sunshine. "In a minute."

Things would change once Fox read the results. With genetic proof, the baby's family couldn't deny responsibility. Although Fox claimed he wanted to be done, his tenderness and care with the infant told a different story.

The Coltons seemed to be a close-knit family. An illegitimate surprise child was bound to put serious stress on the family dynamic. She didn't know if he was procrastinating because he didn't want to find out one of his brothers had lied or if he wasn't ready to let Baby John go.

"Have you decided what you'll do with all the baby gear when he is settled with his family?" she asked.

Fox turned his phone end over end in his hands. "Whatever the family doesn't need, I'll offer to Wyatt and Bailey. If there's anything leftover, I'll cross that bridge later. Unless you want to share it with someone in your family."

He rarely pressed for details about her past. Did he suspect something? Unease prickled along the back of her neck. "No," she said at last. "They have what they need." If not quite everything they wanted. "Is there a women's shelter around? They'd appreciate the donation."

"That's a smart idea." He came around to crouch in front of them, smelling of sunshine and autumn leaves. His shirtsleeves were rolled back and his tanned, muscular forearms flexed as he gently tugged on Baby John's feet. The baby grinned and reached for Fox. "We'd best see how it all shakes out."

"You seem nervous," she said. Not the most tactful observation, especially when he had good reason.

"I am," he admitted. "I don't want to believe the worst of my brothers."

"It's possible the mother didn't tell anyone she was pregnant," she reminded him.

He turned that vibrant, sky blue gaze on her. "You're suggesting that he might be my son after all?"

"You said he wasn't. I believe you." She busied herself with the baby, desperate to hide the longing she felt, the nearly painful need to touch him. Every day she spent with Fox she fell a little harder. It went beyond raw physical attraction. His kind and generous heart was apparently a bottomless pit of compassion. The man had taken in a baby that wasn't his and treated the little guy as if he was the world's greatest gift.

He dealt with the routine and unpredictable moments with an imperturbable ease. No rants or shouting, no threats or demands like so many of the men in her family. She adored the way he got lost in his work and forgot the rest of the world, until the baby fussed. Then, despite it being her job, he was dialed in and offering help. He might not see it yet, but he'd be an amazing father when he did have a family of his own.

Wasn't she the hypocrite? It wasn't her place to put

those values on him. If the end-all, be-all of life was taking a spouse and procreating, she should go back to her family compound right now. How did a couple of weeks playing house with one sexy rancher and a six-month-old change fifteen years of hard-won independence?

"Kelsey?" His hand touched her knee, the contact earning her full attention. He had the most remarkable hands. Rough from the physical demands of the ranch, quick and limber as needed for his research. The contact wasn't inappropriate or unwelcome. The last part worried her most.

"Sorry." She tried to smile as her cheeks flamed. "You were saying?"

The baby threw himself toward Fox. She understood the inclination.

With a chuckle, Fox picked up the baby and stood. Tucking his phone into his back pocket, he swayed side to side. Baby John sighed, relaxing on that sturdy shoulder, his eyelids already drooping.

"I was asking why you so easily believe me." He smiled down at her. "Is it that obvious I haven't been in a relationship lately?"

"Oh." She gathered up the empty bottle and stood as well, draping the cotton blanket over the baby's back. "No," she answered, trying to laugh it off. "It was your reputation."

"Maybe I don't want to know."

Flustered, she explained before the awkwardness got out of control. "It's more the way I interpreted your reputation. *Professionally.*" Good grief, she was making a mess of this. "You're *the* rock star in quarter horses."

"For now." He dipped his head to her. "I have a feeling a younger, prettier star is on the rise."

He thought she was pretty? *Stop it.* Straightening her shoulders, she plowed on. "You're a stickler for the details, analysis and data. When I, um, did a bit of background checking, everyone agreed on that." She sounded like a stalker, even though she knew checking up on anyone she wanted to work with was an essential first move.

"Being a stickler makes me believable?"

At least he wasn't shocked that she'd looked into him. "Being detail-oriented makes it hard for me to believe you wouldn't notice your significant other was pregnant."

He arched one dark eyebrow. "When I'm working I probably wouldn't notice a tornado."

"True, but you also don't have a reputation as a player in the lab or in the field."

"Color me relieved." His features had relaxed. "It's an integrity thing."

"You told me the baby wasn't yours. We might have been new acquaintances at the time, but I know you're a man of your word."

His mouth canted to the side. "Saw both sides of that coin growing up." He twisted, trying to check on the baby without waking him.

"He's not quite out," she told him.

Fox kept swaying, his gaze on the mountains again. "My dad kept his word, usually on the wrong promises. I remember him canceling fun plans more than once, but if he told me to do something *or else*, he always followed through on the 'or else.'" His voice was soothing for the sake of the baby in his arms. It was a weird counterpoint to the story he shared.

Over meals upstairs and through general conversations in the office, he'd shared several stories of his childhood with Russ and Mara. Him sharing something from earlier was rare. "I keep telling you abusive behavior isn't hereditary."

He shrugged.

If he hadn't been holding Baby John she would've given him a hard shake.

"Uncle Russ never struck any of us, and when he made a promise, he kept it."

"It's good that you had positive examples and influences."

"Do you think it's enough?"

"Look at yourself," she said. "I think you're exactly the type of man you're meant to be." Embarrassed by the force of the compliment, she opened the main door and then the office door so he could settle the baby, snoring now, in the portable crib in the office.

"He's a good sleeper," she said, seizing on a change of subject. "We don't have to walk on eggshells."

"I'm still scarred from his arrival," Fox admitted. "And paranoid after meeting Hudson."

She clapped a hand over her mouth to smother her laughter. "Now about those results…"

"We'll get to that." He stopped at her desk. "I hope my reputation is enough to make up for this." His gaze dropped to her lips. "Whenever you laugh, my mind goes blank and all I can think about is tasting you."

"Fox…" She must have dozed off while feeding the baby and was caught up in a daydream. She was thirty years old with a soul-deep crush on her new boss. If he'd declared his undying love for her she wouldn't have been more shocked. She had no idea what to say or do.

Apparently he did. He moved in slowly, giving her room to say no, to scoot away, to do anything but wait, anticipating...him.

His lips met hers lightly. Sweetly. Almost as if neither of them knew exactly what they were doing. Still, her heart pounded as if she'd run up a dozen flights of stairs. Over and over.

He eased back, his breath fanning her cheek, and she caught herself before she grabbed his shirt and pulled him back in for more. Should she ask why or just accept her good fortune that the man could leave a lasting impression with a simple kiss?

"Your background check wasn't flawed. I've never kissed anyone in the office or a lab," he said. His hands enveloped hers. "Never wanted to."

"Wait. Have you kissed someone out in the field?"

"Only a horse or two," he teased.

Somehow the humor steadied her. "Can I ask why me and why now?"

"I tried to wait until we found the baby's father. But I didn't want you to think our first kiss was only gratitude."

"No worries." The man was too honest for his own good. "I know what it feels like to be used."

The humor in his eyes fled and his gaze turned fierce. Protective. She couldn't recall anyone wearing that expression on her behalf before. "Who used you?"

"Fox." She nudged him back so she could breathe deeply, without getting a lungful of his tempting, masculine scent. "No one can go back and right every wrong."

"I'd like to try," he said. "For you."

That was almost as shocking as the kiss. "We barely know each other. It only feels different because we're in a tight orbit while we care for the baby."

He tilted his head, squinting a little as if she was a report he couldn't quite sort out.

"You're about to know my DNA up close and personal," he pointed out. "Whatever we find out, I want more *personal* time with you."

Her heart fluttered. Silly, girlish reaction, but there was no denying it. She was in over her head, logic obliterated with one nearly chaste touch of his lips. That wasn't a good sign. If she let herself get more attached to Fox, would she be able to do the necessary thing and run if her brothers found her?

It was just one kiss. One desire-sparking kiss that made her want so much more. "Why don't we table this?" She circled her finger between them. "And take a look at those results."

"Right." He walked to his laptop, clicked a few keys and the printer started spitting out pages. He pulled the pages from the tray and handed her half. "Your copy."

She watched, mesmerized and more than a little turned on when he donned his reading glasses and studied the report. Biting her lip, she dragged her attention away from her sexy and compelling boss.

Despite the kiss and his thrilling declaration that he wanted to explore their personal connection, she had a job to do. It didn't surprise her that he'd approach this analysis the same way as he did everything else. If the results were clear, his family dynamic might shift dramatically. Since her first day, he'd coaxed her to give her opinion, rather than echo his thoughts or views on a breeding program, a mare's health, or a test result. She'd worked for researchers who only wanted verification of their theories. Any dissenting opinion was argued away if it couldn't be immediately dismissed. Fox's ability to hear other views was refreshing.

The data immediately confirmed that Baby John Doe was *not* Fox's son. No surprise there—she knew he'd been honest with her. The more curious finding was that the baby wasn't fathered by any of Fox's brothers, either. So why had someone put the baby on his doorstep? Rather than answers, there were now more questions.

She flipped from page to page, reviewing the markers between the baby and the samples Fox and the other men provided. The baby was related, likely a cousin to Fox. That information would narrow his search for Baby John's family, but by how much?

"Thoughts?" Fox asked without looking up from his own pages.

"He's not your nephew. I'd say he's the son of one of your cousins based on the data points we have.

"Mmm-hmm."

She took the sound as agreement. Stealing a peek at him while he was distracted, she banked the delicious memory for later. He'd propped his chin on his fist and his elbow on the desktop. Add in the reading glasses and the trimmed beard framing his square jaw, and she was quickly lost to a fantasy of straddling his lap and scattering kisses along his neck, pushing her hands into his thick, dark brown hair and claiming his mouth.

Her pulse lurched into high gear and heat flooded

her face. Not the place and definitely *not* the time. How would they find the right cousin? She reviewed the various DNA markers that matched up between Fox and the men he called his brothers.

Seeing an unexpected result, she paused and stared at him again. Had he expected the data to show his biological father was actually Russ Colton? Was *this* why the nature versus nurture issue lingered at the front of his mind? If so, that didn't explain why he worried about becoming like the father who physically abused him.

At his desk, Fox started muttering. He must be seeing the same thing. "You okay?" she asked, sidling over.

"Yeah." He pushed his hair off his forehead. "Based on the markers from the baby and what I know about the Colton family, I'm thinking my cousin Mason Gilford must be the father."

She counted the sample results. "Did you send a DNA sample from Mason?"

"No." He pushed his glasses to his forehead and rubbed his eyes. Both his elbows propped on his desk, he cradled his head in his hands. "Admittedly, I have plenty of male cousins. Mason and his wife were struggling to conceive. Then she did the unthinkable and kidnapped his pregnant sister, Molly, planning to steal the baby for them."

"That's horrendous."

"It is. The marriage was rocky before that, though Mason didn't talk about it much."

"Rocky enough that he'd have an affair?" she asked.

Fox nodded. "Although that doesn't get us any closer to how the baby ended up on my doorstep."

"Does Mason live nearby?"

Another nod. He turned his head, his expression so forlorn she wanted to cuddle him. "He's head of a new business for the Colton Empire and travels all the time. Maybe the baby's mother tried his place and came here rather than risk that Mason was out of town."

"You are well-known and ranches must be tended," she said.

His lips curved into a weak smile. "And I'm clearly easy to find."

Was he ignoring the rest of the information in the data sets? It wasn't her business. He'd respected her privacy about the skeletons rattling around in her family closet. She should show him the same courtesy. "Is there anything else here that might narrow it down?" she asked. "In case it *isn't* Mason."

He scowled down at the paperwork on his desk and froze in place. Glancing up at the family tree he'd brought up on the wall monitor, he mumbled something as he made a note on the paper.

She didn't want to blurt it out. Maybe he didn't react because it was what he expected to see. When he mentioned his father he usually referred to Russ. Could this be one of those family truths everyone knew and tacitly agreed not to discuss?

"What are you thinking, Kelsey?"

She wouldn't insult him by dancing around it. Pointing to the similarities between Fox and his brothers, she said, "This value is higher than I expected across all four samples."

There. That gave him room to ignore it or explain it.

"That's not looking at the baby's DNA." He frowned at the printouts.

"No. It's your sample next to Wyatt, Decker and Blaine."

She saw the moment it clicked for him. His face went slack and a split second later his gaze narrowed behind his glasses. He swore softly. "That doesn't make sense." Removing his glasses, he pinned her with his intense blue gaze. "If you were looking at a random test, where none of the people behind the samples were known to you, what conclusion would you have from this?"

He was forcing her to say it. "I would say these three men were brothers." She circled the data for his brothers on her printout. "And this is their half brother." She drew a box around his sample.

Fox shoved back from his desk. "And if I say that's impossible?"

She saw the fear flickering in his eyes, the near panic in the pen he held in a white-knuckled grip. This was a revelation he'd never expected. "Are you okay?"

"Just answer the question." His voice, flat and dangerous, didn't scare her. Fox wasn't the kind of man who would shoot the messenger. She wondered if the same could be said for whoever had kept this secret from him.

Science. He needed cold, clinical facts right now. "With such an unexpected result, I would want to verify the samples were collected properly and no cross-contamination occurred."

"You know they were collected properly," he grumbled.

"Yes. The next step is assessing my confidence in the lab and the technicians who processed the samples. Agent Roberts did ask them to rush."

"He ushered those samples through the admin side and made sure they were labeled as a high priority."

"At the FBI lab," she finished. "They make mistakes."

"But not with this." He stalked away from her and back again, rolling a pen between his palms. Then he stopped, staring at the computer. "A reliable lab and clean samples equal a viable, true result."

"Yes," she replied softly, though it hadn't been a question. She could see his world tilting, crumbling. Everything he thought he knew about himself was wrong.

"I wasn't raised with my sister and cousins." He tossed the pen onto the desk. "I was raised with my *half* sisters and my *half* brothers." He landed hard in the chair, his face pale. "Russ Colton is my true father." He leaned forward, elbows on his knees, his ragged breath the only sound.

She'd never felt so helpless, not even the night she'd run away from home. Unlike Fox, she'd known what she was doing, afraid of the worst and hoping for the best. Inching forward, she rested a hand on his shoulder, gratified that he didn't shrug off the offered comfort.

He reached up, covering her hand with his. "Thank you."

"For what?" she asked automatically.

"Not judging."

She wasn't sure what or who he thought she'd judge. Not his fault he didn't know which man was his biological father. Who would hold that kind of thing against a person? "Trust me when I say every family has secrets."

He glanced up, a wry tilt to his lips. "That's the voice of an experienced nanny."

Among other things. "You and I both know the world isn't a perfect place."

"No." She moved as he stood up again. The color was back in his face, but the improvement didn't give her much encouragement.

"You're angry."

"Damn right I am. Someone knew about this." He massaged a fist with the opposite palm. "My mother, obviously."

Kelsey didn't point out the obvious flaw in that assumption. This wasn't the time to throw shade on the one parent who'd loved him so dearly. "If anyone had known, wouldn't it have come out by now?" she asked instead. "You're an adult, out on your own. There's no reason to protect you from mistakes your parents made. There's also no reason to dredge up the past or speak ill of the dead," she added gently.

"Do you think this is why Russ and Mara did the formal adoption?"

"They adopted your sister, too." Her heart ached for him. "From what you've told me, they loved you both. Imperfectly, sure, but sincerely. They made you all a family for the right reasons. I think Russ considered you one of his sons all along."

She gave herself points for tact and diplomacy. If only her mother could see her now, the cursed "big thinker" doling out calm rather than instigating debates that led nowhere.

"I… I have to go." He grabbed the stack of papers and shoved them into his back pocket. "You'll be okay here with the baby?"

"Absolutely." Whatever cropped up, she would handle as she'd been hired to do. "Are you going to see Mason?" She suspected he had a different destination in mind.

"No." He snagged his truck keys from the desktop and stormed out of the office. In the foyer, he paused. "I'm going over to see Russ and Mara. They owe me an explanation."

If the truth of his paternity had stayed a secret this long, she doubted Russ and Mara would agree with him. Still, she sympathized with his need for answers.

She turned back to the office when he stalked back inside. He exchanged one set of keys for another. "I shouldn't take the truck with the baby seat. You might need it."

"We'll be fine," she promised. A man who could think of others while swamped by anger and pain was a rare breed. "Unless you'd like us to go with you?" she offered. Anything to help ease his burden.

"No, thank you. They'll be reluctant to discuss this kind of thing in front of a stranger."

"I understand."

He stepped close and gave her a hard, fast kiss. "You're not a stranger to me."

Before she had a chance to recover or give him a final boost of encouragement, he was gone.

Chapter 8

At the base of the drive, Fox stared at up at Colton Manor, situated just above the valley and backed by the mountain. A massive and gorgeous testament to the success of the Colton Empire, the house had been built after he left for college. He'd never felt at home here, though the stunning showpiece with all its luxurious features and separate wings offered plenty of space for secrets to float around unnoticed.

All these years it had gnawed away at him that Aunt Mara had never accepted him as easily as she had Sloane. Was it because she'd known the truth Fox had just discovered? There was only one way to find out. Another bolt of white-hot anger flashed through him, as uncomfortable and foreign as the idea that his real father was Russ Colton.

He tried again to organize his thoughts as he stalked

to the front door and rang the doorbell. Too many questions and illogical leaps of conjecture weren't doing him any favors. To his surprise, Russ answered.

"Hi..." Fox didn't know how to fill in the blank when "Uncle Russ" didn't come out as it had every other day of his life. A tall man with wide shoulders, he was thicker in the midsection these days. His hair was mostly gray now, but once it had been nearly the same color as Fox's. Their eyes were different, Fox's blue and Russ's a brown that his other sons had inherited.

Which man had had a greater impact on his life—the distracted father or the abusive one?

"You look rough, Fox." Russ stepped back and welcomed him in. "Is the baby keeping you up at night?"

Of course they'd heard about the baby. *That* wasn't a secret. "He sleeps well. Kelsey got him on a schedule that fits into my routine." Days on the ranch started early, so he didn't really mind the 4:00 a.m. wake-up calls.

"Those days are long gone around here. Can't say I miss them," Russ said, leading the way toward the gathering room off the main kitchen. Mara rose from her seat when they walked in.

Fox's palms went damp when he saw his aunt. "Aunt Mara."

He didn't bother attempting an awkward hug this time. Though she'd done her best as a mother, she'd found her calling in business as director of operations at The Chateau. She looked as polished as ever with her blond hair styled up today and a bold dress in autumn colors with a short black jacket.

"Hello, Fox." Her deep blue eyes raked him head to toe. "You look tired."

He shrugged, more comfortable with her criticism than he would've been with compliments. "The baby and I had an early start."

"I can't believe you've taken in that child."

"He's family," Fox replied, suppressing another wave of anger. "You did the same, right? I'm just following your example."

She sniffed, settled back into her chair as aloof and confident as a queen on her throne. "The difference is I *knew* who you were."

"Did you?"

"Of course." Confusion rippled across her features. "You and Sloane were my sister's children." To his shock, her eyes glistened with tears. "You looked so much like Dana when you were younger."

Fox had a sudden recollection of her saying that shortly after they'd moved in. Not to him, but to her husband.

"Have you found the father?" Russ asked, taking a seat near Mara and urging Fox to do the same on the other side of the conversation area anchored by a stone fireplace.

"I think we have. Agent Roberts put a rush on the samples I collected." He met the older man's gaze. "I appreciate you agreeing to submit a cheek swab so we had more data to work with."

Out of the corner of his eye, he saw Mara's fingers dig into the arms of her chair.

"Did it help?" Russ asked.

"It did." Fox pulled the results from his back pocket. "The baby isn't mine. His DNA indicates he's the son of one of the cousins."

"Then why did someone drop him on your doorstep?" Mara queried. "You really should have let child services handle this."

"It may come to that," Fox agreed. "It will depend on what the father chooses."

"Fox—" Mara began.

"Are you worried?" he snapped at her. "Worried about what I'll say next?"

She jerked back as if he'd slapped her and the reaction only made him angrier. "Just like your father. Harrison never could hold his temper," she said. "I warned Dana before they got married. And we did everything possible to give you a better example when we took you in."

"Mara," Russ warned. "There's no need to go there."

"He's an adult now." She turned to Fox. "We never spoke ill of your father back then, but he couldn't have been an easy man to live with."

"You were concerned those tendencies would pass down to me by blood?"

She raised her chin, daring him to contradict her. "You're the expert on genetics, but I know abuse can run in families, whatever the reason."

Of all the times and topics to share his aunt's viewpoint, this was the most awkward. He could leave now and never say a word about what he'd found. He trusted Kelsey to keep the secret. Thinking of her, the way she moved through her yoga exercises and managed to stay calm no matter how the baby fussed, steadied him for what he had to say.

"You know I loved my parents," he began. "They weren't perfect, but I loved them. I love you both and I'm grateful for how you raised us." He met and held Mara's gaze. "You set a good example for Sloane and for me." His sister had found happiness and was raising a lively daughter. Fox didn't want to think how that might be different if Harrison had turned his hard fist to her, too.

"Stop dancing around whatever's on your mind," Russ said. "We're here for you, Fox. Always will be."

He hoped he wasn't about to irrevocably change that. "I looked at the DNA and I noticed a correlation across all of the samples that didn't make sense." He tapped the papers. "When I compared my DNA to you, Wyatt, Decker and Blaine, the results show I'm a half brother rather than a cousin."

A frown worked its way slowly across Russ's brow. Mara's gaze, sharp and accusing, bored into Fox.

"I guess I don't understand what that means," Russ said.

"Your sons are your sons," Fox said. "But it seems I'm your son, too."

Russ shoved to his feet. "You're saying Dana and I… we…" He shook his head. "That's impossible."

"Stop blustering," Mara's voice was as brittle as the first ice over a lake. "I know how you felt about her."

"I married *you*!"

"Of course you did. It's what our parents wanted. And you did your duty by me," she snapped. "I'm truly the *lucky* one."

Russ shifted his attention to Fox. "There's been a mistake," he insisted. He pushed a hand though his hair, scrubbed at his chin. "If you were mine, Dana would've told me. She wouldn't—"

"Of course he's yours!" Mara twisted her wedding band around and around on her finger. "Can't you see it in his face?"

Fox looked from his uncle—*father*—to his aunt. He studied her. "You knew."

"I suspected something from the start." Mara sniffed delicately. "Dying in that hospital, my sister begged me to take in Fox and Sloane, pleaded with me to keep her secret." Standing, she crossed the room and drilled a finger into her husband's chest. "All this time, I've been *faithful* to you, while raising your child without a single complaint. I've stayed when I had every right to leave and take *everything*."

"Well, let me draft a thank-you note right now," Russ snarled. "You had no right to keep this from me, or him."

"I did as my sister asked. Dana told me Harrison had found out about Fox and lost his temper. That was no accident," she said to Fox. "He meant to punish her and was willing to die in the effort."

Fox couldn't move. Dumbstruck, his entire body had gone cold. The accident had been intentional. His heart caught in a brutal vise, his gut twisted. He pressed a hand to his stomach as he clenched his teeth against the sickening upheaval. If he puked on this floor, Mara would never forgive him.

Wait. Shouldn't *she* be worried about *him* forgiving her?

"Mara, stop." Russ was at Fox's side and the strong hand on his shoulder was the only thing that felt real.

"I won't." Her blue eyes flashed. "Harrison was useless and weak and vindictive. He killed my sister." Mara paced, her heels clicking on the slate floor. "Was I angry? Yes. But I honored Dana's last request and raised Fox alongside my sons." Her gaze lashed

Fox. "Every time I looked at you I saw my husband's betrayal."

"That's why," Fox muttered. Overcoming the shock, he shrugged off Russ's support, backing away from the two people he'd always counted on. "That's why nothing I did pleased you."

"That's nonsense," Mara denied. "I loved you as Dana would have done. Your memory is blurred from grief."

"No, he's right," Russ said.

"What do you know about it?" Mara rolled her eyes and threw her hands in the air. "All those years, your Colton Empire took precedent over *our* children. This one—" she sneered at Fox "—moves in and suddenly you're striving for father of the year awards. You'll never convince me you didn't know he was yours."

Fox knew Russ couldn't fake the pain and shock that mirrored his own. What now?

"I didn't, I swear it, Fox," Russ said. "If Dana were alive…" He paused when his voice cracked. "If she were still with us, I would demand some answers." He glared at his wife. "I gave him more attention because I could see you were content to let him flounder."

"You doted on him because he was Dana's!" Mara turned toward the view of the mountains. "You were making up for Harrison's ill temper."

"You knew that, too?" Fox whispered. And no one intervened? "My mom was wonderful," he said. Who was he trying to convince—himself or them? "You, Uncle Russ, were a better dad than the one I started with. I'm grateful for that."

"I hope you're happy," Mara huffed, folding her

arms. "Do you feel better for turning our lives upside down?"

Again, *he* was the problem. That was her stance from day one. "Information and answers are good things, Aunt Mara."

"What will you do now?" Russ asked wearily.

"What should I do?" he countered. The skeletons had crashed through the closet door. "Does anything change? Legally, I still have six siblings." And all of them were *half* siblings now. His real father was alive, not dead. A workaholic instead of an abuser. "We're still family." His gaze drifted to the wall where collages of highlights and school pictures were framed, as if all seven children had been one big happy family.

Mara had allowed for that much at least. It had to count for something. Why did he feel so damned alone?

"Are you going to tell them?" Mara demanded.

"Is there a reason not to?" Fox asked quietly.

"You think I want the public to know that my husband had an affair and forced me to raise the byproduct?"

Fox shook his head. What was he, a cut of pork? He marveled that Mara's sharp words could still slice right through him. His home life could have been worse. He'd grown up, completed school and now owned a successful business. There had been girlfriends and friendships along the way, even if he wasn't yet married.

"I'm going."

Mara raced after him and grabbed his arm, her perfect manicure digging into the fabric of his shirt. "Who do you intend to tell?"

"Who would care?" Russ's other kids might look at

their father with some disappointment, but it was all water under the bridge at this point. "It wasn't your mistake," Fox pointed out. "You're the wounded party. You're the hero for taking me in. Don't you want the world to know?"

She slapped him.

His cheek stinging, Russ compounded the shock and stepped between them. Using only his height advantage, he forced her back. "Apologize, Mara."

"I'll do no such thing!"

"I'm the one you're mad at," Russ said, his voice cool. "Take a shot at me." He spread his arms wide.

Fox walked around them and picked up his coat to make his escape.

"He's an embarrassment," Mara screeched. "Your old infatuation with Dana will ruin me if this gets out."

Fox heard Russ's voice, low and intense, but he couldn't make out the words. Not his business. He kept going, through the foyer, out the front door and to his truck. He'd come for answers and gotten them. Too bad he didn't feel any better.

Driving away, he called his aunt every name he could think of. He hated her, hated the burden she'd heaped on his young shoulders during the worst days of his life. Who would he tell? Everyone who needed to know. A little embarrassment was nothing compared to the doubt and insecurity he had to overcome because of her sniping and neglect.

He'd tell whoever he pleased that Russ Colton was in fact his father. Maybe then the world would stop waiting for him to lose his temper and lash out the way his "father" had. On a wave of indescribable sorrow, Fox pulled to the side of the road. He'd been driving without paying any attention and wound up at the accident site.

Murder site.

He had heard his parents say *I love you*. There had been laughter and cheerful traditions to offset the random bouts of temper. How could a man say those three words to a woman and then kill her?

Fox's stomach rolled. As angry and hurt as he felt right this minute, he couldn't comprehend such a reprehensible choice. Mara had slapped him and he hadn't been remotely inclined to retaliate.

Slowly, like the sun creeping up on the morning, relief seeped through Fox's system. He didn't harbor a genetic predisposition to violence.

Lonely in the office, Kelsey took the baby upstairs to the house for his afternoon nap. She'd brought along the stack of articles she was wading through for the breeding research. With everything on Fox's mind, she thought fleshing out some new ideas would be a positive counterpoint on what had surely been a difficult conversation.

When Baby John awoke, Kelsey changed him and gave him a bottle, then took him out to the backyard for some fresh air and sunshine. The playset Fox had built for his niece had components that could be switched out based on a child's age. Last week, he'd hooked up the baby swing again, though it was still a little early for this little guy to use it.

Kelsey sat down on a full-size swing, keeping John tucked up close. He kicked his feet, and she used her foot to rock them back and forth. The baby laughed and he kicked again. "You'll get the hang of this in no time," she said, kissing the top of his head.

He was the happiest baby she'd ever met, and that was saying quite a bit considering how many little ones she'd cared for before leaving home. Not to mention the babysitting jobs and nanny posts she'd taken to get through school.

When his cheeks were pink from the breeze, she left the swings and carried him around the yard. She pointed out various plants and objects, giving him the names of each though it was too soon for him to either remember or form the words. She was about to walk down to the barn and show the baby the horses, one of his favorite things to do, when she noticed the black sedan parked on the road again.

She should've noticed the car sooner even with the back half of the car in the shadows of the trees. Whoever sat in the front seats would have a clear view of Fox's property. A chill slid down her spine and she shook it off. The car was too far away for her to see anyone inside. The odds of her brothers buying or renting a car that nice were slim to none. At least not before they used her to land the fortune they felt she owed them.

Still, she felt too exposed out here, especially with a baby in her arms.

Kelsey reached for her phone, her first instinct to call Fox. No point. Being watched wasn't the same as being in danger. It could be anyone up there in the sedan. Her brothers, the person who dropped off the baby, possibly a tourist or businessman who'd lost his way. Fox had enough to deal with today, she wouldn't pile on her old baggage and paranoia, as well.

"FAST FIVE" READER SURVEY

Your participation entitles you to:
✱ 4 Thank-You Gifts Worth Over $20!

Complete the survey in minutes.

HARLEQUIN
ROMANTIC suspense
SPECIAL FORCES: THE SPY
Cindy Dees
NEW YORK TIMES BESTSELLING AUTHOR

HARLEQUIN
ROMANTIC suspense
NAVY SEAL BODYGUARD
Tawny Weber
NEW YORK TIMES BESTSELLING AUTHOR

Get 2 FREE Books

Your Thank-You Gifts include **2 FREE BOOKS** and **2 MYSTERY GIFTS**. There's no obligation to purchase anything!

See inside for details.

Boosting John on her hip, she knew it was better to be safe than give Fox reason for worry and she dialed Wyatt and Bailey's house. While the phone rang and rang, she realized just how antsy she was about that car. "Hello?" Bailey answered in a rush.

"Hi. It's Kelsey. Baby John and I wondered if you and Hudson were up for a visit."

"If 'visit' is code for 'this mommy gets a nap,' definitely. Why doesn't my son *ever* sleep?"

Kelsey laughed as she walked inside and up the stairs. "I can give time for a nap."

There was a long pause. "You're serious."

"Well, sure." Bailey didn't know it, but she'd be giving Kelsey a sense of security in trade.

"It sounds divine," the other woman admitted. "But I couldn't ask you to do that. Just come on over. I'm sure adult conversation will be just as refreshing."

She was probably right. Kelsey had seen it often enough growing up. She gathered up Baby John's diaper bag and loaded him into the truck. When she glanced toward the trees, the black sedan was gone.

Pulling up to the house on the other side of the ranch, she found Bailey in a porch rocker, her son snuggled up on her shoulder. They made the cutest pair.

"You and I need to be quiet," Kelsey said to Baby John as she got him out of the car. "Bailey and Hudson need some downtime."

Baby John watched her with wide eyes as she spoke. She liked to think he understood on some level, though plenty of experts would say otherwise.

Bailey gave her a big smile as Kelsey walked up. "Hudson's actually dozing," she whispered.

"Fresh air wipes them out," Kelsey replied. She sat on the top step of the porch with Baby John.

Bailey yawned. "We'll see. You and Fox lucked out, starting with a baby that sleeps through the night."

Kelsey laughed, though the idea of being with Fox as a couple wound around her heart like a blooming vine. It was so easy to imagine a life here with him, so easy to want more than she had any right to ask for.

"He'll be in for a rude awakening when he starts from day one," Bailey said.

"Pun intended?"

Bailey paused, then chuckled. "Definitely."

"Other than the lack of sleep, how's he doing?" Kelsey asked.

"Perfect on all fronts," Bailey replied with a maternal glow. "I've been warned about colic and everything else that can go wrong from head to toe, but he's fine. He just doesn't sleep more than a blink at a time."

"He will," Kelsey promised again. One of her youngest brothers had been like Hudson. She wasn't sure how her mother would've gotten through that first month without Kelsey and her sisters to help.

"You're a comfort, Kelsey, thank you."

"I meant what I said about giving you time to sleep."

"No, thank you. That's silly. Wyatt's been coming home early and giving me a nap before dinner. And we tag-team the baby through the night," Bailey explained. "I'd much rather talk with a grown-up."

Kelsey couldn't help but smile at that. "A grown-up maybe. But a good chunk of my days goes to the care of this little guy." She covered her face with her hands and then parted them, to John's delight.

"Not forever."

"No." And though she'd tried not to get attached, she knew she'd miss the baby terribly when Fox found John's family or an appropriate solution.

When she'd finished college, she'd vowed to leave child care and children behind her. But Baby John had somehow found a way through the wall she'd built around her heart.

"You like him," Bailey observed.

"The baby?" Kelsey asked. "Of course I do. He's a very likable baby."

Bailey rolled her eyes. "You know I meant Fox."

Fox and Baby John together were irresistible. "It's a good thing to like the boss," Kelsey said, deliberately misunderstanding.

Whatever Bailey wanted to say was interrupted by Hudson waking. "Here we go again. Round two hundred forty-two." She sighed. "And that's just counting today."

Kelsey followed her inside the house and they chatted while she changed and fed Hudson. When the baby was full, Kelsey offered to hold him for a bit.

"Let me take him. I can manage both of them," she said. "Go shower or sleep. Take a walk if you'd like." Recalling the sedan she'd seen, Kelsey cringed at the suggestion and hid the expression with a series of silly faces aimed at John.

"You really won't hate me for leaving him with you?"

"I offered. Go on," she urged, cuddling Hudson close. "Shoo."

Bailey flapped her arms. "They're empty. This feels so weird."

"Enjoy it." Kelsey gave the boys her full attention, ignoring Bailey until she darted down the hallway.

"Ten minutes. Fifteen, tops," she called back.

"Mommies need quiet time, too," she told Hudson. The little guy looked just like his daddy. "Colton genes run strong in you," she said. But when she compared Baby John and Hudson, there were differences.

How long would Fox wait before he approached his cousin about the baby? She understood his need to have the whole picture, but once he'd identified the most likely father, Mason, he'd been in no hurry to confront his cousin.

Finding out half your life was a lie could be distracting.

She hadn't been in Fox's employ too long, but it was evident how much he valued family. Leaning close to Hudson, she bumped his nose with hers. "You are a kissable little guy."

Baby John kicked out his feet and hands, gurgling to get her attention. Shifting Hudson, she moved to tickle John's tummy. He giggled, his fingers curling around her hand. "Of course you're my favorite six-month-old," she told him. "And we're making new friends, aren't we? You're a natural."

"So are you."

Kelsey swiveled to see Bailey standing at the end of the hallway watching her. "You've got Hudson mesmerized and John devoted."

"The feeling's mutual."

Bailey joined her, smelling fresh and clean after a shower. "Count me in as one of your new fans. It was heaven knowing I could take my time in the shower."

“And yet, here you are, way too soon.” She rocked Hudson on her up drawn knees. “I’ve got this.”

“Maybe I’m here to find out how,” Bailey admitted.

Kelsey felt the weight of Bailey’s intent study. “I come from a big family,” she began. “Twelve kids.” At least that had been the count when she’d left. “Being one of the oldest, I got plenty of practice with babies.”

Bailey pressed a hand to her tummy. “*Twelve?* I think my uterus just whimpered.”

Kelsey laughed, the sound startling Hudson. He jerked, then settled again. “See?” Kelsey whispered. “That’s progress.”

“I’ll say. Be right back.” Bailey dashed to the kitchen and returned with a bottle of water for herself and a cola for Kelsey. “Is this good?”

“Great, thanks.” She carefully opened the bottle and took a long drink. After her first taste of pop after escaping her family it had become her favorite treat. She hadn’t known a beverage could be so much fun. So many things, away from the strict rules of home, had been delightful discoveries.

Bailey played peek-a-boo with Baby John. “Have you and Fox found his father yet?” she asked in a singsong voice.

“He’s definitely part of the Colton family tree. It’s not Wyatt,” she joked. Dodging Bailey’s theatrical glare, she went on. “Fox thinks the father is one of the cousins.” She wasn’t comfortable sharing any more details of their findings without his permission.

“Do you think his mother dropped him on the doorstep?” Bailey asked.

Kelsey thought about the black sedan near Fox’s place and the active Avalanche Killer case. “That’s my guess, but it's possible someone else had other reasons for leaving him with Fox. Knowing the baby is a Colton, Fox won't hand him over to the foster system until he knows the parents' wishes."

"Not after what happened to him," Bailey agreed.

Kelsey watched John. He was on the verge of sitting up by himself. "You know Fox pretty well."

Bailey smiled. She was ready to catch the baby if he rolled, but she gave him plenty of room to figure out the sitting thing. "He and Wyatt are close."

Closer than Bailey even knew, Kelsey thought.

"It's nice to see Fox happy," Bailey said. "He's always had his work, but with the baby and you..."

Kelsey waited for her to finish. She had no desire to tiptoe through that minefield without a map.

"Did I say something wrong? I thought you liked him."

She'd been well past liking Fox before she knocked on his door the first time. With each passing day, she learned something more about him and her original infatuation simmered closer toward true and substantial feelings. The kiss had only bound the physical and emotional elements, tying her in knots over what to do next.

Still, she wasn't sure this was the right time or circumstance to explore anything she felt for Fox. He was falling for the baby. She was falling for the man and, while she adored Baby John, she planned to leave babies out of her long-term equation.

"I'm just his assistant moonlighting as the nanny," Kelsey said. Heat flooded her cheeks at the denial, her mind relishing the feel of their first kiss.

Bailey wasn't fooled. "You *do* like him. Your cheeks are on fire." She chuckled. "Not that I blame you."

"For blushing?"

"For liking Fox. He's great, though most of the time he seems to get lost in his work."

"He does." Kelsey swallowed, thinking of Fox reading through his reports. Good grief, those glasses did things for her. "We both do." She cleared her throat. "Before you get lost in a matchmaking fantasy—"

"Too late."

"You should know I am committed to the work he's doing with quarter horses. If I have to make a choice, I'll choose the office over the man."

Bailey tilted her head, her gaze narrowing. "I almost believe you."

Hudson fussed, and Kelsey handed him over so Bailey could feed him. She'd been honest and clear. It wasn't her fault if the other woman didn't want to accept it. Baby John rolled to his tummy and pushed up on his arms, scooching backward. He worked himself into a seated position and grinned at Kelsey.

"Look at you!" she praised. The baby giggled. "Such a big boy."

"My goodness," Bailey marveled. "He did it."

"He'll be crawling in another month or two," Kelsey said. Fox would have to find a new solution once the baby was more mobile. The office was no place for an active tyke. Maybe they could partition off more space or adjust her hours—

No. She cut off her runaway thoughts. Fox had promised the nanny role was temporary and secondary to her role as his assistant. She trusted him to keep his word. He would reach out to the father soon and then they could make plans.

"What will Fox do if the father isn't interested in stepping up?" Bailey asked as if reading her thoughts.

"He hasn't discussed any of the options with me," Kelsey replied.

"Fox is serious about strong family ties," Bailey said. "I'm only guessing, but it makes sense that the abandoned baby dredges up all that pain and loss he felt when his parents died. It must have been a dreadful adjustment. Wyatt thinks Fox took in the baby in some attempt at payback."

Kelsey had seen similar indicators in Fox's words and actions. "He hasn't told me too much about that transition. When we're at work, we try to stay on task." Not easy with the baby, and now he was overwhelmed by the secrets his adoptive parents had kept.

"Russ instilled a solid work ethic in all of his kids." Bailey moved Hudson to her shoulder, patting his back gently. "He was a workaholic, but I think his kids are searching for a better balance. I know Wyatt is really conscientious about that. I hope Fox will be, too."

"Does Wyatt worry about repeating his dad's mistakes as a parent?"

"Don't we all?" Bailey countered.

"Guess so." She didn't think her brothers worried about being good fathers as much as they aspired to have obedient wives and children. They surely also wanted a dutiful sister who would guarantee the financial stability of the family for years to come. Kelsey knew she'd never be able to follow the example her mother had set. She needed more in her life than having and raising children.

Kelsey popped up to her feet and brought John back to the center of his blanket. He'd been rolling and sitting and scooting all around. She and Bailey chatted a bit longer about baby milestones and expectations and Kelsey promised to come back for another playdate soon.

When she left a chipper and glowing Bailey with a snoozing baby Hudson, she headed back to Fox's house with John babbling happily in the car seat. In her mind Bailey's question echoed endlessly. What would Fox do if the real father didn't want to raise Baby John?

She couldn't see Fox turning the baby over to foster care. Bailey had been right on target about Fox's commitment to family. However he moved forward, she needed to be clear with him that her primary interest in Roaring Springs was the horse breeding. The baby was wonderful, but she needed more than nanny detail.

Her palms went damp on the steering wheel and she had to pull over for a minute to steady her breathing. There was no reason to stress about any of this. Letting her old issues and insecurities creep in and blot out the joy of her current position was silly. Fox valued her as his assistant and he'd given her no cause to doubt his promises about her future with Crooked C Quarter Horses.

Chapter 9

Fox's mind whirled, his ears ringing with the accusations Russ and Mara were shouting at each other as he'd left. Stunned, frustrated and inexplicably more hurt than he wanted to admit, he pulled to a stop in front of the red barn he called home.

He couldn't go into the office with his emotions so twisted up and his temper running hot. How would he face the innocent baby whose arrival set all this into motion or the woman who'd looked at him with such concern when he'd headed out?

Logically, he needed space and time to process the facts that had turned everything inside out, yet part of him craved Kelsey. More than genetic expert or reasonable colleague, who would listen without judgment, he wanted to lose himself in the sweet softness of her lips.

He stalked into the foyer and was reaching for the

office door before it registered that they weren't inside. They weren't upstairs either, but he found a note that explained Kelsey had taken the baby over to visit with Bailey and Hudson.

Fox crushed the note in his fist, the disappointment and loneliness burning like salt poured into an open wound. Well, if he had the space, he'd best use it.

With some good daylight left, he strode to the barn and saddled up Mags for a head-clearing trail ride. He rode out hard across the property, the mare under him responsive and keen for the action. As he kept his gaze on the western horizon, the recriminations circled in his mind.

He'd torn up his family, wrought havoc on the two people who'd raised him as their own. And for what? He hated admitting Mara was right. Tossing his true parentage out into the light wouldn't change anything.

Out here under the clear, deepening blue of the evening sky, he couldn't remember what he'd hoped to gain.

So what if all of his brothers and sisters were half siblings by blood? They still shared the history of growing up together, a tangle of affection and rivalries and proud and embarrassing milestones. The same holiday traditions anchored by treasured memories.

All he'd really gained was a rational explanation for Mara's reserve and perpetual criticism of him. In her place could he or anyone else have managed a better relationship? He wanted his answer to be a resounding yes, but there was no real way to know.

He supposed he should call Sloane. Hearing this news from anyone else was bound to upset her and he'd dished out enough distress for one day. Slowing the mare, he let Mags meander along the edge of the little-used access road that divided his acreage from Wyatt's. He pulled his phone from the inside pocket of his field jacket and dialed her number.

Sloane picked up with a happy greeting and in the background he heard his niece singing away. "Do you have a minute?" he asked.

"For you, always. Chloe and I are playing dress-up and getting fancy before Liam gets home."

His niece squealed, and Fox held the phone away from his ear, though the sound made him smile.

"Is everything okay with the baby?"

"Thanks to Kelsey it is."

Sloane laughed. "You lucked out there. Have you bought him his first Stetson?"

"I thought I'd teach him to smoke first." It felt so normal to joke around with her. She was the one constant he'd had through every facet of his life. "I'm sorry to take the shine off dress-up time, but there's something you should know."

Sloane gasped. "You *are* the father of that baby."

"I'm not." *I'm also just your half brother.* He couldn't blurt it out that way. "The DNA results gave us a pretty good idea of Baby John Doe's daddy."

"That's great."

"Yes. Kelsey and I also found something else. I wanted you to hear it from me." Best to spit it out quickly, like ripping a bandage off a scraped knee.

"Fox, what is it? You're scaring me."

He turned his gaze to the snow-dusted peak of the mountain framing Roaring Springs. "The DNA also proved I'm your *half* brother. Russ is my real father. I guess he had an affair with Mom."

Suddenly there was only stark silence on the other end of the call. He couldn't hear his sister or his niece. "Sloane…?"

"I'm here." Another long pause. "I… I'm not sure what to say."

"You don't need to say anything. I wanted you to hear it from me," he repeated. "I spoke with Russ and Mara earlier."

"They knew?"

"Russ didn't. Mara kept Mom's secret. I guess, um, our dad found out somehow and that's why the car crashed." He wouldn't tell his sister, not outright, that her father killed their mother.

Sloane hiccupped and started to cry.

Great. He should have gone over and told her this in person or when Liam was around to give her some support. But no, Fox had dumped the news on her out of the blue and wrecked a fun time with her daughter.

Which of Fox's fathers would've done this? He snorted. Both Russ and Harrison had exhibited plenty of selfishness through the years. "I'm sorry, sis."

She sniffled. "Are *you* okay?"

"Not really," he admitted. "I will be, it's just—"

"A shock," she finished for him. "It changes nothing. *Nothing.*" Her voice was so ferocious he smiled. "*You* are still the best brother in the world."

"Thanks. I feel the same way about you." Choked up, he hurried to get off the phone. "Give Chloe a hug."

"Consider it done," she replied thickly. "If you need anything, we're here for you. I love you."

"Love you back," he replied, quickly ending the call.

For the longest time, he just sat there on the back of

the horse, staring at the stunning view but only seeing flashes of his past. Mara's grudging attempt at mothering him. Russ striving to be more engaged and present. Dana's comforting hugs and silly laugh.

He'd never stopped missing his mom. Even as an adult, part of him yearned for his mother. If Mara had been kinder, more maternal or accepting, would he have forgotten his mom? He supposed enough time had passed that the question was irrelevant. Whether or not it had been smooth sailing, his needs had been met. He'd grown up in a stable home and gone on to find a life and career that suited him. He could only hope Baby John would be afforded the same basic comfort and opportunities wherever he ended up.

The sun sank toward the horizon and the faint pink streaks in the sky were a preview of what would be a glorious sunset. He'd been out here far longer than he'd planned, but at last the tumult inside him was calming.

He turned for home, eager to see Kelsey and the baby. Best not to analyze that too much. The most direct route was to keep to the road and cut across his backyard to the stable. Trotting along the roadway, he noticed the fresh tire tracks. This access road was more for service use and he couldn't think of a reason why any of the hands would need to come this way.

He could only assume the sedan had returned. Who kept coming by and why? He'd rather believe it was someone related to Baby John rather than a serial killer in the area.

He'd left Kelsey to cope with any trouble alone. What kind of a father, foster or not, let the nanny deal with a potential threat? Irritated all over again with a past he couldn't change and a future he wasn't sure about, Fox urged Mags into a canter.

He wouldn't feel right again until he laid eyes on Kelsey and the baby.

When Kelsey and the baby got home, Fox still wasn't anywhere to be found. Had he gone to speak with the baby's father, as well?

Baby John had dozed off on the short drive and woken cranky, unwilling to be amused by much of anything. She hurried to fix him a bottle and checked to be sure he wasn't running a fever. Most likely it was the interrupted nap compounded by teething pain. The babies she'd known from siblings to cousins to neighbors had always been grumpy when cutting teeth.

The little guy was drowsy but not quite asleep when Fox finally walked in and called out a hello. At the sound of the deep voice, the baby's eyelids fluttered open and his little mouth curled into a smile.

The same couldn't be said for Fox. His foul mood was evident in the heavy sound of his boots on the floor as he crossed the kitchen. But the hard set of his jaw and the scowl on his face fell away when saw the baby.

"Did I wake him?"

"Not really. He's having a rough evening."

"Makes two of us." He stalked over to the fireplace and started a fire.

She appreciated the thoughtful gesture. "Thanks," she said when the fire was going. "I take it your aunt and uncle didn't take the news well?" It had taken more effort than she anticipating hiding her worry for Fox from Bailey.

Fox dodged the question with one of his own. “Have you eaten?”

“Not yet. If you take him, I’ll throw something together for us.”

Fox hesitated.

Just because the baby wanted to be with him didn’t mean it was the right thing for Fox. “Or you can cook,” she suggested. His willingness to dive in and help with any task had immediately impressed her as they adjusted to the baby’s schedule.

“Do you feel attached to him?” Fox knelt by the chair and let Baby John’s tiny fingers curl around his. “Could *you* send him to foster care?”

“As the nanny, it’s counterproductive for me to send the baby away.”

He gave her a sidelong glance. “You know what I’m asking.”

She did and answered accordingly. “If Baby John landed on my doorstep I would’ve felt compelled to relinquish him until his parents could be found.”

“I guess I should be thankful I was taken in by the Coltons,” Fox muttered. “But you didn’t answer my first question. Are you *attached* to him?”

She thought there was an obvious difference between taking in an articulate and grieving child and caring for a helpless baby. Admittedly, in either case, she would’ve opened her heart and home. “I’m fond of him, yes. He makes it easy to get attached, being such a sweet and happy little guy. What do you really want to know?”

The baby reached for Fox and he gathered him into his big, strong arms. Kelsey felt a little stab of envy, misplaced as it was. It seemed dinner was up to her.

"Can we talk it out once he's down for the night?"

"Sure." Once she mixed up a casserole and got it into the oven, she and Fox managed the baby's bedtime routine. Yet once John was down for the night, Fox seemed reluctant to share what had happened with Russ and Mara.

"I enjoyed my visit with Bailey today," she said, hoping normal conversation would put Fox at ease. "Hudson's aversion to sleep is running them ragged."

"Guess we're pretty lucky with Baby John."

Being included in that "we" made her smile. "We are." She slid a glance his way. "Want to tell me how things went with Mara and Russ?"

"I don't know where to start," Fox admitted as he cleared the dishes.

She stowed the leftovers in the refrigerator and grabbed a beer for him. "The beginning works for me."

He took a long drink. "You saw the beginning."

She had and she'd been concerned for him for hours now. "Why not start at the beginning of your conversation with them."

"I went over there mad." Fox sighed and sank onto a stool at the island. "It wasn't a good way to start the discussion."

In her opinion, he'd gone over there hurt and confused, but she didn't interrupt.

"I walked them through it. Turns out DNA results are one hell of an icebreaker. Russ had no idea I'm his son. Aunt Mara? She's known all along."

"You're kidding." Kelsey couldn't imagine keeping such a crucial detail from Fox, especially as an adult. Anyone who bothered to look could see that he worried about being too much like the man he thought was his father. Apparently Mara hadn't bothered.

"I wish. Mara said my mom confided in her on her deathbed. She never confronted Russ about it." He took another long drink. "She also said my dad planned the car crash, using it as a murder-suicide."

"Fox, I'm so sorry." It was all Kelsey could do to keep her hands to herself. The man needed a hug, some tangible and comforting reminder that he was valued and appreciated.

Loved.

Her heart wouldn't be denied this time. Circumstances or not, she'd fallen hard for the man she'd admired, the man who'd become her boss and moved her into his home. The man who needed a friend more than anything else right now.

"If my mom had lived, Russ would want to wring her neck. Not that he'd actually do it." He crossed the room and sat down on the hearth, stretching his legs out in front of him. "I left them raging at each other about their relationship. They're both furious. I may have ended a marriage today."

She couldn't picture it. Divorce wasn't allowed where she grew up. At least Mara wouldn't be forced to leave everything behind if she ended the marriage. "Whatever they decide has nothing to do with you," she said softly.

He cocked an eyebrow.

"You know what I mean. Your parents made those choices, not you."

"I chose to confront them."

"Mad or not, that's a reasonable choice." She sat down beside him. "I'm sorry it didn't go as expected."

"I'm not sure what I expected, but it wasn't that." He set aside the beer. "It does help to understand *why* she treated me differently."

"You were a kid." A grieving kid. "There's no excuse for making you feel uncomfortable or unworthy."

"Mara was shouting at Russ. I heard her claim she'd held the family together and should be sainted for not dumping me on foster care."

"Sainted?" Kelsey was furious on Fox's behalf. The woman had treated Fox like an outsider from the start. "I can think of better words."

"Thanks." He raised his head, and she caught the faint flicker of a smile. "I want to hate her," Fox admitted gruffly. "But I can't. She took us in when she would've been within her rights to abandon us, at least me, to foster care." He pushed to his feet, restless. "The affair hurt her. Her sister and her husband. I can't imagine the betrayal she felt on both sides. And facing me every day? It had to be the worst kind of pain."

Maybe, but taking it out on an innocent boy was inexcusable. Kelsey picked up the beer bottle and took it to the recycling bin in the kitchen. Returning, she caught Fox staring down the hall. The baby did force him to look at the most uncomfortable moments in his past. Unlike Mara, he kept lavishing the boy with affection, making sure all his needs were met.

She was thankful she hadn't burdened Fox with her worries about her brothers. He had more than enough family drama on his plate. If her brothers had been in the sedan, they would've shown up or called or started ugly rumors about her in town by now.

Her life changed so dramatically when she'd finally escaped her family. She'd slowly discovered a world where love was rooted in kindness and stability rather than harsh discipline and rigid standards. She'd found a place where her strengths were celebrated instead of muted. In her first week of freedom, she'd cried herself to sleep every night—tears of joy, hope and relief.

"Neglect can be as hurtful as outright abuse," she murmured, pausing at the end of the couch. She hadn't known what she'd been missing and she would never go back.

"Well, I've had a bit of both." His voice cracked. "I've had good and bad parental examples." He walked toward the fireplace and stirred it to life, adding a fresh log that sparked and crackled. "Why can't I focus on the good and forget the ugly?"

There was no easy answer to that question. It had taken years of watching how other people interacted positively in relationships for her to understand how much she'd been denied. She tried an appeal to his scientific side. "Wanting love, approval and attention from our parents is a natural biological response, Fox."

He shrugged.

"You know the basic needs," she continued. "When those aren't met, it changes how we see and value ourselves."

"I'm a grown man," he protested. "Russ is really the only father I know. These skeletons are old news."

"Not to you," she pointed out. "You need time to adjust."

Fox leaned a forearm on the thick, rough-hewn mantel and stared into the fire, looking forlorn and wounded. She went to him. The man needed a hug. Several, really, to make up for the slights he'd suffered as a child. Slipping her arms around his lean waist, she rested her cheek against his back. “Parents aren’t perfect and never will be. You’re an incredible, kind, accomplished man despite the tragedies in your past.”

“Kelsey—”

“Just listen.” She gave him a gentle squeeze, her palms pressed over his heart. She couldn’t say this to his face, not yet. “I haven’t known you long in person. I knew your reputation as a geneticist and breeder. Now that I’m here, I’ve discovered you’re a nerd.”

He chuckled. “As expected?”

“A little, yes,” she replied. “You’re also one of the smartest, most generous and compassionate men I’ve met.” She’d save *drop-dead sexy* for a better moment. “Those traits and strengths aren’t simply a by-product of DNA or upbringing. Those traits are all *you*. Inherent in the way you’ve chosen to live your life.”

He covered her hands with his, trapping them against his hard muscles. “Thank you.”

She pulled back, feeling inexplicably exposed and shaky. What now? She stuffed her hands into her pockets and when Fox turned around, she couldn’t quite meet his gaze. It hadn’t been her place to say any of those things, and now she was floundering.

“Well, I should—” She took a step backward and tipped her head toward the bedrooms. “He’ll be up early.” Maybe her embarrassment would be manageable by morning. She’d meant every word, though she should have kept them to herself.

He took a step closer and the raw desire in his eyes startled her. Suddenly the room felt too hot, her clothes too tight.

Fox was too close. Too deliciously close. The scent of the fire was layered over the darker, tantalizing spice of his skin. He pulled her hands from her pockets and held them loosely. His gaze dropped to her lips, rested there while her heart pounded.

Was he going to kiss her again? Would it be even better than last time? She licked her lips, anticipating, hoping.

"Can I kiss you?"

She nodded, afraid if she tried to speak she'd tell him he could do whatever he pleased.

His mouth touched hers in another sweet, not-quite-innocent kiss. Then it changed, ignited from one heartbeat to the next. On a gasp of pleasure, she parted her lips to the sensual slide of his tongue against hers.

She laced her fingers at the back of his neck, toying with his thick hair. The awareness, the surety that this was where she belonged overwhelmed her, turned her knees weak. She must have wobbled or swayed because his hands splayed across her hips as he pulled her closer to the strong security of his body.

"Kelsey." His fingertips skimmed under the hem of her sweater. Her skin pebbled with the contrast of his hot touch and the cooler air of the room. "I want you, Kelsey."

The thrill of being wanted this way, wanted by Fox, made her dizzy. "It's mutual," she managed.

"You've given me so much already." His lips traced the curve of her ear.

"Same." This was different and she'd deal with the consequences later. If she missed this chance with him, she'd never forgive herself. One night with Fox wouldn't mean a shotgun wedding or a life bearing his children.

"I'll still be your assistant in the morning," she

promised. Pressed close, she felt his low laughter more than she heard it. The vibration from his torso teased the stiff peaks of her breasts.

"Then there's nothing to lose." He leaned back and waited for her to meet his gaze. "I'd be lost without you."

She believed him. Worse, she suspected she'd be equally lost without him. Fox wasn't perfect, but he was sincere. Genuine. Trustworthy. She surrendered to the moment and the demands of her body as they stripped away layers of clothing and reveled in the discovery of each other.

He laid her down on the thick rug in front of the fireplace, where the warmth of the flames was no competition for the heat he stoked with his mouth and hands. The feel of skin on skin nearly brought her to a climax.

She nudged him back, eagerly exploring all the lean lines of muscles toned from keeping the ranch running well. *This* was everything. *He* was everything. She trailed kisses across his chest, breathing him in, daring to venture lower still, until he sucked in a breath and hauled her back up to claim her mouth with a soul-searing kiss.

His hands speared through her hair, scattering the last of the pins holding up her long tresses. He nipped at her lower lip, ran kisses along her chin, the column of her throat, murmuring her name over and over. Shifting her higher still, he ran his tongue over one nipple and she arched, crying out as pleasure coursed through her. She wanted—needed—all of him. *Now.*

He dug a condom from the pocket of his jeans and rolled it over his erection. Braced over her, the firelight cast highlights through his hair. Breathless, she touched his features, surged up to kiss him.

Gripping her hips, he glided deep in one smooth thrust, and she gasped at the exquisite sensations of him filling her, surrounding her. *Cherished* was her only thought as he stared down at her. He flexed his hips, she responded and they found a pace that carried them both to a shattering release. She held him close, her body cradling his as her pulse eased and they floated back down to earth. To reality.

A new reality in which she'd just made love with her boss.

"You okay?" he asked when he returned from disposing of the condom.

She shivered at the stunning view of him, his body golden in the light of the fire.

"Cold?"

With the fire at her back and Fox at her front? Not a chance. "I'm perfectly content." She traced the slope of his shoulder as he stretched out beside her.

"Makes two of us."

His languid touches at her waist, her hip, her hair, kept her just awake enough to want more. If only she had the guts to ask, or the skills to flirt and tempt him into round two. She hadn't come into this a virgin, but her experience with sex was limited. She didn't want to be clingy, but she wasn't ready to retreat to her bedroom.

"Kelsey?"

"Hmm?" Her eyelids had drifted closed as she rested her cheek against his shoulder.

"Will you sleep with me tonight?"

That roused her. She pushed up onto an elbow to be sure she'd heard him. "Here?"

"I'd prefer my bed," he said, lips tilted in a smile.

Her heart dropped, then skipped right back up into place. It seemed like a big step, but was it really any bigger than making love in front of the fire?

He twirled a lock of her hair around his finger. "Is that too much too fast?"

"I think it's just right." She leaned in to kiss him, her body stirring.

In the next instant, she was in his arms and he was carrying her down the hallway. She didn't even care that they'd left clothing scattered in front of the fireplace.

Fox woke to an empty bed, the soft patter of rain on the roof and the sweet scent of Kelsey lingering on his pillow. He breathed it in, smiling as he heard her and the baby through the monitor on the nightstand.

He wasn't sure what he'd done to bring a woman as amazing as Kelsey into his life, but he was grateful. Well, he supposed science had brought her to him, with his reputation as a quarter horse breeder. He nearly laughed, imagining what Wyatt would say about his brain being the magnet. Eager to see her and the baby, he hustled through a fast shower and then tugged on clothes for chores.

Not even the fact that they needed to talk to Mason today could knock him off the high of being with Kelsey last night. Twice.

He found her in the kitchen, feeding Baby John cereal. Her hair was damp and already twisted into the familiar bun at the nape of her neck. She wore loose cotton pants printed with sugar skulls and roses and a moss-green top that did amazing things for her eyes. Here was the balance he'd been searching for all his life and he hadn't even known it. A woman who appreciated his focus, could discuss horse traits for hours, and who beautifully dealt with both the mundane and the unexpected.

Happier than he could ever remember feeling, he kissed the baby on the head as he walked by.

"Good morning," she said, spooning another bite into John's open mouth.

"It is." He tipped up her chin and lingered over her lips. Her eyes were dazed when he pulled back. "It definitely is."

He poured coffee for himself, refilled her mug, as well. "We should go see Mason today," he said. "I'd like you and the baby to come along."

She drew the cereal and spoon out of the baby's reach as she studied him. "You're sure?"

"Absolutely." He didn't want to go anywhere without her anymore. Maybe it was too much, too fast, but he'd take that chance. She wasn't just a nanny or his assistant, she was the woman he wanted beside him through whatever came next. "If you'd rather avoid a scene, I understand."

"You'd take the baby on your own?"

"If necessary."

An expression he couldn't decipher clouded her hazel eyes before she gave Baby John her full attention. "We'll be ready when you are."

"Thanks." His spirits soaring, Fox went out to the barn, whistling through the routine work.

When the chores were done and he and Kelsey had

finished breakfast, Fox called the sales office and learned Mason was working from home. It was a courtesy extended by the Colton Empire due to the Gilford family troubles with the murder of his sister, Sabrina, and the recent crimes committed by his wife.

Fox had never visited his cousin's custom home nestled in an upscale suburban neighborhood. As they drove along the wide, tree-lined streets, he appreciated the simplicity of his ranch and the wide-open spaces.

At Mason's house, Fox carried the baby in his seat up to the door and shoved the unclaimed newspapers aside so Kelsey wouldn't trip. He already knew the other man was going through hell, but the shabby state of the house and overgrown lawn told the story. Ringing the doorbell, Fox prayed for the right words. Maybe having a child, an adorable little boy to care for, would pull Mason out of the sorrow and darkness and shine a light in his life again.

The man who answered the door dashed Fox's hopes. Normally perfectly groomed, today Mason's blue eyes were red-rimmed from too much alcohol or not enough sleep. His jet-black hair stuck out in clumps and he needed a shave. Despite his scruffy appearance, Fox could see something in the shape of his eyes and cheekbones that were clearly echoed in Baby John's face.

"Hey, Mason," Fox said with gentle cheer. "This is Kelsey, my new assistant. She and I need to speak with you for a minute."

Mason leaned on the partially open door, not inviting them in. "Why? I'm not in the market for a new horse."

"We found something else you might be interested in."

Mason's gaze sharpened. "Did you find a lead on Sabrina's killer?"

Another rain shower started and there was a bite in the wind. Kelsey shivered. "Could we come in for just a minute?"

"Yeah, sure." He stepped aside, opening the door wider. "Place is a mess."

"We won't stay long," Fox said. The soaring foyer felt stuffy and in the front room the air was heavy with sweat and booze and what might have been stale pizza. Fox wondered what they were exposing the baby to. With the blinds closed and curtains drawn the only light came from the television, tuned to a twenty-four hour news network.

Fox couldn't help judging his cousin. He'd been hollowed out, gutted, when his parents died but he hadn't been old enough to indulge in the self-pity and wallowing going on here. Maybe he'd hire a cleaning crew for Mason as a gift. Breathing carefully, he decided to make this quick as he and Kelsey found seats.

"So talk." Mason turned on a lamp and muted the television. His eyes raked Kelsey head to toe and his eyebrows arched at the sight of the baby in the carrier. "You knocked up your assistant?"

"I haven't," Fox said through gritted teeth.

The vow he'd made years ago not to get too deep in a relationship for fear of becoming a partner or father seemed pointless now, his first rule of his personal life shattered under the weight of new evidence. Although being Russ's biological son was a relief, he had to consider the impact of being a victim in Harrison's household.

Kelsey's encouragement last night was helping him

put things into perspective, but speedy adjustments weren't his strength. Fox cleared his throat. This wasn't about him and Kelsey, it was about Mason having a kid and stepping up.

Kelsey balanced the baby carrier on her lap as if she was afraid to set it down on this floor. He didn't blame her. "Luckily for both of us, Kelsey has experience in child care, too."

"What are you talking about?" Mason snapped.

Fox pointed at Baby John. "That's your son."

"Not a chance. Elaine went off the deep end because we couldn't have kids."

"Let me assure you, the fertility trouble was on her side. This little boy was left on my porch, but the DNA points to you."

"Not a chance," Mason repeated.

Fox ignored the denial. "Let's start with why his mother or whoever left him on my porch."

"Probably because he's yours." Mason stalked to the kitchen and returned with a beer.

Fox rolled his eyes. It wasn't even noon. "We ran the DNA. He isn't my child, Mason. He's yours."

Mason stared at the baby for a long, disbelieving minute. "That can't be my kid." He set down the beer and pushed his hands against the air, as if he could nudge the three of them out of his door. "I can't have a kid."

"But you do," Fox insisted. "Do you have any idea who the mother could be?" he pressed.

"How the hell do I know who you sleep with?" At Mason's outburst the baby started to cry, and Kelsey rocked the carrier from side to side. "Sorry," he said, quieter. "Kids were Elaine's obsession."

Despite the grief, Fox couldn't allow Mason to wriggle off the hook. "Why would the mother of *your* child leave him at my door?"

Mason's hand fisted and Fox braced for the blow. Something must have shown in his eyes because Mason backed down instantly. He slumped on the edge of the nearest chair. "I don't care what your results say. I can't take care of a kid."

Fox waited him out. It was common knowledge that Mason and Elaine had been having trouble and Mason's reputation with women before his marriage hadn't changed much after the wedding.

"Ah, hell, Fox." Mason scrubbed at his face with both hands. "I guess it could be mine. Once in a while I used your name when I traveled."

Incredulous, he glanced at Kelsey. "What?"

"As an alias," Mason confirmed. "I'm married. I couldn't use my name when I picked up women during business trips."

Fury blasted through him like a summer storm, hot and electric. He could spit nails. "You used *my* name to cheat on your wife?"

He had the grace to look ashamed. "The mother must have done her homework and found your address."

If she'd done her homework online, wouldn't she have noticed Fox Colton didn't resemble his cousin? "This *is* your son." The DNA had been enough for him, but Mason's admission sealed it. "Who is the mother?"

"How should I know?" Mason flopped back in the chair, hands covering his face. When he sat up again, his cheeks were damp.

Fox was out of sympathy. He and Kelsey had been

giving the baby every ounce of care and compassion and love they had and Mason just kept feeling sorry for himself.

Unlike his father—the father he'd thought had sired him—Fox had never struck another person. Scraps and squabbles with his brothers didn't count. However, at the moment, he wanted to haul Mason out of the chair, shake him until his head rolled and dump him in a cold shower until the man came to his senses. "You'll step up and be a dad," he ordered. "You'll do the right thing here."

"I can't," Mason protested. "Fox, look at me. I *can't*. I never even wanted kids. Take him back to his mom."

If only it could be that simple. "Based on his appearance at my door, it seems his mother thought *you* should have him," Fox pointed out.

"On paper I'm sure Fox Colton is pretty appealing," Mason sneered.

Fuming, he didn't trust himself to speak.

"Who do you think is the mother?" Kelsey's question hung heavy in the stuffy air.

"I don't know!" Mason shouted, setting the baby off again. "Damn it." He shoved out of the chair and pulled his wallet from his pocket. "I used the same escort agency most of the time." He flipped through a stack of cards until he found what he was after. "Here."

Fox reluctantly took the offered business card.

"You want to find her so bad, start there."

"Do you have a name?" Fox demanded.

"There were a few." He stared at the baby. "How old is it?"

"Not *it*. He," Fox said. "Your *son* is around six months old."

Mason swore, squinting as though thinking about the timeline gave him a headache. "Candace. She and I had a good time until…"

"Until?" Fox prompted.

"Until the agency told me she wasn't available anymore. She stopped answering my direct texts." He flung a hand at Baby John. "Apparently because she was pregnant. The timing fits. How could she even know it was mine?"

"I'll ask her when we find her," Fox promised. "What do you want to do?"

"About what?" Mason appeared baffled. "You have everything under control. Why upset a good thing?"

"You have rights as the father."

"I never asked to be!" his cousin roared.

The baby burst into tears, and Kelsey stood up. "We'll wait in the truck," she said, hurrying out of the house.

"You need to pull yourself together," Fox said when they were alone. "I know grief is hell. You're not the only person to suffer. You have people who would like to help you, people who need you. Including your son."

"Stop saying that. I can't be a father. Do whatever you think is best, Fox. Just get out."

"In a minute." Fox quizzed Mason on his travels over the past year and where he most frequently met Candace.

Walking out, he drew the rain-washed air deep into his lungs. The rain had subsided, and Kelsey was walking under the shade of a big maple tree in full autumn color, the baby quiet in her arms. She was playing peekaboo with a bright orange leaf, making John giggle.

Joining her, he wrapped his arms around both of

them, holding on until the frustration and anger finally melted away.

"You're so good with him," he whispered against her hair. "Thank you."

She leaned into him. "Please tell me you didn't convince him to take the baby."

"No." Fox was exhausted in heart and spirit. "He's not in a good place. Come on." He wanted to get as far as possible from Mason and his overwhelming sorrow.

"What now? Will you tell the sheriff you found Baby John's father?" Kelsey asked as they drove away from Mason's house.

"I'd rather try and find the mother first if you're up for it."

"We're game." She twisted in her seat, settling the pacifier in the baby's mouth. "Aren't we, little guy?"

Fox didn't have the courage to ask if she was stunned, appalled or smothering laughter at the mess that was this chapter of his life. No, Kelsey wouldn't laugh *at* him. She was too compassionate for that. They drove back to the ranch in silence.

"You must be ready to bolt." He took her hand, tried not to hold on too tightly. "I haven't forgotten the real reason you're here."

"Don't worry about it." She leaned across the seat and kissed him softly. "Let's go in and you can tell me how to help locate the baby's mother."

"It's going to take some web searching and probably a few awkward phone calls," he said.

"Then let's get started."

She sounded eager. Because she wanted to be done with the nanny gig…or because she enjoyed solving puzzles as much as he did?

He carried the baby as they went into the office, feeling more like a part of a family than he should. She didn't seem to want children any more than he did. So why did it feel like finding Baby John's rightful family would rip out a piece of his heart?

Chapter 10

Kelsey thought she and Fox were being remarkably productive considering their splintered focus. Between the analyses of last year's losses and tending to the broodmares, the ranch and the baby, she and Fox had tracked down Candace in only two days.

More remarkable, the woman agreed to meet with them today at her apartment this side of Denver.

Fox was obviously nervous. Who could blame him? With every layer they peeled back on the mystery of Baby John Doe, another skeleton fell out of his closet. Hopefully today would answer the last of his questions and he'd have enough information to present a plan, with parental consent, to the sheriff.

"Can we stop for groceries on the way back?" she asked as they left the ranch behind. "We're running low on formula and I'd like to pick up some ingredients for cookies."

"What kind of cookies?" There was a boyish tilt to his lips when he glanced her way.

"Whichever is your favorite," she said. He needed something fun and normal to chase away the heavy stuff. She wanted to do something nice for him, something that didn't have strings or secrets attached.

"Chocolate chip is a classic," he said. "I love those."

"But..." she said, hearing a hesitation in his voice.

"Oatmeal raisin cookies are the best."

"How so?"

"It's a treat that's practically health food."

She laughed, helpless against such an outrageous claim. "Lucky you, I make an excellent oatmeal raisin cookie."

"Hmm." He arched a brow. "I look forward to being the judge of that."

Unlike the day of their visit to Mason, today was clear and unseasonably warm. They cracked the windows to enjoy the fresh air on the drive out of the Roaring Springs valley, through terrain flanked by rugged mountains.

"This is it," Fox said, following the last instructions from his navigation app on his phone. He parked in a space marked for visitors and stared up at the three-story apartment building.

"Looks nice," Kelsey said. She didn't know what she'd expected, but it hadn't been something this normal and middle-class.

"I guess business is good," Fox muttered.

"You thought it would be a sketchy neighborhood?"

"I did," he admitted. "If she can afford a nice place, why not hire a sitter? Or find a new career?"

"We should go on up and ask her," Kelsey said.

Fox closed his eyes. "It's not *her* fault."

"Not yours, either," she reminded him. She was battling her own urge to judge why a mother would give up her baby. "We're only here to get the rest of the story."

"And her opinion on how to proceed. What if she wants him back?"

Kelsey squeezed his hand. Whether he wanted to admit it or not, he'd grown incredibly attached to the baby. "We'll figure it out."

Fox carried John, asleep in his car seat, up the three flights of stairs. She knocked on Candace's door.

A woman with copper-colored hair styled in a sleek chin-length bob greeted them. Her skin was nearly as fair as Kelsey's without the freckles.

In jeans and a chunky cranberry-red sweater, she might have been a model. Her dark brown eyes flitted from Kelsey to Fox and finally landed on the baby.

Everything about her softened when she saw him. Kelsey knew they'd found the baby's mother. "Candace?" she asked, since Fox had yet to do anything but stare.

"Yes." She stepped back. "Come in, come in."

The apartment was cheerful and tidy, the furniture out of date but in excellent condition. Far better than some of the places Kelsey had stayed in recent years.

"I'm Kelsey," she said. "I'm, uh, Fox's friend."

"Where is he?" She wiped her palms on her jeans and looked past them as if she expected another person to join them.

Fox introduced himself. "I'm Fox Colton. My cousin used my name when he, um, called on you."

"Oh!" Candace instantly relaxed and closed the

door. "I should have known, but he— What's his real name?"

"Mason."

"Mason was so sincere. Convincing. Still—" she tapped her knuckles to her head "—I should have known."

Candace's gaze kept drifting to the baby with unmistakable longing. She kept her hands clasped tight at her waist as if she was afraid to reach out and touch him.

"Would you like to hold him?" Kelsey asked quietly.

"No." Candace's eyes brimmed with tears, though none fell. "No, I can't. He's yours now. Well, Mason's I guess."

"What happened?" Fox blurted out the question and then gentled his tone. "I mean, I know the obvious part of what happened." He looked around. "Why give him up?"

"Babies aren't an asset in my line of work," Candace said. "Please, sit down. Do you want anything?"

"We're fine," Kelsey replied, tugging Fox down beside her on the love seat. The man was stiff as a board, clearly out of his element. The baby continued to doze in his carrier at their feet.

"He looks good," Candace murmured. "Bigger."

"He is good," Fox said.

"Your baby's doing fine." Kelsey smiled. "He's a charmer. Sitting up now, too. What was his name?"

"Baby boy," Candace confessed in a whisper. "I couldn't name him. He was too precious from the start. I put John on the birth certificate, but it felt ugly to me, y'know, because that's kind of shorthand for clients. What do you call him?"

“Baby John Doe is on the police report,” Fox said.

Kelsey elbowed him. “We’ve been calling him Baby John.”

“Figures.” Candace shook her head, her copper red hair swinging. “How did you find his real dad?”

“DNA tests,” Kelsey supplied. “Fox was sure the baby wasn’t his, but since you left him on Colton property, he had his brothers give us samples to develop a genetic pool. We’re equine geneticists,” she explained when the other woman’s eyes went wide.

“From the results, it was a matter of legwork,” Fox said. “Mason admitted using my name when we confronted him.”

“Fox suits you,” Candace murmured. “Never fit him.” She bit her lip. “See, I just couldn’t abort the baby. Some girls do and that’s fine for them. It wasn’t my thing. With some finagling I was able to have him, even though I knew I’d never be able to keep him.”

As she spoke, the baby woke and turned toward her voice. Clearly he remembered his mother. Kelsey sympathized with Candace’s struggle. She’d left home determined not to care for another child, and here she was caring for a baby whose mother loved him enough to let him go. “We don’t mean to make this difficult.”

“It’s okay. Mason, right?” At Fox’s nod she continued. “Mason was a regular client at that point. We were careful most of the time. Still, mistakes happen and, well…” She flared her hands toward the baby.

He started to fuss, and Kelsey reached for him. “He wakes up hungry.”

“I swear he had a hollow leg,” Candace joked. She watched every move Kelsey made until the baby was settled with a bottle. John's gaze locked onto his mother.

"You're sure you don't want some time with him?" Fox asked. "He seems to remember you."

"Today's hard enough." She sniffled. "Are you mad?"

"No."

His answer surprised Kelsey, though she knew it was the truth. "My suddenly having a baby has raised a few eyebrows, but I'm not angry. Though I am worried about you."

"Oh, I'm good now," Candace replied. "If I could've done right by him, I would have. Even if I dropped him on the wrong doorstep, he lucked out."

"He did," Kelsey agreed.

"I didn't do it to cause anyone any grief, but once I looked you up, I knew you could give him more than I could. Doesn't his real father want him?"

"His real father isn't sure yet. He's full up on family crises right now."

Candace frowned.

"Are you willing to let us continue to care for the baby?"

"Sure. He seems to like you guys. Do you plan on keeping him?"

"If you're relinquishing your parental rights, it will depend on Mason's decision," Fox said. "But it would smooth the way for all of us if you could put it in writing that you're surrendering care of him to me."

"Whatever you need," Candace said. "It probably sounds crass or cold..."

"Not at all," Kelsey interjected. She shifted the baby

to burp him. "No one's judging you," she added. "It's just keeping things clear. Legal."

"We'll make sure he knows he's been loved from the start," Fox said. "And we'll make sure he's well provided for even if Mason can't deal with fatherhood."

"Thank you," Candace whispered. "I'm the first girl from the agency to handle this kind of trouble this way. It's good to know he'll have a happy and safe life."

"He will," Fox promised. "Roaring Springs is a good place to grow up."

"Not as safe as it used to be," Candace mused. "My friend Bianca was in the wrong place at the wrong time."

"What do you mean?" Kelsey asked.

"I heard the Avalanche Killer got her. I was already out of the rotation when she disappeared, but we texted a couple times that night. Her regular didn't show up, so she went to The Lodge to try and get some off-agency cash." Candace reached for her phone. "I haven't cleared out the texts. I miss her." When she found the old messages, she handed her phone to Fox. "See. She called him Blue Eyes."

Kelsey watched him skim through the messages. Candace's career was full of inherent risks. "Have you ever considered another line of work?" she ventured.

"Well, Bianca dying made me reassess, for sure. But it's kinda too late for me to change things up. All my friends are in the business. We stick together."

"Would you be willing to share this with the Avalanche Killer investigation?" Fox asked.

"If you think it'll help. I don't want Bianca to be forgotten or her killer to think he can do whatever he wants to working girls."

With her permission, Fox forwarded the text messages to his phone. "I'll pass this and your contact information to the deputy in charge of the case."

When they were ready to leave, Kelsey buckled the baby into the carrier again and let Fox do the heavy lifting. At the door, Kelsey caught Candace in a hug. "You're a good mother," she said, "whether you're actively in his life or not."

Candace's eyes were glistening as she closed the door.

She knew Fox had heard the exchange when he secured the baby and came around to her side of the truck. He opened the door and just stared at her for the longest time.

"Are you okay?"

"Yes," he said, gaze locked on hers.

"Do you need me to drive?" she asked when he didn't move.

"You're amazing," he rasped. He caught her hands and his thumbs caressed her knuckles. "I'd be a frantic mess without you, Kelsey."

She wanted to blow it off, to say something casual or silly to make him laugh, but she couldn't. She could only admire that rugged, handsome face, the shoulders broad enough for any burden and the wide-open heart. "I think you, Mr. Amazing, should look in a mirror," she said at last.

He reached up, his big, warm hand stroking the back of her neck, and slowly drew her mouth to his. The bold kiss, right out here in public, shocked her. No, they weren't in Roaring Springs, but Kelsey was used to being followed, watched.

She gripped his shoulders for balance and let herself fall into the moment. There was sweet music in the sounds of the baby gurgling happily behind them. Her heart pounded as he eased back and heat swept through her, radiating out from where his palms came to rest on her thighs.

"*You're* amazing," he repeated. "I wouldn't have survived this without you." He nudged her legs forward and closed the door.

She pulled herself together and buckled her seat belt as he walked around to the driver's side. She'd thought love was a single fall, a singular moment. Instead, it seemed to be more like a spiral slide, each curve carving deeper into her heart.

"You don't have to come in," Fox said. They'd driven straight from Candace's place to the sheriff's station. Going in alone would be difficult, but he couldn't keep relying on Kelsey to keep him steady through every ugly moment. She was supposed to be his assistant, not a life coach or security blanket. He opened his door. "I won't be long."

"It would be nice to stand for a bit," she replied. "And Baby John loves meeting new people. We won't get in the way."

"You couldn't possibly," he said, meaning it. "Do you want the carrier?"

"No, thanks. I'll just get the diaper bag. We'll be right behind you."

He waited to walk in with her anyway. Stalling? Probably better to get it over with, but he was suddenly reluctant to relinquish care of the baby. He couldn't do this indefinitely, even with Kelsey's help. Despite the family unit the three of them appeared to be, they weren't one. This was someone else's child in the arms of a woman who should only be a professional associate.

A voice in his head scoffed. However she'd come into his life, he was growing more comfortable with her by the hour. More reliant. More enamored. He never would've looked in the mirror and called himself clingy, but he had a need for Kelsey that showed no signs of easing up.

He held the door for Kelsey and the baby and stepped inside to see Trey coming out of his office. "Got a minute?"

"I do," the sheriff replied. "Come on back."

Fox glanced at Kelsey.

"We'll be right there," she said with a wry smile and a pat on the baby's bottom. "He needs to be changed."

Fox watched her go for a long moment before joining his cousin.

"Have a seat," Trey said, settling into his chair. "You have news?"

"And a lot of it. The baby's mother is a woman who goes by Candace. She works with an escort service and lives near Denver.

The sheriff's eyebrows arched. "Never pegged you for the escort service type."

"You know I'm not," Fox said, trying to laugh it off.

"So why did she pick your porch over all the porches in Roaring Springs?"

"The father of her child used my name as an alias when he called on the service." Trey's wide grin halted his explanation. Following his gaze, Fox turned to see Kelsey standing in the doorway, Baby John on her hip. They made an adorable picture of happiness. Of normalcy. However, seeing it that way didn't make it true. Life wasn't so simple.

"Don't let us interrupt," she said.

"Not at all." The sheriff bounded to his feet again and invited Kelsey and the baby to join them. "So your little tyke isn't a John Doe anymore?" he asked, propping a hip on the corner of his desk and making faces at the baby.

"No. His mother granted permission for me to raise him for now." Fox reached into his back pocket for the letter. "She's agreed to sign whatever legal paperwork is necessary to complete a formal adoption."

The sheriff leveled that stern gaze on Fox. "Is that the way you're leaning?"

Yes. His heart nearly overrode common sense. "No."

He wanted Kelsey to stay on with the breeding program, plus a chance to have a relationship with her. That would be easier for all concerned if they weren't also juggling the added responsibility of a baby.

"The father then? Who was out there using your name?"

"Mason Gilford," Fox answered.

Trey gave a low whistle and the baby stared at him. He did it again, chuckling at John's wide eyes and slow smile. "I suppose I can see a bit of his daddy in that face."

Fox could too, now that he knew the truth, though when he saw the baby with Kelsey, he found a resemblance, as well. The mind was a strange and powerful thing. Maybe nurture could sway nature. If so, it didn't bode well for him.

"Mason led you to Candace?" Trey confirmed. "That man's been through hell and back."

"Is he back?" Fox wondered aloud. "He didn't seem eager to take on his role as father."

"So I assumed, since the boy's still with you. Still, he has rights." Trey moved to pace behind his desk. "Should I call in child services?"

Fox sat up straight as that pinch returned between his shoulder blades. Baby John was family, though they weren't related in the way he'd expected. "We told Mason we'd keep the baby with us for now. Give him time to think it over."

"That's generous of you, Fox. Knowing you have means and support and the mother's endorsement, that works. For now. Just let me get a copy of this letter for the file."

"Sure thing."

Alone in the office, Kelsey reached over and covered his hand with hers. Her skin was creamy and fair, though not flawless. His was tanned and weathered from riding. Her slender fingers might give the impression of frailty or weakness, but having watched Kelsey in the barn and with the baby, learning every inch of her body, he knew she was neither of those things.

"Thanks for being here." In the office, at the ranch, in his life. This wasn't the place to express all the feelings that came over him when he looked at her.

The baby reached for him, eyes wide, and he welcomed that sweet innocence. Were his days playing father to this baby numbered? There was no telling how long it would be before Mason made a decision.

"Before we go, I need to track down Deputy Bloom," he said as they exited the office.

"Absolutely. We'll wait here."

Deputies and police officers, hearing the baby, were

coming up to say hello. “That kid sure knows how to make friends.”

Kelsey grinned. “Definitely a charmer. Before long, the girls will be swarming.”

“Too late.” He winked as a woman walked up behind Kelsey to coo at the baby.

With Kelsey’s quick laughter in his wake, he went to find the deputy in charge of the Avalanche Killer case.

Approaching Deputy Bloom’s office, he saw her speaking with FBI Agent Roberts. Fox stopped short when he realized they were in a heated discussion, but he was too close not to overhear.

“I tracked an Ava Bloom to Arizona,” Roberts was saying. “She gave birth to a girl who’d be your age.”

“Ava,” Daria echoed. “Can I talk to her?”

Fox tried not to assume how the women were related. Their conversation wasn’t his business.

“She died,” Roberts said. “About ten years ago. Cancer.”

Fox heard Daria’s sound of frustration. “Thanks, Stefan. It’s more than I had, even if it’s not the news I’d hoped for.”

Agent Roberts walked out and did a double take when he saw Fox. With a lift of his chin he kept on going.

Fox moved to speak with Daria. “Deputy Bloom?”

She looked up and the sadness on her face slowly faded. “Fox.” She smiled. “Where’s the baby?”

“He’s entertaining the masses near the front door.”

“I’ll have to get in on that,” Daria said.

“Before you do, I have some information about the Avalanche Killer. Did you ever talk with a woman at the escort service agency named Candace?”

"The name doesn't sound familiar." She flipped open the case file and skimmed through the long list of names. "I don't have anyone on this list by that name. You think she knows something?"

"She might." Fox took a deep breath. "I met her today in the process of tracking down Baby John Doe's parents." He passed along Candace's contact information and the text messages she'd shared.

Daria sat back, lips pursed in thought. "I can't believe we didn't know about her. Thanks."

"Candace was so sad that Bianca was in the wrong place at the wrong time. She told us she'd just left the agency to deal with her pregnancy. From what she told me, when a regular doesn't show or something, the girls frequently try to earn some cash on the side."

"Right." Daria leaned forward. "Did Candace say anything more?"

"Just that she got a voice mail from Candace about landing a good-looking older man she called Blue Eyes. She only had the text messages saved."

Daria's face lit with excitement. "This is excellent news. Thanks again, Fox."

Kelsey didn't have any trouble keeping Baby John happy or amused while Fox went in search of Deputy Bloom. The baby drew people with his adorable smile and inquisitive nature. She'd never seen a baby so adept at making friends.

The front door opened with a blast of crisp October air, sunshine glaring off the floor. Mason stalked in, bringing the mood down in an instant with his grief-stricken glare. In her arms, John went still, his smile gone as he watched Mason approach.

It seemed his biological father was the only person he wasn't happy to see. She'd been around enough babies to know they had preferences, even among the people closest to them.

Mason glowered at everyone in the area until his gaze landed on the sheriff. "Have you made any progress on Sabrina's case?"

"We're working on it," the sheriff assured him.

"Right." Mason flung out an arm, gesturing to the room at large. "You're laughing it up while my sister's killer walks free. Sabrina, a Gilford, has *never* been your priority, Sheriff *Colton*."

The baby whimpered and Kelsey cuddled him close. There was nowhere to escape this time.

"Mason, lower your voice," Trey said. "We can talk in my office."

"For all the good that'll do," Mason shouted.

Baby John cried in earnest, and Kelsey swayed from side to side as she tried to melt out of Mason's sight. The people nearest her stepped between her and Mason.

On the other side of the lobby, Fox and Deputy Bloom hurried forward. "Mason," Fox said. "Take it easy."

"I won't!" He whirled on Fox. "You have Skye back. You can't convince me you give a damn about seeing justice done for Sabrina."

"We're family," Fox told him. "Of course I care."

"Bull—"

"We're *family*," Fox repeated.

Mason was a loose cannon, making the people around him uneasy. Fox was a rock, grounded and utterly unmovable amid all of the antics surrounding him.

Kelsey watched him seek her out across the room. With a quick exchange of glances, he asked and she answered that she and the baby were fine. This awareness between them was an oddly comfortable phenomenon. All her life she'd felt a step out of sync with everyone else. Not the right fit in her family, a bit too naive when she joined the rest of the world. Too fascinated by science and math to make friends quickly in high school and too worried about staying out of her brothers' traps to trust people in college or the workforce. But with Fox she felt accepted and understood. Cared for and valued.

Like she was finally on solid footing for the first time in her life. "You have Skye back," Mason roared. "I will have justice for Sabrina."

"Mason, we're doing all we can," Deputy Bloom promised. "We need to handle this properly—"

Mason lunged. Fox grabbed his shirt, pulling him aside before he tackled the deputy.

"If my last name was Colton you'd show some hustle."

"Mason, that's enough," Fox said, backing him into the nearest wall. "You need to calm down before you say or do something you'll regret."

The man seemed to deflate like a popped balloon. He yanked free of Fox and covered his face with his hands.

"Mason," Trey said calmly, "let's talk for a minute." He gestured to his office and Fox and Deputy Bloom ushered Mason inside.

At the tilt of Fox's head, Kelsey followed.

Mason and the deputy took the chairs in front of the

sheriff's desk. Fox stood with her at the door, his arm around her waist. "Need a break?"

His touch steadied her and she leaned into him, much as the baby sought solace in her. Although she couldn't see his face, she knew Baby John wasn't asleep. "I'm okay." It didn't seem smart to throw gasoline on the fire by letting Fox hold Mason's son right now.

"Mason, we have active leads," Deputy Bloom assured him. "Just because we can't advertise those leads doesn't mean we're not working to find Sabrina's killer."

Mason glared at the floor. Kelsey didn't know much about how the law worked, but she had a feeling if the sheriff shared information with Mason, he'd interfere with their case.

"We have another matter to discuss, if you'll excuse us, Daria."

Kelsey's hold on the baby tightened as the deputy walked by. This wasn't her child or her family, but she couldn't bear the idea that the sheriff would hand the baby over to Mason. Not while the man was so volatile.

"Fox has told you you're a father," Trey began.

"So now you're going to lecture me on parenthood and responsibility?" Mason snarled.

"No."

Fox's hand moved across her shoulders, keeping her grounded, which in turn kept the baby calmer. She peeked up at him to see a muscle in his jaw jumping. He wasn't looking forward to this conversation any more than she was.

"Mason, you have a son, currently in the care of

your cousin. I know you're grieving, but you have rights. Do you want to take custody of your child?"

"What will I do with a kid?"

The sheriff only cocked an eyebrow. "Taking your current distress into account, I'll allow you some time to think it through before you surrender your paternal rights. You've lost a great deal, but that baby is a ray of sunshine."

Mason shook his head, his gaze still on the floor. "I don't want him."

Kelsey's heart broke, though the baby would never remember this dreadful meeting.

"Nevertheless, you'll have time to get your head clear before we make it official."

Beside her, Fox exchanged a nod with the sheriff.

"In the meantime," Trey continued, "I'd like to hear you give permission for the baby to remain with Fox."

"Yes. Let Fox handle it."

Over Mason's head, the sheriff shooed the three of them out of his office.

Kelsey didn't breathe easy until they were loaded into the truck and backing out of the parking space. "Trey wouldn't have done it, would he?"

Fox arched an eyebrow. "Given the baby to Mason?"

"Yes," she said through the knot of emotion lodged in her throat.

"Not while Mason is in that state of mind," Fox assured her.

"He can hardly look at Baby John," she choked out.

"Hard to blame him," Fox allowed. "As he said, he didn't want a baby. His wife went off the deep end in her effort to start a family."

She reached back, caressing the downy hair on the

baby's head. "I can't help thinking he's the luckiest little boy in the world to have landed at your door."

"And I'm convinced he really hit the jackpot when you walked into his life," Fox said. "Let's grab a bite to eat and then we can run through the store before we head home."

Home. She loved the way he said it, the way he included her in the meaning of it. "Sounds like a plan," she managed around the emotions clogging her throat.

She was being foolish, especially with her brothers most likely nearby, but she couldn't seem to keep her heart in line. Better to soak it up, to add it to her bank of positive experiences. Should her brothers force her to run again, she would have one more example of how good families operated.

Keeping the baby in his seat, Fox carried John into the restaurant. Her stomach growled at the savory scents of chili and French fries while they waited for a table. Within minutes they were situated at a booth in front of a window where she could watch the town move by. She liked Roaring Springs and the blend of locals and tourists.

She studied the menu, though it was a challenge while Fox interacted with the baby. These moments made her realize how much she enjoyed the simpler things in life. Would she ever find a peaceful balance between her work and her heart?

"Mason really rattled you," Fox said.

She dragged her gaze away from the window and found him watching her as if she was a new genetic marker he'd just discovered. "He's so sad." It made her wonder if her mom or siblings grieved for her. Not publicly, that wouldn't have been allowed, but in the privacy of their own hearts and minds. "I hope they can give him closure about his sister."

"Deputy Bloom is on it. The sheriff, too. They'll figure it out."

The waitress stopped by the table with water and took their order, cooing over the baby.

Kelsey adjusted the baby seat in the booth once they'd ordered. "I know I have no say or stake it any of it, but I'm relieved the sheriff didn't hand over Baby John."

Fox's blue eyes turned somber. "That makes two of us. He's not mine and can't be, but I like him."

"He's a likable kid." Lovable, though she wouldn't use that word. Those attachments were far too risky in a situation as precarious as this one. "How much time do you think the sheriff will give Mason?"

"However long it takes."

"Spoken like a true rancher," she teased.

"We know what we can't control." His smile lit up his handsome face. "I realize it's been an unconventional start, but do you think you want to stay?"

"For the baby?"

"For the *work*," he clarified. "Both, for as long as we can manage it."

She wished he'd bring up whatever was building between them, as well. "The work you're doing is so important." She sat on her hands for a moment to keep them still as her excitement mounted. "I'm thrilled to be part of it and yes, I want to stay."

"You have no idea what a positive difference you've made already."

She felt the heat rising to her cheeks and didn't even mind this time. Sipping her water, she turned to the window again as a banged-up van sporting primer drove by. *That* was the kind of car she'd expect her brothers to be driving. They didn't waste a penny on luxuries. Not yet anyway.

"You know your horses and your ranches," Fox was saying. "Did your family focus on food or cattle?"

Isolation. Rules. "My dad's goal was to be self-sustaining, off the grid," she said. "We had a herd of cattle and a big garden."

"Big enough for fourteen counting your parents?" he asked.

Most of the time. She looked at the baby so she could smile and mean it. "We appreciated the food we harvested. My mother would say the effort added flavor."

"You disagree?"

She shrugged. "Work, chores and responsibility are important."

"Builds character."

"It does." But choices were important, too. Fox said it almost every day in the office, that she was an asset. Her mind, her skills, her analytic ability. She would have withered under her father's plan for her life. The risk was still there, if she couldn't find a way to drive her brothers home for good.

How could she explain the situation without burdening Fox with an embarrassing amount of information he didn't need to worry about? He had enough on his plate. She should have told him on the day he'd hired her, but it had seemed foolish to invite trouble when she hoped to avoid it.

"I'm prying." He reached across the table to touch

her hand. "I only want to know you better. If you're comfortable sharing."

A completely fair request considering how intertwined they'd become. They cared for the baby like a parental team. The DNA work might not be all about the horses in recent days, but they were a well-oiled machine there, too. And at night she slept in his bed, sated and content, her body wrapped up with his.

Her early visions of an ideal life paled next to the fabulous reality of living and working with Fox.

"Okay. I'm the third-oldest girl." She smiled, thinking about the days that had been closer to happy. "Most people can't fathom being in a family that big. It was just my reality. We all loved and laughed and pitched in from one day to the next."

"Until you had to leave." His blue eyes, so serious, held hers. "That took remarkable grit. I can't pretend to understand how you made the choice, but I'm grateful you wound up here."

The food arrived, saving her from having to reply. She'd barely taken a bite of her cheeseburger when the baby started to fuss.

Fox was out of the booth first. "I've got him." He hitched the diaper bag over his shoulder and lifted John from the seat. "You eat while it's hot, we have man-business."

She laughed as he walked toward the restrooms. The man was a marvel. None of the men from her childhood would've done that. Whenever a baby in her house had interrupted dinner, her mother or one of the girls had handled it without complaint. Seeing men and women doing what needed done without thought to gender had been one of the most startling revelations when she'd left home. As her aunt Greta had told her time and again, escaping the family closed one door forever, but it opened a wealth of others.

And Kelsey had walked through those open doors with varying amounts of courage.

This one, this door that opened on this priceless time with Fox, felt like the best yet.

Chapter 11

By the time they walked out of the grocery store, Fox was feeling normal again. Though the baby posed an ongoing predicament, he figured Kelsey's help bought him some time to figure out the next step. Beside him, she laughed when the baby scrunched up his face and sneezed against the sudden blast of late-afternoon sunshine.

"My mom, Dana, would've said he's allergic to sunshine," Fox said.

"Your mom sounds wonderful."

"She was." He wondered what she'd think of the baby landing on his doorstep or the woman who'd shown up at the perfect time to save him from his doubt and insecurity. "Sometimes it makes me sad how much Sloane missed out. Then I remember Mara tried harder with her than with me."

"It isn't easy when a parent of any variety demonstrates a preference," Kelsey said. "Every kid is different, so material things might not always be exactly even, but time and love should be doled out equally across the board."

Something in her tone had him asking if her mom had played favorites.

"Both of my parents were clear that boys of any age outranked the girls. Boys were assets and we were viewed as…support."

She'd previously called the setup archaic and he found himself agreeing.

The baby spit out his pacifier as they crossed the parking lot and Fox was again grateful for the little clip and leash Kelsey had insisted on during that first trip for baby gear. The kid was too cute and on a day like this one it was too easy to imagine doing errands like this every week.

Family life. He'd been afraid of the risk he posed for so long. Now, though he couldn't claim complete confidence, he found himself wanting more. Maybe wanting family was contagious. He wouldn't have given it any further consideration before the baby landed on his doorstep. Even in those long hours before Kelsey had shown up, an angel among nannies, he hadn't pictured a future with children constantly around. Being an uncle was enough pressure.

He used the key fob to open the truck and lifted Baby John, car seat and all, into the frame buckled into the rear seat. Kelsey unloaded groceries from the cart and tucked the diaper bag on the floor behind her seat.

"We need to go," she said, her voice quaking. Her

gaze darted furtively to the other side of the parking lot as she fumbled to open the front passenger door.

"What is it?" He looked around, trying to see what had made her so jumpy.

"That man." She pointed in the direction, using the truck to hide the gesture. "He's one of my brothers."

He looked around for the black sedan she'd seen at the ranch and didn't spot one. The man wore a faded Denver Broncos ball cap and the sunlight showed the red in his thick beard. He was definitely staring at them, although they were hardly the only people in his general line of sight.

"I'll go over and tell him to leave you alone." The urge to protect her roared to life.

"No!" She pressed her lips together. "Let's just go. He won't follow us onto your property."

Fox disagreed. Hadn't her brothers already done that? Refusing to waste time arguing, he boosted up into the driver's seat and started the engine.

She fumbled with her seat belt, and he reached over to click it into place. "Thanks." She sat on her hands.

"I can't just do nothing when you're this scared."

"I'm scared for you and the baby. I'm used to taking care of myself."

What the hell did that mean? "We'll call the sheriff and wait for him here."

"No, not here," she argued. "If I confront my brothers in public, they'll make a scene. Whenever they find me, they try to embarrass me or discredit me so any friends or support I have is gone."

"What?"

Her hazel eyes pleaded with him. "Please, Fox. I'll

tell you the whole story, I promise, just get us out of here."

He noticed a tall, burly man with dark red hair striding toward them, his eyes shaded by dark sunglasses. Fox backed out of the parking space as if he hadn't seen the man or the anxiety he created in Kelsey.

"He'll follow us," Kelsey warned.

The grim certainty troubled him.

"You should drop me at the sheriff's station," she continued. "With your endorsement, one of the officers can mediate for me. That will put you and the baby in the clear and give me a head start."

"Not a chance, sweetheart." He reached for her hand, squeezed. Now that he'd found the woman he wanted in his life, he wouldn't let her run away. "Talk to me."

"Fox, it's a mess. *My* mess. Just drop me off and extricate yourself while you can."

"No. You're staying. And not just because I still can't cope when Baby John cries."

The joke fell flat. He reached up and rubbed her shoulder. "Come on, Kelsey, you've been on hand for all my family drama." She should have someone in her corner...and he wanted her to realize that someone was *him.*

Fox checked his rearview mirror as they drove through town. On a hunch, he took a turn where he might normally go straight and a beat-up van with a primer-gray door followed.

Kelsey swiveled around in her seat. "I knew the black car I saw at the ranch was too nice for them."

Then who had been in the car watching his house? One problem at a time. Fox pulled into the gas station nearest the sheriff's office, ignoring Kelsey's miserable groan. The van cruised by, close enough for him to confirm the man in the seat was one of the men from the parking lot.

He went ahead and topped off the gas tank and as he drove off, the van trailed behind them.

"You won't reconsider?" Kelsey asked.

"Would you in my place?"

"No," she admitted, dejected.

"Start talking," he said. He wanted to know what he was up against.

"My family history is a long, ugly story. I was born into a separatist community way up north. Rural, isolated. It might as well have been a different country." She spoke quickly, listing off bullet points that should've been supported by a slideshow. "I am one of twelve children in my family, and I did help Mom with the babies younger than me. That's all true. And I did run away from home when I was fourteen because I wanted to be more than a mother."

He'd never thought she'd lied. "That's fair." The way her mind worked, he couldn't imagine her happy if she couldn't learn and explore.

"Not where I'm from."

"Meaning?"

"I ran away," she repeated. "I broke rank. My brothers have been trying to take me back ever since. If you let me go, they'll leave you and the baby alone."

"You're afraid of them." He glanced over. She was steadier now, calmer.

"More accurately, I don't look forward to another confrontation. I don't want you and Baby John getting tangled up in this. I can handle them." She said it like an affirmation. "I have handled them before. It's how I made it this far."

"How old are you?"

Her auburn eyebrows snapped together. "Why is that relevant?"

Because it distracted her. "Twenty-eight or so?"

"Ha. I'm thirty and I know you know that."

He managed to stifle the smile. "All I'm saying is that you've done a great job evading your persistent family on your own. I'm happy to lend a hand this time." And in any future attempts, as well.

"What about the baby?"

He'd thought the same thing. "We'll let him sleep through it." Fox had to keep the mood light or she'd see exactly what he thought of her brothers scaring her this way.

She thumped her head back against the headrest a few times. "I didn't think they'd catch up with me so quickly. I never would've agreed to help as a nanny if I'd known."

"That might be my fault." If he'd brought this on her, unwittingly or not, he'd fix it.

"How?"

"Do your brothers know what you do?"

"Pretty much. They've followed me everywhere and they've been in the real world enough to know girls *can* do math."

Fox cringed at the backward mind-set. "I've mentioned you by name at the ranch and in town. This is on me."

She shook her head. "I doubt it. They know how to hunt and track. We were in town for the baby, to deal with my car, and for plenty of other reasons these past few weeks. I worked my way through school waitressing or babysitting. That's where they look first."

Her assessment didn't ease his guilt. If he'd kept her in the office as an assistant—the job she'd come for—this might not have even been an issue.

She reached over and patted his thigh. "Seriously, Fox, they always find me. I create escape plans every time or I wouldn't be here now. If you pulled over, I could straighten them out."

"Does straightening them out include leaving the Crooked C?"

"That would be the best thing for you," she said softly.

He admired her honesty, though his chest constricted at the thought of her walking out of his life as easily as she'd walked in. "If you keep doing the same thing, you'll keep getting the same result, Kelsey."

"I'm aware." She sighed. "Same goes for them."

"True." Fox decided he wouldn't take no for an answer. "We're almost to the ranch. If they come onto the property, we'll stop. You'll call Trey and I'll press charges for trespassing."

"That's a bad tactic, Fox."

"Just tell me who's behind us."

"My older brother, David, is the redhead in sunglasses," Kelsey replied. "He brought Saul along this time."

This time? He bristled. This would be the *last* time. "Is that good or bad?"

"Well, David has a mean streak. Saul keeps his cool and usually keeps David calm, but he can be sneaky."

"Good to know."

The van with her brothers boldly followed when

he made the turn onto ranch property. He drove far enough to leave no doubt about the property lines or intentions before he pulled over. Shoving the gearshift into Park, he turned to her. "I'll talk to them while you call Trey and drive on to the house."

"Fox, it should be me doing the talking," she protested.

Her voice cracked. It might be her family drama, but she needed an ally. Kelsey was a grown woman. She'd put herself though a rigorous college program and become a respected equine geneticist. How had she accomplished so much with a threat like this looming over her?

"Go." He climbed out of the driver's seat. They could argue later. "Get to the house and take care of John." He glanced toward the battered van. "I'll deal with this."

"But—"

"Go." He turned away, had to trust her to do the right thing for the baby if not herself.

The van slowed and stopped several car lengths behind his truck. Grateful they hadn't tried to run him down, Fox gave her brothers a point for common sense.

He walked closer to the van as Kelsey eased away. It felt like a victory already that she was doing as he asked, trusting him to handle this.

"You lost?" Fox asked the driver, Kelsey's brother David. He seemed a bit thicker through the shoulders than Saul.

"We know exactly where we are," Saul replied.

David's mouth slanted into a sneer. "You have something that belongs to us. We're here to collect."

"I can't imagine what that would be," Fox replied.

"The woman raising your kid is our sister," David snapped.

"Easy," Saul said to his brother, then turned back to Fox. "We don't expect you to know or understand the whole story."

David drummed his fingers on the steering wheel while Saul spun a tale of Kelsey being abducted and brainwashed.

The story was so outrageous, the picture they painted of her so bizarre, it seemed only her name had been kept the same. Though he wanted to challenge them, Fox thought better of it. He was currently outnumbered and unarmed. Despite this being his property, he couldn't risk hoping that the brothers weren't carrying weapons of some kind.

"Interesting," he said. "Bottom line, you're on private property. You need to turn around now." He pulled out his phone. "I'll have to call the sheriff if you refuse."

"We just want to take our sister home where she belongs," Saul told him. "We've missed her."

David's sneer returned. "I'm sure she's great with your brat, but she has family responsibilities elsewhere."

A voice in Fox's head clamored that Kelsey was *his* family. And Baby John was not a brat. He struggled to keep his hands loose while a vision of pounding this jerk into the ground hazed his vision. "Where can Kelsey reach you?"

Saul handed Fox a business card from a cheap motel outside of town. "My number's on the back. We look forward to hearing from you."

"Have her call soon," David snarled. "Or you'll regret it. I'd hate to see this nice spread torn up for no reason."

"Is that a threat?"

Saul's smile was oily. "No," he said smoothly. "We don't want trouble. Just our sister."

David rolled up his window and backed away. His tires kicked up dust and debris when he made a U-turn and hit the gas.

Fox dusted himself off once they were out of sight. Then he checked his phone and smiled—he'd managed to get good pictures of their faces and van along with the entirety of the license plate. That would help both the sheriff and Wyatt when he reported this pair of annoying trespassers.

Quickly adjusting the driver's seat, Kelsey drove away, her eyes on the rearview and side mirrors for as long as possible. Her brothers weren't killers, but that didn't make them safe people. She called the police, reporting trespassers on the ranch without naming her brothers.

Coward.

What lies would they tell Fox? Would they try to convince him she was married? Her father had drawn up a marriage contract on her fourteenth birthday and scheduled the wedding for the weekend after she turned eighteen.

No choices for her. No chance to fall in love with a boy her own age. The contract was only binding within the confines of the community. That was small comfort when her brothers were feeding Fox lies so they could take her home.

They'd gotten her fired before. During her sophomore year in college they'd nearly cost her the scholarship she'd busted her butt to earn. Without her aunt's intervention at that time, who knows where she'd be now.

Her palms went damp and her anxiety returned with a vengeance, pulling tight across her shoulders. She focused on her breath, leaning on the earliest lessons of the martial arts classes she'd taken to protect herself. Parking in front of the big red barn, her thoughts skittered like the colorful leaves in the autumn breeze.

The baby's safety was paramount. She should call Wyatt and the ranch manager. Maybe it would be better to drive over and ask Bailey to keep an eye on Baby John so she could go back for Fox. As she reached for the key to do just that, the baby started fussing. The sound snapped her out of the tizzy. They would be safe upstairs and she could make more calls from there.

She was familiar enough with the ranch now to have a good idea of how long it would take Fox to walk back. With that timer running in her head, she lifted the baby from his car seat and headed inside, locking the doors behind her. Heading straight back to the nursery, she rocked him back to sleep and then tucked him into the crib.

She peered through the windows after bringing in the groceries, but there was still no sign of Fox. Her heart heavy, she walked back to the room she'd initially shared with the baby.

Packing now meant less of a delay when he kicked her out. She had faith in Fox, but it was nearly impossible to believe things would work out. Her brothers were master manipulators.

She'd miss this place and the man who'd built it. His

breeding program was an excellent fit for her interests and skills. She pressed her hands to her eyes, refusing to cry. There were other places she could be useful but she'd never find another ranch as beautiful as this one or a boss as smart and dedicated and sexy.

Not that *sexy* was a trait she actively sought in a boss. Fox was the exception. This was the first and only time she'd trampled on the line between personal and professional activities.

She heard someone pounding on the door and her body braced for battle a moment before she heard Fox calling her name. She rushed downstairs to let him in before he woke the baby.

She flung open the door, the urge to jump into his arms immediately quelled by the thunderous expression on his face.

"They told me you'd be gone."

"I'd never leave the baby." She pointed to the monitor on her hip. "I'm sure they told you a lot of things." She stepped back to give him room, pleased when he turned the dead bolt, locking them inside.

"I didn't believe them," he said, his voice ragged.

She glared up at him. "Right. That explains why you were so happy to see me answer your door." She shook the tension from her hands. Being angry with him solved nothing. He wasn't the first person her brothers had fooled. Resigned, she started up the stairs.

"Kelsey, wait."

She didn't.

He caught her at the landing and turned her around. She was prepared to quit, to spare him the hassle of firing her, but then her resolve slipped as he gathered her close. He was shaking all over, his heart hammering under her ear. She stroked his back, trying to soothe him.

"Fox?" His reaction shocked her. "What is it? What did they say?"

"Hush." His arms banded around her, making it hard to breathe. Then he kissed her with a needy desperation. "You…you're here," he said, easing back. He traced her jaw with his thumb, tucked a wayward strand of hair behind her ear. "That's all that matters."

She looked up into his face and knew better. "What did they tell you?" He kissed her, his lips trembling, and she knew she was in for an uphill battle. "Do I need to pack?"

He nudged her into his home. "Only if you want to go back with them."

"Never." The idea of returning to her original family held no appeal.

"Then stay."

"That's it?" It couldn't be that easy.

"I'd like *you* to tell me the whole story, but only when you're ready."

She owed him that much and sooner rather than later. No matter what he'd said to make her brothers leave, they would be back. "I'm ready."

Fox fixed himself a cup of coffee and a cup of hot cocoa for her and set both on the kitchen island. "If I could, I'd pack up all three of us and head out of here tonight," he said.

Her mouth dropped open. "You can't," she protested. "Your entire life is here."

"Well, if I can't go, then neither can you," he said. "You're an indispensable part of my life here."

"If you're worried they'll be back—"

"I sure of it," he interjected.

"Take comfort that they only want me," she finished. "They won't hurt the baby."

"That's not any comfort at all," he said. "They struck me as motivated enough to ignore any collateral damage."

She dunked a miniature marshmallow into the cocoa with her spoon. "I'm sorry."

"Talk to me," he urged gently. "I've spoken with Wyatt and the sheriff and we're all on alert to their threats, but you know them best."

The chocolate turned bitter in her mouth. "What threats? They tell lies about me and why they're trying to take me back, but they've never threatened anyone before."

"Why, Kelsey?"

"Money." She yanked out the band and pins and let her hair unwind. Massaging her scalp, she gathered her thoughts. "If they take me back, they can profit when the marriage contract is fulfilled." There, the worst of it was out.

Fox's lips pursed. "You said you left home just before your fifteenth birthday."

"I did. My brothers told you I was abducted?"

"They did," Fox confirmed. "It was quite a tale."

"A few months before I escaped, I was in town with my mother, running herd on my siblings. I bumped into a woman who looked familiar. It was my mother's oldest sister. I hadn't seen her in years. She left the family after her husband died in an accident. Her father had been arranging her second marriage during the funeral."

"Cold."

"Normal," Kelsey corrected. "Where I grew up that

was normal." It was so hard to explain it to outsiders. "Aunt Greta told me she'd come to love her first husband. They'd only had one child, a girl, and the man her father wanted her to marry next was much older. He had no use for little girls. She left to make sure her daughter wouldn't be taken from her."

Kelsey sipped her cocoa. "When she and her daughter left, they were written out of our family history. My mother never mentioned her name again. I figured out Greta helped others who wanted to leave our community. When I escaped, I ran to her."

"So not everyone is tracked down and harassed the way your brothers hound you?"

She shook her head. "What else did they tell you?"

"They blustered."

There was plenty he left unsaid, but that was secondary. Fox couldn't find the right solution without all of the information. "They won't give up on me because of the marriage contract my father negotiated when I was fourteen," she said.

"Fourteen?"

His shock rolled over her and he shot to his feet, outraged.

"The wedding was delayed until I turned eighteen," she added quickly. "Money changed hands, though, so time is irrelevant. Based on what Aunt Greta learned, it comes down to mineral rights. A major deposit spans both properties. My brothers won't profit unless both families agree to let the developers in."

"Which is why your marriage was arranged in the first place." Scowling, he braced his hands on his hips. "This is appalling."

She agreed. "My father died a few years ago but the

contract is considered binding within the community. My brothers are determined to get rich."

"And you left right away." He rushed forward and hugged her again.

"No," she confessed. "I left when my father pulled me out of school." She was so embarrassed she could barely get the words out. "My friend, another boy, was sneaking me math and science books and assignments. We were caught."

"Kelsey."

She didn't realize she was crying until Fox brushed the tears from her cheek. "It was bad." She'd never told anyone just how bad. "My brother David found us. He refused to keep his mouth shut. They punished both of us."

He tightened his arms around her and she held on until the worst of those ugly memories passed. "What happened to your friend?"

"He died." Fox's body stiffened. "The elders didn't kill him intentionally. He died of internal bleeding from his injuries."

Over her head, Fox muttered an oath. "I sent pictures of the van and your brothers to the sheriff. They threatened to destroy the ranch if I didn't let you go," Fox said.

She moved out of his reach. "I'll leave. They'll follow me and forget you."

"You will *not* leave," he said, his tone hard as the granite countertop. "You're not in this alone anymore."

"I can't ask—"

"You didn't ask." He massaged his knuckles with his opposite palm. "But sweetheart? Maybe you should have. What do you think they'll do?"

She rubbed her forehead, the shame pressing in on her. "In the past they've vandalized my car or apartment, but they've never done damage to other property."

"They're desperate now."

"Seems like it," she agreed. "I'd expect them to harass and annoy, maybe spread some lies or try to drum up some bad blood in town. Saul is the more logical of the two. He won't let David do anything dumb enough to land them in jail."

"All right." Fox gave a gusty sigh. "I'll tell everyone on the Crooked C to keep an eye out and to report anything suspicious."

"I really am sorry, Fox."

"None of us can choose the family we start with," he said.

Through the monitor, they heard the baby waking up. "I'll get him." She started down the hall, relieved for a break from the hardest conversation of her life.

"I'll fix a bottle," Fox told her.

While she fed the baby, she answered more of Fox's questions about where and how she was raised and how she'd adapted to life in the real world. It was almost fun sharing more normal high school and college moments. She felt as if Fox was leading them out of the wilderness and back onto a smooth path where they could be comfortable with each other again.

But when she looked up, the deep, contemplative shadows in his eyes worried her.

"Fox, listen." She propped the baby on her shoulder and patted his back until he burped loudly. "I can handle my brothers."

"They make you nervous."

She didn't bother denying it. "That's why I've trained hard to protect myself. Why I have plans in place just in case they do overpower me."

Fox's face turned red, his fingers curling into his palms. "Have they done that before?"

"Not with any success." His eyes narrowed and she rushed on. "When I walked away from my family, it was forever, even if they can't accept it."

"What will make it clear to them?"

"Nothing short of a husband," she joked, though it was true. "Or plastic surgery," she added to lighten the mood. "I stay in touch with my aunt. If she doesn't hear from me at regular intervals, she knows to take my sworn statement to the state police so they can search the family compound for me."

His mouth set in a hard line, she knew he was still searching for a better solution. "Marriage would make them go away for good?" he asked.

Had he been listening at all? She had it under control. Staying alert at the ranch should be enough to protect all of them.

Done with the bottle, the baby arched toward Fox and he obliged, sitting on the floor with the baby.

"Taking me from a real-world husband is too close to stealing in my brothers' minds," she explained. "I'm trying to be clear that if, by some misguided miracle, they do nab me they won't have me for long."

He looked up as she walked back in. She'd never seen such a hard, cold edge in his blue eyes. "I want your aunt's contact information."

"You already have it."

He frowned. "I do?"

"It's in my phone and in my employee file."

"You have an employee file?"

She grinned. "I set it up for you on my first day in the office."

His eyebrows arched and he laughed. She appreciated a man who could admit his weaknesses. The baby reached for the buttons on his shirt and when he smiled into that perfect little face, her heart melted a little more.

Fox appreciated her confidence that she could handle herself, but he couldn't settle down. Kelsey's brothers struck him as dangerous and money often made people desperate enough to do stupid things. Regardless of her martial arts training, there were two of them and only one of her.

The best solution was obvious to him. He just didn't know how to bring her around to the idea of marrying him. It would keep her safe and keep them together. He wanted both.

Why did the woman who'd essentially rescued him from his baby-care ignorance have to be in trouble? Why now? And good grief, the whining voice in his head was annoying.

He needed a fresh perspective. Though he didn't want to leave her alone again, he wanted to get an objective opinion. With dinner done and the baby content, now was as good a time as any.

"I'm going out," he said. "I won't be gone long. You'll be okay?"

Her smile didn't quite reach her eyes. "We will."

"I know we planned to work tonight." Confronting her brothers had ruined his concentration.

"Better to hit it fresh tomorrow," she said. "We'll be right here, safe and content when you get back."

It sounded so perfectly domestic, he nearly changed his mind. "I'm only headed to Wyatt's. Call if you need me."

"I promise."

He kissed her cheek and headed out. Only the baby kept him from slamming the doors on the way. He made up for it outside when he climbed into the driver's seat of his truck and slammed that door closed. Recognizing the tantrum rolling through him, he felt more like Harrison than ever.

He wasn't mad at *her.* She'd had no say in the family she'd escaped. She had no control over her two hotheaded brothers.

But should she have told him sooner? Would he be this worried if John wasn't in the mix?

By the time he reached Wyatt's place, he'd regained some self-control. He walked up and caught himself before he rang the doorbell. He took a seat on the top step of the porch and sent his brother a text message.

The front door opened a few minutes later and Wyatt stepped out, carrying two longneck bottles of beer. "You've had a rough day," his brother said, planting himself in one of the porch rockers.

"Rougher than others," Fox admitted.

"That's saying something. Come up here and be civilized," Wyatt said, holding out a beer bottle like a carrot. "I'm a dad now and I feel lost if I'm not swaying or otherwise in motion all the time."

Fox took the offered beer and a rocking chair. "Kelsey does that with John," he murmured. Standing, he realized he too had made a habit of the parent-sway. "Did you ever worry about becoming a dad?"

"Be a fool not to," Wyatt said. "You didn't get months to adjust to the idea. How are you holding up?"

"Haven't hit him yet," Fox muttered.

Wyatt kicked Fox's boot. "And you won't, you idiot. Your dad's issues were his own. You're the science guy, but I doubt that kind of thing is hereditary."

"Wouldn't matter if it was." Fox debated the wisdom of sharing the DNA results with his favorite brother. "Most authorities on the topic think that kind of thing is learned by example."

"Nurture over nature?" Wyatt mused. "Then I'm glad you came to live with us, though I know you'll always miss your mom."

"True enough." Fox took a long drink. "Russ was way different than my dad."

"Not perfect," Wyatt allowed. "One hell of a provider."

Also true. "But at what cost to the family?"

Wyatt's rocker stopped creaking and he sat forward, elbows braced on his hands. "We know we want more balance. Knowing it means we'll take better care to make it happen."

"You sound so certain."

"Good. Maybe I'll convince you. I admit Bailey is a big part of my attitude on this," he said. "Having that partner in the trenches with you, one who shares your vision of family, makes it easier to stay the course."

"Even when you're not getting any sleep?"

"Even then."

Fox wanted Kelsey as his partner. It defied logic and reasonable timelines, but it was as much a fact as the earth under his feet. "Those two men in a beat-up van will be back," Fox said. "They're Kelsey's brothers and focused on harassing her, but be alert."

"We'll keep an eye out. Do you know why they're hassling her?"

"Her family is more messed up than ours." It was her story to share, not his, but Wyatt deserved an explanation. "She was raised in a separatist community. She escaped years ago, but they want her back."

"What does *she* want?"

"To stay right where she is," Fox replied. "Helping me with the breeding program."

"Huh." Wyatt sputtered and Fox kicked him this time. "Come on. A baby's not a bad way to hook a woman."

Maybe if that woman hadn't raised her siblings and a few of the neighbor kids, as well. "That's not exactly what happened," he protested.

"Isn't it? Even I appreciated your brilliant efficiency in moving a beautiful, competent woman into your place."

"Baby John is temporary." Fox tapped the bottle against the arm of the rocking chair. "His dad will come around." Eventually. Hopefully?

"If he doesn't?"

Fox only grunted. He wanted Kelsey to stay and he wasn't sure she would if the baby was part of his life, too.

Wyatt stopped rocking. In the dark Fox couldn't see the speculative glint that was no doubt in his brother's eyes, but he felt exposed. "What do you want to hear?" Wyatt asked.

Fox shoved himself out of the chair and leaned

against the porch rail, his back to Wyatt as he stared up at the stars winking into view overhead. "I don't know. There's a woman in my house, caring for a baby that isn't mine. I think she's in real trouble."

"You think you can help?"

Fox nodded. "Yes," he added, allowing for the poor lighting.

Wyatt's rocker resumed the soothing pace. "You're too smart to mix business and pleasure."

Clearly not. He tried to put it into words his brother would understand without poking fun. "I see her with the baby and it's…it's like…"

"Easy?" Wyatt supplied. "Uncomfortable?"

"Both," Fox snapped. "More. I didn't want a family. How can that change on a dime?" he demanded, turning around.

Wyatt's laughter carried out into the night. "You're the data guy," Wyatt replied. "Analyze."

"You're no help."

"Seriously, Fox. Only you have those answers. Make a theory or hypothesis and find some evidence."

"This isn't science, it's personal. How can I trust this mash-up of feelings?"

Wyatt's rocking chair creaked for a few minutes. "How do you know which horses to breed for the traits you want?"

"Science," he said.

"And?" Wyatt asked with infinite patience.

"Instinct."

"Exactly. Trust your gut."

"She's a person. There's a reason I deal with horses." Other than Sloane, the people he'd trusted most, loved most, had been taken from him. To survive, he'd made a habit of treading carefully, never stepping out of line so he wouldn't offend anyone.

Or, more accurately, so he'd be worthy of love. Fox couldn't say definitively that the tactic had worked. He had his siblings, but he'd been reluctant to let anyone else get close enough to hurt him. Until the baby. And Kelsey.

She needed a husband to escape the trouble her brothers posed, but he wanted to be her husband because he'd fallen in love. He *loved* her. Although the work was central to his life and her interests, he also had a baby that was the exact opposite of what she wanted.

"If only there was a formula for the personal stuff." Wyatt stood and clapped him on the shoulder. "Once you make quarter horses perfect you could work on finding the people formula."

"Maybe I will," Fox muttered. "Thanks for the beer."

"Anytime. Us dads need to stick together."

Was he a dad? He sure felt like one, thanks to Kelsey. Every time the three of them were together it felt like family. Could he convince her to take the leap with him?

Kelsey refused to dwell on Fox's departure. He had a great deal on his mind and she'd just added to the burden. Technically, he'd needed the details of her past, but it did not alleviate her guilt.

Instead, she focused on the baby, enjoying his happy personality while she made herself a sandwich and stirred up cereal for him. Though she'd done this countless times for her siblings, often with a whip of resentment, with John it was different. Pure joy.

She was older, sure, but it went deeper. She'd established her career and made positive changes. This time around, she didn't feel stuck or pigeonholed by taking on a nanny post. It helped too that Fox made it clear how much he appreciated her efforts with both the baby and the horses.

During bath time, she was no match for the memories that bubbled up. She thought she'd be ready for them after talking about her family as much as she had. Her mother had rarely asked for help, simply assuming her girls wanted to learn and pitch in and be useful around the house and garden.

For a time it had been enough. She hadn't known to want more. Then her father started keeping her home from school more often with a variety of excuses. Tears blurred her vision as the baby splashed, trying to catch the washcloth. Those days were done. She wasn't going back no matter what her brothers tried next.

"Why can't they accept it?" she asked John. "They'd be happier if they did." She couldn't shake off the shame of Fox stepping into the breach and dealing with the stickier parts of her past.

She finished the baby's bath and got him into clean pajamas. In the guest room turned nursery, she sat down in the glider and rocked, singing an old hymn as a lullaby.

If she hadn't already been in love with Fox, she would've fallen when he reminded her that no one could choose the family they were born into. "It seems he's chosen you, little one," she murmured to the baby, now sound asleep. "Eventually you'll know how lucky you are to have a man like Fox ride to the rescue."

Restless after tucking the baby into his bed, she wandered the house. It didn't seem right to just go to sleep or turn on a movie after her brothers had pulled that stunt. She wandered, looking for something to fill her time while she waited for Fox to come home.

Baby monitor in hand, she changed clothes and cleared some space by the hearth to stretch. Yoga had become her go-to technique to settle her nerves and stay limber as she'd progressed from standard self-defense to Krav Maga classes. Letting her breath move through her, she felt empowered, free and safe. She moved slowly while her muscles warmed up, helping her forget her brothers and reinforcing who she had become despite her start in life.

This time she wouldn't run. She'd stick. Her brothers would not steal one more hour of her hard-earned happiness and joy. Fox might have his doubts, but she *was* capable of defending herself and protecting the baby.

And she would do so at all costs.

The sound of a car outside startled her. Her body primed for action, she listened to the smooth rumble of the engine. Fox, not her brothers.

Her heart kicked again, this time with pleasure when she heard him walk into the house.

"Kelsey?" he called softly.

"In here," she replied. Grabbing the baby monitor, she met him in the kitchen. "Did you eat?"

"No." He pressed a hand to his belly. Her palm tingled, remembering the feel of his skin and taut muscles.

"We can fix that." She smiled, trying to ease them closer to normal. "We have plenty of food." As she came around the island, he caught her around the waist, drew her close.

Her yoga pants and long-sleeved T-shirt were no protection against the tantalizing heat of his body or the rasp of the heavier fabric of his oxford shirt and jeans. Her body molded to his in an instant, need pulsing through her veins. So much for her soothing yoga session. She was ready to climb him like a tree. Keeping her gaze on that space between his collarbones, she struggled for composure.

He tipped up her chin, his vibrant blue gaze hot on hers. "You don't have to cook for me."

"I don't mind." She meant it. In his embrace, she felt her earlier tension slip away. With him she didn't have to be tough or aloof. She could relax and let down her guard.

Even knowing her brothers were lurking close by, Fox gave her a sense of peace and security. Here, she had a purpose beyond the miracle of bearing children. Doing something nice for him was her choice, her pleasure, rather than an expected tithe.

"Come on," she urged, though she didn't move out of the circle of his arms. "Do you want a hot or cold sandwich?"

His hooded gaze dropped to her lips and it felt like forever before his mouth covered hers. The hot, frenzied contact wrapped around her, them, a silky cocoon she didn't want to escape. When he lifted his head they were both gasping.

What *was* that? Off balance, she clutched his shoulders until the world righted itself. She couldn't ask. Not until she was ready to hear the answer.

His stomach growled and they both smiled. While

she fixed a hot ham and Swiss sandwich for him they chatted about Wyatt's cattle and Fox's horses. She set the plate in front of him and poured a tall glass of water for each of them before taking a seat.

Talking with him, exchanging ideas on everything from the breeding to John to the ranch operations in general, had become one of the highlights of her day.

"The baby went down okay?"

"He did."

Fox's brow flexed. "And you're feeling all right?"

"Better than," she said. "You haven't changed your mind about having me here?"

He pinned her with a look that left her breathless. "I haven't changed my mind, Kelsey."

"Good." Something in his voice left her unsettled, as if she'd missed a topic change or the punchline of a joke. "Do you want anything else?"

He stared at her for a moment, his mouth curving into a sexy grin. Pushing his plate aside, he boosted her up onto the island and stepped between her open thighs. She welcomed his ravishing kiss, sliding her hands up under his shirt. She could almost hear the click as her world snapped back into place.

Chapter 12

The next morning in the office, Fox tried to put Wyatt's advice to work. With his monitor full of data on horses, his mind worked full-time on a Kelsey analysis. More precisely, he was working on a solution to address the undeniable connection growing between them.

He couldn't be objective. Every assessment and review cycled back to the same conclusion: he loved her. Bigger than proximity or lust, this went into completely new territory. He'd known the love of family. That began with his mother. And he'd lay down his life for his sister or any of his other siblings. That was a love he understood with or without DNA markers.

Granted, he'd only been a temporary dad for a few weeks, but he'd jump in front of a charging bull for Baby John, too. Seeing Kelsey with the baby added yet another layer of love every time. He hadn't known his heart could hold so much joy.

Clearly, love had nothing to do with the quantity of the genetic material involved or the duration of a connection. No, his initial analysis indicated love was more reliant on the *quality* of the connection. The X-factor, he thought with a snort.

"Did you find something?" Kelsey asked.

He glanced across the office to where the baby played on a colorful blanket while she continued her reading.

"Time will tell." What would she do if he blurted out an *I love you* or shared his top solution to send her brothers packing? He wrote those three powerful words on a notepad instead, staring at them. How could he convince her he wasn't infatuated with great sex and a convenient arrangement?

She hadn't given him any verbal indication of her feelings, either. If there was a rule about who should say it first, he didn't know it. No way would he do an internet search on that topic while she was right here in the office.

After the run-in with her brothers he worried that she'd feel cornered if he told her how he felt. She'd overcome so much to shake free of her rigid expectations and make her own way in the world.

Wyatt would tell him to man up. If the woman he loved had been courageous enough to blaze her own trail, she deserved a man courageous enough to risk rejection.

Fox had muddied the waters with Kelsey. Why would she believe he loved her when the scales were so unbalanced? She was giving him and the baby so much more than he was giving her. He just had to put it all out there, had to be clear about what he wanted and listen to what she needed.

What if she didn't want him?

He fought against a flurry of insecurities. His father had been a hard man, and Mara had done everything but shun him. Russ had raised him as his own, yet even that relationship had its pitfalls.

"Fox?"

His head snapped up, eager for the distraction. "What do you need?"

"Do we have more highlighters?" She held up a neon yellow marker. "This one's dry."

He rooted around in his desk drawer until he found what she wanted and walked it over to her.

"Thanks." She immediately put it to use. "This could be helpful when we finally dig into your losses last season."

"I'm pleased that we're at zero losses so far this season." It wouldn't last, but it was an excellent start.

One of the brightest minds in the field had sought him out and Kelsey's enthusiasm and insight had sparked several new ideas already. He would change at least two of his breeding plans because of her. Whether or not she stayed, with him personally or professionally, he'd see her for years to come in the foals that resulted from those changes.

He poured himself a fresh cup of coffee and watched her with the baby. John sat up and squealed, then rolled down to his belly again. Kelsey, engrossed with her reading a moment ago, gave him a big smile and heaped on praise. Satisfied, they both went back to their tasks.

Great. The baby could articulate his feelings better than Fox.

He opened his mouth to start the conversation about hiring a nanny and the baby made a sound of frustration, his little hands grasping for something just out of reach. Patiently, Kelsey helped him retrieve the toy. Baby John gurgled and tossed it out of reach again.

In a corner of his mind, Fox could see the three of them bobbing along on a soft cloud of happiness. An unexpected family, but a family rooted in love. If he wasn't careful, he might break into song. He was assuming too much, getting too tied up in what could be. Better to wait on any declarations, at least until they knew what would happen with John.

Calling himself a coward, Fox returned to his desk and hid behind his monitors and his coffee. He'd find a way to convince Kelsey of his plans and his feelings just as soon as he had the words sorted out in his head.

Kelsey wasn't sure if it was being inspired by Fox or having the built-in mental breaks between study and baby care, but she was making great progress catching up on the Crooked C breeding history. Of course, she couldn't discount the effect of working with a sexy scientist who was so focused he rarely caught her staring.

Sitting on the floor next to John, she highlighted another passage on managing mare breeding cycles while keeping him amused. He was winding down and soon she'd take him up out to the barn before his midday nap. She'd learned the short walk and some time with the horses helped him sleep more soundly.

"Hey, Kelsey?"

She glanced up, expecting to find Fox staring at a

monitor. Her heart skipped when she caught him staring at her, his reading glasses hooked in the placket of his Henley shirt. "Did you find something new?"

A shy smile curved his lips. "I'm not sure how to do this the right way." The smile faded and a small frown puckered his brow. "We've crossed a few lines along the way, but I want this to be clear. I want you to hear me."

Her stomach clenched. Was he firing her? He didn't have a reputation for sleeping with assistants and dumping them. It was her brothers—it had to be. She couldn't blame him for wanting to eliminate the risk she posed to his business and his family and friends. She'd fallen in love with Fox, just in time for her past to wreck everything.

The baby fussed, as if sensing her distress. She picked him up and bounced him gently on her knees until he giggled. "Just say it, Fox."

"Right, sure." He had a dopey grin on his face. "You're so good with the baby." He cleared his throat and the furrow returned. "I wish you could be his nanny full-time."

"I don't understand." Was he unhappy with her work? She had no idea if the loose feeling in her belly was a good or bad sign. The heat rising in her face she understood. That was frustration exacerbated by the small, mean voice in her head screaming at the unfairness of life.

Years of running and working and scraping by only to wind up as a nanny to the man she admired? She adored the baby, but she couldn't do that. She couldn't put her dreams and plans on hold, not even for Fox.

"No," he murmured. "No, I botched that." He was

across the room before she realized he'd moved. He plucked the baby from her arms and reached out to help her to her feet. "You're so good with the baby and even better with the work you came here to do. I doubt we'll find a nanny half as good as you, but we have to try. Whether it's another week or a month, I don't want your focus divided anymore."

"You're putting the priority on me? Professionally." That was more than she'd hoped for at any of stage of her career.

"Yes. I should've done it right away," he said.

"Wow." She looked around the office. "This isn't because we're, um, sleeping together?"

He gave her a knowing grin that sent a sizzle along her skin. "No."

The baby, tired and growing fussy, leaned for Kelsey. Fox had a good hold on him, but she reached out automatically. The little guy snuggled in, his downy hair soft against her neck. She swayed from side to side and pressed a kiss to that sweet-smelling head.

"What do you say?" Fox braced on the desk, his long legs crossed at the ankle, his arms folded as well, as if he was protecting himself from her answer. "I just want someone who can watch him for us during business hours. We can handle him the rest of the time, right?"

Yes! Yes! Yes! A satisfied smirk teased the corner of his mouth and she gave in to the urge to kiss him.

"You know, if we have a nanny, it's possible we could connect on a personal level, inside the office, too."

As his meaning registered, she felt her cheeks flame.

Her fair skin was useless at hiding her feelings. "You're ridiculous."

"Am I?"

Not a bit, but she shouldn't encourage him. She distracted herself with the baby for a moment, trying to maintain some professional decorum.

"Kelsey, you're a talented geneticist," Fox said. "We're a good team and we'll do good things."

She tucked the baby's pacifier into his mouth. "I agree."

"I also care about you. Us."

She lifted her gaze to his, deeply moved by the sincerity she found in his blue eyes. The man could talk science for hours, but the personal side of things seemed to muddle him up. She couldn't read too much into it or make any big assumptions. What he'd learned about his family history had to be affecting him. The news he'd faced would rattle anyone.

However awkwardly they'd begun, they were on solid footing now. He reached out and touched the baby's hand.

The stark love on his face when he looked at the baby filled her with wonder. Longing. And a little worry. What would he do when Baby John was settled with his father or a permanent family?

"You're amazing," Fox said. "With him. With me. But you're even more talented with genetics."

The compliment sent a shock wave through her system. It was like the Fourth of July and Christmas rolled up into one giant explosion of giddy happiness. "Thanks," she murmured.

He moved in, brushing his lips over the baby's cheek, and then kissed her with more intent, the tender contact full of sensual promises. Her lips tingling, she carried the baby out of the office and into the crisp autumn air.

Alone, Fox pumped a fist, proud of himself for recovering from the rocky start. He didn't know how to label their current relationship, but he didn't let that mute the high of knowing they had time to figure it out.

He returned to his work, only moderately distracted by visions of Kelsey's fair skin blushing with pleasure at his compliments. She was so smart and competent, he forgot she was still building up confidence after her unusual upbringing.

He ignored the sounds of a car outside. Ranch business meant vehicles came and went throughout the day. If anyone needed him, they'd find him in due time.

A piercing scream sounded outside and shattered his concentration. Kelsey and the baby had gone for their daily walk to the barn. He grabbed his cell phone and dialed 911 as he bolted out of the office.

Had her brothers returned? Was it the Avalanche Killer? No. He couldn't lose her. *Not her, not her*, he chanted in his head, while he frantically gave his address to the emergency operator.

He saw the van first, down the road from the barn. Then he saw her.

Kelsey, her hair a trail of pale fire streaming behind her, fought off two men. Both much bigger than her—everyone was bigger than her. One had red hair and the other wore a Broncos ball cap.

Her brothers. Damn it.

For a moment, he marveled at the way she moved,

the speed and strikes. She was holding her own. Ducking low, she rolled away from David and into Saul.

David recovered and grabbed her in a choke hold, thumping her against the side of the barn. "You're coming home."

"You've had enough time to play," Saul added, straightening his shirt.

Somewhere in the barn, the baby cried.

"Stop right there," Fox shouted. Why had he grabbed his phone instead of his shotgun? "You're trespassing. The sheriff is on the way."

"She's coming with us," David snarled.

John's cries ratcheted up, as if he too protested that statement.

Fox inched closer. "Only if I hear that from her."

David gave her a shake. "Tell him."

"Let me go," Kelsey rasped.

"Tell him."

Her brother screamed as she became a flurry of motion, stabbing him in the eye and turning him until he was trapped between her elbow strikes and knees to his groin and the unyielding wall of the barn. David slumped to the ground, choking on a nosebleed as he tried to crawl away.

Saul raced to intervene. Fox lunged, tackling him from behind. Fox didn't have Kelsey's impressive skill, but he had the experience of brothers and fought dirty, driving Saul's face into the dirt and pulling his arm up behind his back.

By the time Trey and Deputy Bloom arrived, amid blaring lights and sirens, he and Kelsey had her brothers subdued.

"Where's John?" Fox asked Kelsey.

"Tucked into the dry three-foot tank near the tack room," she replied.

The sheriff secured David and Saul with plastic zip tie handcuffs, and Kelsey rushed to comfort the baby while Fox gave a statement. When she returned, holding John, she'd never looked more beautiful.

"Warrior," he murmured, taking the baby. "The sheriff needs your statement."

Shaking out her arms, she walked Trey through the attack. Fox listened to her explain how the van rolled up, interrupting her walk with the baby. Her brothers had let her put the baby in a safe place, then David dragged her toward the vehicle.

Goose bumps rose on Fox's arms and he stopped swaying. The baby whimpered enough for him to resume the motion as she continued her story. "I slipped his hold and ran. That way." She pointed to the spot where Fox had found her. "I had just enough time to scream."

It would be a long time before Fox forgot that scream.

"This time they came at me together."

"This time?" the sheriff and Fox asked in unison.

"They've tried to abduct me before." Her chin lifted in defiance. "Usually one lies in wait and the other harbors delusions of grandeur as a getaway driver."

"How many times?"

"This makes three direct attacks in the past two years."

Fox recognized Trey's temper nearing the flash point. "All in this state?" Trey asked, glaring at the cuffed men.

"No, sir," Kelsey replied. "This is their first attempt in Colorado."

"Did you file complaints on those occasions?"

"No, sir. In the past, after escaping, I went into hiding or moved."

Fox suppressed a chill. He would not allow Kelsey to run away this time.

Trey stalked backed to David and Saul. "You two have harassed this girl enough."

"She's our sister. It's our business."

Furious, Trey and Deputy Bloom read the brothers their rights and loaded them into the car. "Someone will be by to tow the van," Trey said to Fox.

"Great." Fox shook his cousin's hand. "We appreciate this." Though Kelsey's reasons might differ from his, he knew they were both delighted and relieved to see her brothers in cuffs, facing charges for assault and attempted kidnapping.

Beside him, Kelsey took a slow, deep breath. He put his arm around her shoulders, the quiver of nerves and adrenaline almost imperceptible now. The woman blew him away. "You can take care of yourself."

She leaned her head on his shoulder as they watched the sheriff drive out of sight. "I appreciate the backup."

It didn't matter to him that Kelsey was an expert in hand-to-hand combat and could hold her own in a fight. He would not take any more chances with her. His heart couldn't take this. She had nine more siblings who might try to force her into fulfilling the hope for a family fortune.

"That's it," he said, making his decision as they walked toward the house.

"I'll take the baby," she said. "Make a bottle."

"You can make the bottle. I'll feed him while you pack a bag for him and you. We're leaving."

She paused, staring up at him. "What are you talking about?"

"We're leaving, all three of us, right now." He ushered her upstairs. "That narrow escape calls for a changeup. I'm not taking any more chances with you or the baby."

"Fox, I'm fine. My brothers—"

"I'm not taking chances," he repeated. The baby wriggled in his arms.

When John had his bottle, Fox sent her to pack and started making calls. There was a great deal to do if he was going to orchestrate a wedding worthy of the woman he loved.

From his vantage point he kept a close eye on the action at the Crooked C. His next target had put up one hell of a fight. She would be the perfect challenge. The sheriff had come and gone, taking away the two men who could have interfered.

He was mentally adjusting his timeline and ideal point of attack when he realized Fox was taking both the woman and the baby.

Not a drive to town, based on the luggage.

He lowered the binoculars and swore at the sky. All this time invested and no reward. But he had another target in mind. He would move swiftly so he didn't lose that opportunity.

Chapter 13

"Where are we headed?" Kelsey asked.

Fox had been a blur of action since he'd declared they were leaving town. She caught the deep scowl on his face as she buckled the baby into his car seat and Fox loaded up suitcases and the baby's portable crib.

"Las Vegas." He glanced up and met her gaze, the glower of a moment ago replaced by a warm smile. "We're getting married."

She felt her chin drop. The shock kept her rooted in place, hovering over the baby's seat, half in and half out of the car. The baby patted her face, nudging her back into motion.

"What?" She couldn't have heard him right. Fox was the opposite of impulsive and until now hadn't shown any dictator-like tendencies.

"Marry me, Kelsey. It solves everything."

Does it? As proposals went, it lacked finesse and was devoid of romance, and sparked a host of other concerns. Starting with the fact that she was in love with him.

Being in love should've smoothed out the rough edges of his imperfect proposal. This could be a joyful moment if he loved her back, if that was truly the catalyst for this trip. But that was wishful thinking on her part. Her brothers had spurred him into this uncharacteristically rash action. A fear response.

And knowing Fox, he wouldn't give up. Once he made a decision, he went all in.

"Come on, Kelsey." Apparently, she'd frozen again. He boosted her into the passenger seat and closed the back door. "We can hash out the details on the way."

They were going to Vegas to get married. His way, his terms. It seemed she was just along for the ride.

Her temper made her throat tight, her palms itch. "Details?" she asked as he climbed into the driver's seat. "What are you thinking?"

Had she even agreed to this wacky scheme?

He put the car in gear and the baby chortled. "John's up for it."

"Two out of three is good enough for you?"

He glanced her way, and she caught the smirk on his face. "It'll be fun, I promise."

"Fun?"

"Or romantic," he said quickly. "If that's what you want. Whatever kind of wedding you want, we'll do that."

"In Las Vegas."

"Best solution on short notice. Have you ever been?"

She didn't want a short-notice solution, she wanted

to be desired. She'd decided years ago that when she did marry, she'd be a valued and equal partner in the arrangement.

"Once." She'd gone with friends from college to watch the bull riding championships. "For a weekend."

"We can stay a few days and enjoy ourselves. We'll have to deal with some necessary publicity, although that too should put an end to your family's stunts."

She couldn't wrap her head around it. Marrying Fox Colton was a fantasy. One of those wispy dreams that teased and tantalized before it was obliterated by the alarm clock.

"Fox, have you really thought this out?" She hated the idea of causing him more trouble that he'd have to wade through. "A whirlwind wedding is absurd. Marriage is serious."

"I'm serious about you," he replied. "I'm surprised you haven't thought of this before."

Not once had she considered a marriage of convenience as a viable solution to her family drama. It wouldn't be fair to the fake husband and she couldn't get past the idea of being subject to a man. In the community where she'd been raised, a woman was still considered her husband's property. Kelsey rubbed the unexpected chill from her arms. She'd watched marriage douse the light of so many women, including her mother and older sisters.

She had to reel him in. "Fox, really. I appreciate the gesture, but—"

"It's not a gesture. It's a wedding, Kelsey. A marriage. Real and legal. You told me getting married would get your brothers off your back."

"I did." And now she wished she could take it back. "That doesn't mean you have to be the sacrificial groom."

"I don't feel sacrificial at all." He reached over and covered her hand. "It's true this is a sudden step, but we're a good team in and out of the office."

Yes, they had complementary strengths. Even with the baby, though that wouldn't be a permanent part of his life. She wondered if Fox realized how much he'd miss the baby when Mason made his final decision.

"We like and respect each other and we're compatible." He glanced back as if he expected the John to pick up on the innuendo.

They were definitely compatible, she thought as her cheeks heated. "Just tell me if this is because of the skeletons that tumbled out of your closet or mine."

He tilted his head. "Both," he admitted. "Getting married, with the requisite public announcement, protects you." He glanced her way, his blue eyes alight with possibilities. "This marriage will empower you. Think about having the freedom to follow your career wherever it takes you, without the worry that your brothers will jump out of the shadows."

She shook her head. "You noticed I held my own."

"More than," he agreed.

Was that pride she heard in his voice? "But what about you?" He must have other plans for his life than wedding an assistant he'd only known for a few weeks.

"Well, I get to call the best equine geneticist on record my wife for as long as she'll have me."

It sounded so cold even as his words gave her a little thrill. She'd be Fox Colton's *wife*. "Will you draw up a contract or something?"

"Why leave a paper trail? I think we should stay married for a year at the very least, but whenever you want out of the marriage, just say the word."

She wanted to believe him, yet those dreadful memories from her childhood reared up, whispering warnings that this was a trap.

More noise from the back seat drew his attention and when he checked John in the rearview mirror, his smile melted the last of her reserve.

"All right," she agreed. "A real, legal wedding with the necessary publicity that will get me shunned and my name blotted from the family record."

"Which leaves you free to do whatever you please."

"You really mean that?"

He turned, winked. "I do."

She wanted to argue, but it was true that being married would render her damaged goods and break the contract she'd been avoiding for half her life. Her family would have no reason to come after her and she really would be completely safe.

If he was going into this wedding with his eyes wide-open, she'd be a fool to talk him out of it. Even if he didn't love her.

Vegas swirled around them in a riot of color and sparkle and glitz. Fox couldn't whisk her to Paris, but he'd done the next best thing by booking a two-bedroom suite at the Paris Las Vegas Hotel. Of all the places he expected to marry, it wasn't here, where nothing was quite what it seemed.

Until Kelsey mentioned it, he hadn't given marriage much thought at all. Though the Coltons expected him to settle down, he'd planned to put it off as long as possible.

More than anything he wanted her to enjoy an unforgettable and romantic weekend. The hotel happily arranged for them to meet with a wedding planner and connected them with an outstanding child care service.

All he really wanted from the ceremony was a happy and safe bride. He'd brought her here to protect her, to rescue her, though her rescuing him was a better description of what had happened. Would he have come through all the shocking upheavals of these past few weeks without her?

Well, physically, sure. He had his work and the baby to keep him going. Unlike the man he'd believed to be his father, he wasn't a brute, but having Kelsey close made all the ugliness easier to bear.

Kelsey slipped her arm around his waist as he continued to stare at the glittering strip several stories below their balcony. "Having second thoughts?"

Her voice and touch were soothing. No wonder Baby John had taken to her so quickly. The little tyke had recognized a caring and competent source of security. "Not one. Your safety is paramount and I don't want you to live in fear ever again."

"Are you adding that to the vows?"

"It doesn't sound romantic, but I mean it." Fox glanced down at her heart-shaped face to find her hazel eyes sparkling brighter than the strip. Her hair was down, a soft fall of rose-gold silk. As her lips curved into a warm smile, he felt like the luckiest man alive. Marriage of convenience or not, he was proud the world would know him as her husband. "You don't think it's implied with the traditional vows to love, honor and cherish?"

"Cherish?" Tears welled up in those big hazel eyes and she didn't blink quite fast enough.

Cupping her cheek, he brushed the teardrop away. "Kelsey? What did I say?"

"You said everything right." She gave her head a tiny shake. "I need a second."

Instead of walking away, she pressed herself close, both arms banding around his waist. "I've always heard *obey*," she said at last. "Every wedding I sat through as a kid, *obey* was nonnegotiable. I've been in the real world long enough to know there are options, but that word was stuck in my head, ruining the moment, even when I tried to imagine my own wedding."

And yes, she'd agreed to this stunt. It couldn't be a quick ceremony for show. Thanks to his last name, it would be a public announcement that would make national news. The trust she'd put in him landed like a kick to his heart.

All her life, she'd been locked down by restrictions and attitudes and a hard community. Her only chance at freedom had been to run away. He'd been stuck as well, afraid to be himself in either of his childhood homes. Kelsey changed that, forced him to look in the mirror and own not only his fears but also his hopes and dreams. Being with her was a different kind of safe for him, but he assumed the relief was similar for both of them.

"This wedding is for you, Kelsey. Fast or not, there won't be a single word or song or flower that doesn't suit you."

"I'm being silly," she murmured into his shirt.

He stroked her back, marveling again at the strength packed into her petite frame. "You're not." He loved her, *desperately*, and wanted to tell her just how real the upcoming ceremony would be to him.

The thought alone was too selfish to speak. How could he tie her down just when she'd found her freedom? Publicly becoming his wife gave her the ability to grow in her field, to conduct research, and eventually find the man she wanted to cherish for the rest of her days.

But oh, what he wouldn't give for that man to be *him*.

"You're sure this will be enough to keep you safe from your family?"

She stepped back, linking her hands with his. "I am. Giving my vow to you is something they'll respect even if they don't like it." She flashed him a brilliant smile. "I'll be damaged goods."

"Nothing damaged about you, sweetheart." Fox bent his head and brushed his lips across hers. She kissed him back with a tenderness that left him undone.

In the other room the baby giggled and the sitter's laughter followed. Fox felt her lips smile with his.

"Baby John makes new friends wherever he goes," she said.

"Seems that way," Fox agreed. He checked his watch as he steered her toward the central room of the suite. The wedding planner would be here any minute. "Are you ready to finalize the details for tomorrow?"

She grinned up at him. "I don't know how you've coordinated all of this, but it's wonderful. All the best parts of a real wedding without the turmoil and angst I've seen other women go through. I feel cherished already."

"You are." They'd start with cherish and move on to the *L* word when she was ready to hear it.

With his arm around her waist and the baby playing peekaboo with the sitter that love surged through him. Better if he waited until they were back on the ranch to tell her. They still had to work out the situation with Baby John. After spending her childhood raising babies, he couldn't ask her to repeat that cycle now that she had the freedom to be or do anything her heart desired.

He'd get to say *love* during the ceremony tomorrow. It would be enough, for now. Reaching into his pocket, he pulled out the ring he'd chosen for her. The diamond wasn't huge, but the emerald-cut stone was top-quality and gleamed in the platinum setting between two cushion-cut rubies.

He cocked an eyebrow when she gasped, pressing her hands to her lips. "Fox."

One more daring move. Was it right or wrong?

"I meant it, Kelsey. You get the final say on every detail. If you want something different, speak up."

"It's too much. Where did you get that? When?"

"I met with the jeweler while you were distracted with something else." Seeing this ring, he'd immediately envisioned it on her finger as she worked in the lab or played with the baby, or rode out with him on the ranch. She had yet to give him a chance to slide it on her finger.

"We might have to adjust the sizing." He'd guessed at that, was hopeful he'd come close.

"Fox, it's beautiful." At last she extended her hand, her fingers quivering.

Or maybe it was his hand shaking as he slipped the

ring onto her finger. *I love you. Today, tomorrow and always.* The words burned where he kept them locked away in his heart.

"It's perfect." She held up her hand, letting the light dance in the stones. A moment later, she launched herself into his arms, and he caught her, gave her a quick spin as she peppered him with kisses.

He took that as approval, the last of his doubts about making their wedding memorable floating away.

When had her life turned into a fairy tale? Kelsey was drenched in a wonderland of luxury with her own personal hero. He wasn't wearing shiny armor, but his sexy reading glasses and the dazzling rock on her hand made up for that. He could definitely ride to the rescue better than any fantasy hero from her dreams. She'd tried to articulate the difference last night and failed. Fox didn't seem to have any idea how his actions affected her.

Running away had been the hardest thing in her life, second only to dodging the traps her brothers set. No more. In a few hours she'd be completely free of her past.

Fox had truly given her the world with this crazy wedding. Long before he'd slipped the engagement ring on her finger, before he'd suggested this whirlwind trip, he'd given her more than she'd known to ask for.

While she and the wedding planner chose her dress and marked the alterations, Fox agreed to whittle down the cake design and floral options. With the dress marked with minor alterations, she returned to the main room to find Fox and Baby John looking at pictures of flowers.

Her heart plopped at Fox's feet. How could she feel so content and so unsettled all at once? Admiring the man and his work was one thing. Could she live with affection rather than love?

She was about to find out. She pressed her lips together and forced her feet to carry her forward. It was too late to back out and no matter what she *felt* for Fox, the reality was she *needed* this wedding to be free of her family.

Cherish.

The word echoed in her mind as guilt prickled, cold and ugly, under her skin. She would find a way to make this up to him.

"Kelsey?"

He was watching her over his reading glasses and all that tenderness was eclipsed by pure lust that burned hotter with love added in. She forced a smile to her face. "The dress is going to knock your socks off. Thank you."

"Can't wait to see it." He dodged John's curious grab for his glasses and filled the baby's hand with a crumpled catalog page.

"Do you have a favorite flower?" he asked.

"What's in season?"

"It's Las Vegas," he replied. "Anything you want can be in season."

"True enough." She scooped up the baby and spun in a circle, making him giggle. "How much do the flowers matter to you?"

The bright and happy sound settled her like nothing else. She'd miss the little guy if Mason decided to raise him. More likely, she'd miss the little guy when she and Fox embarked on their separate lives.

His eyes went wide. "This isn't about the ceremony, it's a Marriage 101 question."

She chuckled. "Expecting to be in the doghouse?"

"You've seen how I get lost in my work." He tugged off his glasses. "It's bound to happen."

Her heart did another happy dance when he smiled. "In that case, I want flowers that sparkle and never die," she joked, flashing her engagement ring.

"I'll make myself a note." He stood up and hooked his glasses on his back pocket. "I'll trade," Fox offered, holding out the floral catalog in exchange for the baby.

After a brief discussion, they made their final selections and the wedding planner left to put everything into motion. This was good practice in case they had to throw a reception for Fox's family when they got back to Roaring Springs.

After everything Fox had done for her, the least she could do was leave him breathless when he saw her walk into the chapel tomorrow. When they returned to the Crooked C, her focus would shift to being the best assistant possible.

Leaving the baby with the sitter, she and Fox went out for dinner and on to watch a professional hockey game. Kelsey couldn't recall ever feeling so relaxed. With Fox by her side, John in expert hands and miles of distance between her and any threat, she marveled at her first taste of pure freedom.

But by the second intermission, they were both missing the baby and laughing at themselves as they agreed to go back to the suite. In John's room, they stood for several minutes, just watching him sleep.

"Thank you for this," she whispered as they left the baby's room.

Fox skimmed a hand over her hair. "You keep saying that, but I promise, you've done more for me, Kelsey."

His sincerity was etched on his face, gleaming in the depths of his gorgeous blue eyes. "Your hair is lovely down."

"So you've said."

"I love—"

Her heart stuttered.

"—the way it warms in sunlight." He twirled his fingers into a lock of her hair and followed the wave of it to her shoulder.

Her breath caught in her throat. She'd debated cutting her locks short while they were here, but she couldn't do it now. A few more weeks storing up the way he gazed at her with that stark longing and blatant appreciation would hold her for the rest of her days.

If her father had ever looked at her mother with more than dutiful respect, Kelsey had never seen it. Fox was so much more than she'd ever known to hope for. "Take me to bed. Please?"

"Isn't that bad luck?" he teased. He bent close, his lips grazing her temple, the shell of her ear, the column of her throat.

"Fox," she begged. "We make our own luck."

He scooped her up and carried her into the bedroom where they put the honeymoon ahead of the wedding ceremony in the best possible way. Every woman should know the joy and pleasure of being loved with all her gifts and flaws.

Kelsey came awake the next morning to the sweet sounds of Baby John happily playing in his crib. The baby monitor was better than any alarm clock.

She rolled over, but Fox was up and out, the sheets and pillow cool to the touch.

Today was her wedding day. No matter the method or madness, she would leave Las Vegas as Mrs. Fox Colton. The notion was a dizzying prospect and for a moment, she just basked in anticipation.

"It's my wedding day, John."

Kelsey rolled to her side, smiling as Fox's deep, mellow voice came through the monitor. The baby cooed. She often wanted to do the same thing when Fox spoke.

"I'm the luckiest guy in the world," Fox continued. "She's a beauty and smart as a whip. And a great baby-care teacher," he finished with a laugh.

She smothered her own chuckle as she listened to Fox changing and dressing John. "You think she'd like it if you joined us today?"

Yes! She would. It would make for an interesting story when they shared the wedding pictures with friends and family.

The conversation faded as Fox left the baby's room for the kitchen to fix Baby John's first bottle.

She listened to the normal sounds, as familiar here as they were at the house on the ranch. It was so hard not to beg him for the forever they would promise each other in just a few hours. What would Fox say if she told him she'd fallen hopelessly in love with him? The baby too, though that was even more treacherous territory. Mason might still claim his son.

What would it do to Fox if he did?

She knew he was as attached to the child as she was. More, probably, although Baby John's sweet and easy-going personality made him irresistible to her.

After a quick shower, she dressed in jeans and a cable-knit sweater and wound her hair into a messy bun. The baby, in the bouncy seat, saw her first and kicked his legs, a big smile on his round face. His tiny fists opened and closed as if he could pull her to him.

"Good morning, handsome." She planted a kiss on the top of his head.

Fox turned, his smile warming her from the inside out. "Good morning. How are you feeling?"

"Uncaffeinated." She looked over and noticed he'd set out a mug for her, along with a spoon and saucer for her creamer. "You're a saint for letting me sleep in."

He shrugged. "Just call me the smartest groom of the day."

"Maybe." She filled her cup, added cream and let the aroma swirl around her for a moment. This was heaven. "I know we have a head start on traditional couples, but I think we've got this morning routine down."

"Almost," he said, aiming a spoonful of cereal at Baby John's mouth.

"What did I miss?"

He tapped his cheek, still shadowed with overnight stubble. "You skipped me."

She obliged, then nudged him aside to take over the feeding. "Go on and clean up." The coffee always got Fox going in the morning, but nothing woke him up like a shower.

"But you'll get messy."

"The salon will fix me." She made a silly face at the baby and he laughed, cereal oozing down his chin.

It was her wedding day and she was happily feeding a baby. Not an ounce of resentment or frustration in her heart. Strange that with Baby John she was willing to go the extra mile while raising her siblings had felt like crushing responsibility.

"Maybe it's maturity," she said to the baby in a sweet singsong voice. "Or the company." More likely it was the awareness that this little guy had options in life and however he'd come into the world, he was cherished now.

Did all brides have this weird mix of nostalgia and hope on their wedding day? A fake bride should probably just focus on playing her part. Especially one who couldn't drum up the courage to ask the groom about making it real.

Fox stood at the front of the chapel with the minister he'd met yesterday. The man reminded him of Santa Claus with the white hair, robust build and a rosy-cheeked smile. Quick with a joke, he kept Fox's heart rate closer to normal.

Then Kelsey walked into view and the world just went still. Every cell in his body riveted onto the vision of his beautiful bride.

She'd had her pick of dresses from elaborate to fanciful. He assumed all of them would have looked lovely on her. But the warm, ivory-colored lace that left her shoulders bare and flowed with the graceful curves of her body stole his breath. Her hair was a mass of curls piled high on her head, with luminous pearl drops scattered through.

Like a moth to flame, he took a step toward her before the minister stopped him with a word.

The baby, perched on the sitter's knee in the first row, bounced up and down, delighted to see her. *Yeah, buddy*, Fox thought. *I agree 100 percent.*

With the soft melody of classical music carrying on the air, Fox nearly called a halt to her short walk down the aisle so he could tell her he wanted their marriage to be real from the start.

Every step brought her closer to him and his heart swelled with joy. At Baby John's happy gurgle, her gaze moved to the infant and her face glowed when she saw him in a tuxedo that matched Fox's.

"You're quite a pair," she said as she took her place.

"You approve?"

She nodded, her smile brilliant as the minister began the ceremony. When it was time, they vowed to love, honor and cherish each other. He willed her to hear the heart-deep promise of his words. When she said her vows to him, he believed she meant every word, as well.

He was still wishing it was true when the minister declared them husband and wife and invited him to kiss his bride. He did, pouring all the promises he intended to keep into that sizzling meeting of lips.

They were officially married and his wild, impromptu wedding idea was complete, just like that.

Fox held the baby for a few pictures, wondering how much time Kelsey would give him before she used her newfound freedom to move on to greener pastures.

He didn't wallow in the "what next." It was impossible to be melancholy when she was beside him, beaming at him, at the baby and at the camera that would soon splash this news on outlets around the world.

She played her part to perfection and he followed her lead. No matter that his heart was already breaking in anticipation of her walking out of his life.

Chapter 14

By the time they boarded the plane the day after the wedding, Kelsey knew something was off. Fox was increasingly polite and more distant with every minute since the champagne toast that had followed the ceremony.

She adjusted Baby John, dozing on her shoulder, and tried to sort fact from the rising panic in her heart. She was terrified he was having second thoughts. Except every time she replayed that moment when he'd spoken his vows, she knew he'd meant it. It was a strange concept, to treasure someone, and it made her wonder about the layers of love she'd never considered.

She'd seen mothers cherish children and she'd watched fathers glow with pride. Protection was love in action, filtering down in various ways. Fox had elevated protection when he'd married her, effectively laying the world at her feet.

There was a hum of happy energy coursing through her system that she couldn't quite harness. Underneath it was the skeptic she'd learned to be, waiting for all that happiness to be yanked away.

Working side by side with Fox she'd fallen in love with the way his mind worked. Strange to dissect it that way, but it was true. She'd been raised to be a wife, to defer to and support and obey her husband in all things.

After escaping the confines of her family, she hadn't expected those early ingrained lessons to leap back to the fore as soon as she said *I do.* Yet here she was, eager to do whatever she could to ease the burden currently weighing on Fox.

Their first kiss as husband and wife had curled her toes, nearly eclipsing the remarkable pleasure of their first kiss. She chalked it up to the awareness and significance of their decision. They were officially tethered for life. Even if they divorced in the future, he'd be her first husband for the rest of her days. Was there any hope that this relationship, what they shared right now, would be enough?

"Did you hear from Mason?" she asked as another explanation for his somber mood occurred to her.

"Not yet," he replied without looking up from his cell phone.

"Have I done something wrong?" She cringed, hearing the echo of her mother's defeated voice in the question.

His gaze snapped to hers over his reading glasses. "No." He deliberately set aside his phone and took her hand. "You're perfect."

"We both know I'm not," she said.

"We'll have to agree to disagree on that. Why did you ask?"

"You've been increasingly quiet since the wedding," she told him. "And not in your typical work-distracted way."

"I'd rather have this conversation when we're home," he replied. "Privately."

She fought the sting of tears, just to keep from upsetting the baby. "I'm sure you would."

When her father had said those things, they would get home and the moment the door closed, the punishment landed. Fox was not her father. She repeated it over and over. Fox had overcome a similar father. His temperament was completely different.

"Kelsey." He stroked the length of her arm and she realized she was shaking. "Let me take the baby."

"No."

On her shoulder, Baby John squirmed in his sleep, restless because she was struggling with a well of emotion she hadn't prepared for. But she couldn't bear to feel that alone, set apart from both Fox and the child. It would be too much like her childhood, where her father dictated everything from thoughts to emotions to discipline.

"I… I…" When his hand touched hers, she clung.

"Easy," he murmured in the soothing voice he used with the horses. "Talk to me."

"You first." She prayed he'd open up while she gathered the bits of her shattered composure.

"Here?"

She nodded. "Please."

"Fine." He dropped his head back on the seat, his

gaze on the panel overhead. "I can't stop wondering how soon you'll move on."

"You want me to move on?"

"Of course."

Her heart dropped like a stone. That should be music to her ears, her soul. The freedom to go and do as she pleased. It was central to why she'd agreed to this marriage. What was wrong with her that a stunning ring, a few words and some publicity photos changed her entire mind-set?

"You can't be my assistant forever."

No, I'm your wife. She longed to be his partner in life and work. Apparently marrying Fox had snuffed out her wanderlust. She didn't want to move on.

"There's more for you to do and learn, more you want to do," he was saying.

"Yes," she said when he paused. His face clouded over, though not in anger. She wanted to keep growing in her field, but given the chance, she thought she could do that and be his wife.

Kelsey rocked John gently on her shoulder. And raise his children. She could hardly believe she'd had such a thought, but when she turned it around, she knew nothing else could make her happier.

"Sweetheart..." He lowered his voice, leaned in close. "We don't have to set hard dates right here and now."

A measure of relief whispered through her. That would give them time for love to grow.

"I want you to have choices, to be fulfilled. To be safe wherever your dreams take you." He gave her fingers a squeeze, brushed a soft kiss across her temple.

Her dreams had led her to *him*. A brilliant man who

understood the science of building a better quarter horse. A kind and generous man who had been totally stressed out and uncertain about caring for a baby but had stepped up like a champ.

"I'm overwhelmed," she admitted. "I didn't expect to be."

She hadn't expected any of the emotions tossing her about like a leaf on the wind.

With his hand joined with hers and the baby snoring on her shoulder, she relaxed, heart and mind. Fox was right. What she had to say and what she needed to hear were best handled in the privacy of his home.

Fox couldn't get Kelsey's reaction on the plane out of his mind. Her tear-filled eyes, the quaking and the unsettling questions. He suspected her past had reared up. His own rocky upbringing had informed his recent choices, as well.

Primarily, Baby John. A child should grow up knowing love and stability, having the opportunity to make mistakes without fear of violent repercussions. Good grief, he and Kelsey were living and breathing proof of the long-term effects of living in fear.

He could breed the best horse possible, but that horse would never reach its potential if hampered by fear of pain.

He didn't want to hold Kelsey back or make her feel obligated to stay, but keeping his feelings locked down was making him quiet in a way that clearly distressed her. He had to get the words out there, where she could analyze and assess. He couldn't expect her to decide anything without all the facts out in the open.

And loving her was an irrefutable fact.

While she settled the baby down for what remained of the night, he checked his email and put the phone on speaker to listen to the messages.

"Fox? Mason. Look, I just can't take on the kid. Parenting was Elaine's dream." His next words were muffled, but Fox was sure the sentiment wasn't kind. "I'll sign off on the paternity rights and you can do whatever you need to do with the baby."

The line went dead, and Fox stared at the phone.

"Do *whatever*?" Kelsey echoed. "Glad Baby John is too young to hear that."

"Me, too." Fox went to her. "I'll erase the message as soon as I talk with Trey. I didn't hear you come in. How's the little guy?"

"Down for the count."

"You have a way with him," he said before he thought it through. To his relief, she smiled.

"True. You do, too." She held up her phone. "We made it home before the story hit the news."

"That will make it easier to field calls from the family," he said.

She ducked her head, trying to hide the grin and then simply let it burst free.

"Imagining how your family will react?"

"Yes." She flung her arms wide and turned in a circle. "How can I ever thank you enough? I'm so happy and relieved."

He crossed the room. When had holding back ever worked in his favor? They wouldn't be legally married now if he'd kept the idea tucked away in the "she wouldn't go for it" column.

Slowly, giving her room to react or retreat, he wrapped her arms around his waist and linked his hands at the small of her back. Only when they were holding each other did he let the words tumble free. "I love you, Kelsey Lauder Colton. Whether you live here as my wife for a year or for always, I love you. That won't change."

"Fox..." she breathed.

He interrupted her with a soft kiss. He had to get everything out. "You heard Mason's message. If he won't step up as Baby John's father, I plan to." As he spoke, the excitement of being a father rushed through him. "That boy won me over on my doorstep, but you smoothed out what was sure to be a rocky path. Hell, it's likely to get sticky again on occasion.

"More than anything," he continued, "I'd like the three of us to be a real family, to build on what we've started. That's only what *I* want." He brought her hands to his lips. "To me, loving you means giving you time to spread your wings. I won't hold you back. I'm not asking you to be the baby's nanny or mother if you want something else..." His voice faded at the sheen of tears in her eyes.

But this time the smile on her lips filled him with hope.

"Fox Colton, I love you, too." She hugged him tight, giggling when he boosted her up and spun her in a circle. "You've set me free to be everything I've dreamed of. Over the last few weeks, everything I've dreamed of has come true, right here with you."

"You're agreeing to a real marriage? With me?"

"With you." She laid a hand over his heart. "You and the baby boy sleeping in the nursery."

"I won't let you regret it," he promised.

"Not a chance, my love." She drew his face close and kissed him deeply.

"Having a wife should make the adoption process easier," he teased.

"I guess we'll find out together." The joy glowing on her face lit an equally brilliant fire inside him.

Together.

At last they both had a family to treasure and nurture, family to lean on and support. She could sink roots here, the baby too, and they would all grow stronger day by day. Love was the X-factor that healed old wounds and made room for new hopes and dreams.

His heart soaring, Fox carried Kelsey back to their bedroom to celebrate their first night at *home*, together as husband and wife.

* * * * *

Coltons of Roaring Springs miniseries:

Colton Cowboy Standoff *by Marie Ferrarella*
Colton Under Fire *by Cindy Dees*
Colton's Convenient Bride *by Jennifer Morey*
Colton's Secret Bodyguard *by Jane Godman*
A Colton Target *by Beverly Long*
Colton's Covert Baby *by Lara Lacombe*
Colton's Mistaken Identity *by Geri Krotow*
The Colton Sheriff *by Addison Fox*
Colton on the Run *by Anna J. Stewart*

Available now from Harlequin Romantic Suspense.

And don't miss the next chapter of
the Coltons of Roaring Springs,
Colton's Secret Investigation *by Justine Davis,*

Coming in November 2019!

COMING NEXT MONTH FROM

HARLEQUIN®

ROMANTIC suspense

Available November 5, 2019

#2063 COLTON'S SECRET INVESTIGATION

The Coltons of Roaring Springs • by Justine Davis

As the liaison between local law enforcement and the FBI, Daria Bloom is hell-bent on catching the Avalanche Killer. But her FBI counterpart, Stefan Roberts, is a gorgeous distraction in the fight of her life...and a shocking discovery about her family.

#2064 COLTON 911: CAUGHT IN THE CROSSFIRE

Colton 911 • by Linda O. Johnston

In Cactus Creek, Arizona, murder and cattle rustling bring Deputy Sheriff Casey Colton to OverHerd Ranch, where he meets lovely ranch hand Melody Hayworth. Neither is looking for love, but a sizzling connection sparks between them, putting them directly in harm's way.

#2065 CAVANAUGH STAKEOUT

Cavanaugh Justice • by Marie Ferrarella

When the Cavanaugh patriarch is attacked, his grandson Finn Cavanaugh is on the case with an unlikely accomplice, Nik Kowalski, a feisty investigator. As they chase down leads, Finn and Nik can't deny their attraction, no matter how hard they try.

#2066 HER DARK WEB DEFENDER

True Blue • by Dana Nussio

Burned-out FBI special agent Tony Lazzaro is desperate to leave his task force, but his boss delays his transfer until a murder case is closed. Tony's progress is slowed while training new task force member Kelly Roberts, who sees her assignment as a chance for redemption. As danger mounts, they must rely on only each other for safety...and love.
